THE
PLAYDATE

BOOKS BY VICTORIA JENKINS

THE DETECTIVES KING AND LANE SERIES
The Girls in the Water
The First one to Die
Nobody's Child
A Promise to the Dead

The Divorce
The Argument
The Accusation

THE
PLAYDATE

Bookouture

Published by Bookouture in 2021

An imprint of Storyfire Ltd.
Carmelite House
50 Victoria Embankment
London EC4Y 0DZ

www.bookouture.com

ISBN: 978-1-80019-506-6
eBook ISBN: 978-1-80019-505-9

ONE

DANI

Eve was dead. Somehow the enormity of the news was hard to process amid the normality of life: Layla on the carpet eating dry Cheerios with her fingers while watching Daddy Pig try to rescue Mummy Pig from a blackberry bush; Dani's mother vacuuming in the front room, the Dyson's hum interspersed with its thuds against the skirting boards. For once Dani was grateful for the noise of the house, competing as it did with the screaming of her thoughts as she stared at the headline in front of her. She felt detached, the words not quite real.

The message had pinged onto her phone half an hour earlier, but she had only just had a chance to look at it. Getting Layla ready for playgroup was a time-consuming process – wrestling reluctant, rigid limbs into leggings and a T-shirt, trying to grapple a toothbrush past clenched teeth, dragging a hairbrush through a tangle of knots while Layla refused to sit still – and by the time her daughter was finally ready, Dani no longer felt like going anywhere. If it wasn't for her mother's burst of daily cleaning, she would have stayed at home. Caroline's obsessive vacuuming had increased with the cat's age, his hair moulting onto every available surface. There had been times Dani felt convinced her mother had some form of obsessive-compulsive disorder, though Caroline would never have got rid of Dylan, who was as much a part of the family as the rest of them.

Dani hadn't heard from Kelly Thompson in years, and if she hadn't remembered the name, she would never have recognised her from the thumbnail photograph that sat alongside the message. Kelly wore a beanie hat that covered most of her head, but from the wisps that escaped it, her fringe windswept across her eyes, it looked as though she had dyed her hair silver blonde. Behind her loomed a mountain, and her arms were stretched out wide in a gesture that screamed, 'Yes, I'm here… I've made it.' Dani felt the twist of envy in her chest like a knot of indigestion and tried to swallow it down, reminding herself that social media didn't always portray lives as they really were.

She and Kelly had been friends in primary school for a while, but during secondary school they had drifted apart in the way that many friendships distanced themselves over time, gradually and without either party seeming to notice. Dani had attached herself to Eve almost immediately upon meeting her, in awe of her confidence and the fact that she seemed so much older than everyone else in their year group. She had befriended Eve to the exclusion of all others, which had later proved to be a poor decision. She tried to remember the last time she had spoken to Kelly. Everything had ended in such a rush.

Hi Dani. Hope everything's okay with you? You may have already heard about this, but I thought I should contact you in case you haven't and you see it somewhere else. Big shock! Her poor parents x

Beneath the message there was a link. A report from a Bath newspaper. *Young Woman Found Drowned in River*, read the headline. Dani scanned the words repeatedly, getting caught on the name every time, its letters jumping at her from the screen.

*The body of a young woman found drowned in the River
Avon at the weekend has been identified as that of 22-year-old
Eve Gardiner, who was last seen on Saturday evening after
leaving a friend's house. It is believed that Miss Gardiner,
who was unable to swim, slipped and fell into the water.*

She had always expected to see Eve's name in print one day.
She had imagined a tabloid article about a date with a famous
footballer, a string of photographs capturing Eve toned and sun-
kissed, just returned from a fortnight's holiday somewhere exotic
and expensive. Maybe she would read about her running for
election as a local MP, or as the spokesperson for some charitable
cause, her glossy hair and whitened teeth shining for the camera.
Her name was always going to be known in some way or another.
But never like this.

It wasn't a case of it all seeming more real the more she read it,
because in fact her thoughts just strayed further, as though she was
clinging onto them by her fingertips, reeling them back in before
they escaped her. She was taken back four years to a classroom she
hadn't spent enough time in and a life that already felt as though
it belonged to someone else. Mrs Preston, the history teacher, was
talking final exam preparations, but Dani wasn't listening – she
hadn't really been listening for months – and instead was texting
Eve, her phone hidden beneath the desk.

Send me a photo of the dress x

'Dani! Dani!'
Her mother called her from the front room, and Dani was
yanked back to the present. The vacuum cleaner was muted for a
moment, Caroline standing with one hand pressed to her hip, the

other clutching the handle of the Dyson as though she was about to film a TV advertisement for carpet cleaner.

'You haven't left yet then?'

'Apparently not.'

'Grab us some fags on the way back, love. There's a tenner in the pot on the microwave.'

'I thought you were giving up?'

'I am,' she snapped, then smiled apologetically, her head tilting into a look that aimed to win her daughter over. 'But you know what they say... Rome wasn't built in a day.'

'You know what else they say? Smoking gives you lung cancer.'

Caroline pulled a face. 'Thank you, my little ray of sunshine. Enjoy your morning.'

She turned the Dyson back on and Dani headed to the living room to fetch her daughter, who had lost interest in the television and was about to drag a red crayon across her grandmother's silver wallpaper. They did a search of the living room for Layla's trainers, the ones with the light-up heels that had cost Dani almost a full day's pay. When Dani tried to put them on, Layla pushed her hands away, insisting she could do the Velcro straps by herself. She wailed with frustration when she couldn't pull the shoe past her heel, and Dani grabbed it from her. 'For God's sake, Layla,' she snapped. 'Just let me do it.'

Layla looked at her and her lip quivered, and when she burst into tears, Dani felt like the worst mother in the world, which some days she thought she might be. She loved Layla with the kind of love that felt as though it might burst out of her chest – a love she didn't think she could ever feel for anyone else – yet there were days when she felt like walking out of the house, catching the next train to the first destination that made itself available and never coming back. She never would – it was just a thought, like all the other thoughts about what her life might have been had she made different choices.

She put her arms around Layla for a hug. Her daughter resisted at first, but then allowed herself to be pulled into the embrace. Dani said sorry for shouting, which she was. It wasn't Layla's fault. It was that bloody link on her phone. What had happened to Eve was shocking, a tragedy, but she couldn't let Layla see how it had affected her. Eve was a part of Dani's past, and she knew she must keep her that way.

'Come on,' she said, and grabbed Layla's coat from the back of one of the kitchen chairs. 'Let's go.'

In recent weeks, Layla had hit a phase of independence, getting frustrated with every simple task and bubbling over into anger when she couldn't do something on the first attempt. Her tantrums were full-blown – no one else's child seemed to lose control of their emotions on the same scale – and though she had only recently turned two, Dani was already counting down the days until she hit her third birthday, praying there would be an overnight change when her temper would just evaporate.

She zipped Layla into her coat before grabbing the tenner from the pot – her mother's cigarette fund. Caroline was asthmatic, but that hadn't stopped her smoking like a disposable barbecue since Dani's dad died over nine years earlier. She had given up a little while before that, the fags replaced with chewing gum, but when their lives were upended by the accident, suddenly all bets were off.

'Come on,' Dani said to Layla, reaching for her hand. 'We'll be late.'

The church hall was just a short walk from their house, so they never bothered with the pushchair; Layla walked half the way and Dani carried her the rest. The little girl was getting heavy, but Dani figured her days of being allowed to carry her anywhere were numbered, so she should make the most of them while she could. The women at the playgroup – the grandmothers especially – were forever telling her to enjoy this time, that before she knew it Layla's childhood would be over and she would be gone. Dani supposed they knew what they were talking about, though it was hard sometimes to feel grateful when Layla was crying at 3 a.m. for no apparent reason or throwing a strop because Dani had put her dinner on the wrong-coloured plate.

When they arrived, the group had already started, toys strewn across the floor, and one of the playgroup leaders was arranging biscuits on a plate and waiting for the kettle to boil. There was, as always, a clear divide within the group, though no one ever seemed to mention it – the women who sat at one side of the room, and those who gathered at the other. The two never really seemed to mix, as though some unspoken guidelines had been accepted by everyone, with no explanation ever offered.

Elaine was already there. Her grandson, Josh, was standing at the plastic kitchen in the corner, shoving as many toy plates and utensils as he could into the microwave. Layla wriggled down from Dani's arms when she spotted him, and Dani made a grab for her, taking off her coat before Layla ran over to join him.

Elaine was sitting with another woman, someone who had started coming to the group a couple of weeks before. Dani wasn't sure of her name – it might have been mentioned, but she didn't remember – and the woman had kept herself to herself, sitting on her own near the door while her daughter played on one of the mats at her feet. Dani smiled at them both as she took off her jacket and slipped it over the back of a chair.

'All right, love?' Elaine greeted her. 'This is Adele. You two met already?'

Adele shook her head. She was wearing jeans and a long-sleeved sweater that was loose around her narrow shoulders, and she was older than Dani had thought her from a distance; close up, the fine lines around her eyes were visible and there were the slightest flecks of grey at her temples. The thought that she seemed a bit old to be the mum of a toddler crossed Dani's mind, but she reminded herself that people often looked at her and thought she was too young.

'What's your daughter's name?' she asked. The little girl was sitting nearby, playing with a wooden tractor.

'Ivy.'

'Pretty name.'

'Shall I get you a cuppa?' Elaine offered.

'Thanks,' Dani said.

'You had a cup yet?' Elaine turned to Adele. 'Have one now while you've got the chance. I didn't get to finish a cup of tea while it was still hot until my youngest started school.'

She got up to fetch two cups of tea, then went back for a plate of biscuits. Adele took a rich tea, which Dani thought a strange choice when there were chocolate digestives right next to it.

'Thanks. I shouldn't really,' she added, moving her hand self-consciously to her waist.

'Christ,' Elaine said, 'there's nothing of you.'

She was right; Adele was pencil thin. Perhaps that was why she looked older – being skinny did that to some people. She was just one of those types it was hard to put an age to: anywhere between thirty and fifty depending on the lighting.

'What's *your* daughter called?' she asked Dani.

'Layla.'

'That's lovely.' Adele put the biscuit on the table beside her. 'How old is she?'

'Turned two last month... Layla!' Dani made a grab for the biscuit Layla had just taken from the table, but it was bitten into before she could reach it. 'I'm so sorry,' she said to Adele, rolling her eyes. 'I'll get you another one.'

'She's fine. And no, thanks though.'

Adele smiled at Layla, watching as the little girl's mouth stretched into a biscuit-coated yawn.

'She didn't sleep well last night,' Dani explained. 'She's not a fan of sleep. I mean, it's quite easy to get her off, but it's the staying asleep that's the problem. Is Ivy good?'

She wondered why she used the word 'good', when Layla being a terrible sleeper didn't make her bad. But that was how people seemed to talk about children, especially when they were babies. *Is she a good baby?* people would ask her when Layla was newborn, and she was sometimes tempted to ask them what a bad baby looked like.

Adele nodded. 'She's pretty easy-going at night.'

She meant nothing by it – it was only an honest answer to the question – but Dani felt the words like a sharp elbow dug into her side, as though they suggested that she had gone wrong somewhere.

'I've tried everything with Layla. Crying it out, comforters, co-sleeping… nothing seems to work.'

Elaine rolled her eyes.

'What?' Dani asked with a small smile, knowing her admissions were about to be met with scepticism.

'There's too much pressure now for everything to be a certain way. As though there's some sort of one-size-fits-all solution to everything. I've got three boys, and they all survived without Google telling me how long they should be sleeping, or where they should be doing it. I reckon that's the problem these days, you know – there's too much pressure on parents to be everything. Especially mothers. You should be doing this in this way, you should be doing that in that way… it's all crap, as far as I'm concerned. Every kid is different. No one knows a child the way its mother does.' She stopped and turned her head, giving a not-so-subtle nod to the women at the other side of the room. 'Too many experts in everything these days. I blame the internet.'

She concluded her speech with a celebratory sip of tea, and Dani cast a glance at Adele. This was what she loved about Elaine.

She was the sort of woman she wished her mother was: honest and surprise-free.

'How old is Ivy?' she asked.

'Twenty months.'

'She's so pretty.'

And she really was – it wasn't said just to be nice, in the way that people often did when there was a child involved. The little girl was genuinely beautiful. Big blue eyes and a mass of white-blonde curls, the kind of face used to advertise no-tears shampoo.

'Do you live local then?' Elaine asked Adele.

'Not too far, but there don't seem to be many groups for toddlers over our way.'

They chatted a while longer, and then it was time for art and crafts, which involved a ten-minute break from the toys and a chance for the children to cause as much chaos and mess as possible. At the end of the session, after they'd helped pack everything away, Dani collected their jackets and retrieved Layla's personalised drink bottle from underneath a chair. She was zipping Layla into her coat when Adele came over to say goodbye. Ivy was wrapped up snugly in a thick winter jacket that looked as though it had cost more than Dani's entire outfit.

'See you next week?' Adele asked, tightening her grip on her daughter's hand as Ivy tried to pull her towards the door.

'Yeah, we'll be here.'

Adele put her free hand in her pocket, then let go of Ivy's hand to drop her bag down her shoulder. 'Ivy, wait a minute, please.' She crouched to unzip the bag before rummaging through its contents. 'Not again,' she mumbled.

'Everything okay?' Dani asked.

'I can't find my phone. I'm always doing this. Well, I say *I…*' She gestured to Ivy, who was now amusing herself by trying to pull a sticker from the back of one of the chairs. 'She's fascinated with the thing. I should keep it out of reach.'

'Have you had it since you got here?'

'I don't know. I used it on the bus, but…' Adele stood as she gave up her search. 'Great. I've probably left it there.'

'Do you want me to call it for you?' Dani offered. 'Just in case?'

'Would you mind?' Adele waited for Dani to retrieve her phone, then recited her mobile number. A moment later they heard ringing from somewhere at the back of the room. The phone was behind one of the chairs, underneath a radiator.

'Must have fallen out of your pocket,' Dani said. 'Panic over.'

'Thank you so much. I'm sorry… we've held you up now.'

'It's no problem.'

'It was nice to meet you. Say bye, Ivy.'

The little girl waved, and Dani prompted Layla to wave back.

After leaving the church, Dani managed to get her daughter to walk most of the way home. It was only as they turned onto their street that she realised she had forgotten to pick up her mother's cigarettes. She would say nothing and wait for her to mention it. Perhaps Caroline would realise Dani's forgetfulness had inadvertently done her a favour.

She set Layla down on the doorstep as she searched in her jacket pocket for her key. 'Come on,' she said, 'let's get you some dinner.'

TWO

ADELE

Adele left the playgroup feeling better than she had in weeks, possibly months. She knew she should have done this a long time ago, and she felt a sadness for the time she had wasted, just a little more to be added to all the time in her life that had been lost to the worry of everything that might go wrong. Simply being out of the house and around people had made her feel as though anything was possible. She had grown too set in her ways, fearing the unknown and dreading the uncertainty of change, but the world seemed less frightening when she was in it, amid people. Perhaps she wouldn't have to hide herself away any more. This feeling of possibility had been unfamiliar to her for quite some time, and she wanted to hold onto it, to embrace all the what-ifs the future might hold.

On the bus on their way home, Ivy reached for her hand. It felt warm and comforting pressed against her own, the child's skin offering safety, as though transferring to Adele a reassurance that everything was going to be all right. For a moment, she allowed herself to believe the silent promise. Maybe it wouldn't happen yet, but yes, everything *was* going to be all right.

They got off at the bus stop nearest home and walked through the village, along a high street characterised by Victorian buildings and independent shops that sold hand-stitched clothing and locally produced cheese, a small block of which cost more than some people earned in an hour. Coxton was fifteen miles east of Cardiff, popular with wealthy city workers who didn't want to live amid the noise and bustle of the capital, and families who sought a slice of rural living without being too remote. The high street was lined with bunting, though Adele wasn't sure why: there had been no street party, no festival; it was a permanent decoration, as though the community was in a constant state of celebration. She supposed that living in such an affluent area merited this level of optimism for some, but the feeling had yet to reach her. This place would never be home.

Ivy wriggled in her pushchair, pulling it to the left, distracted by something in one of the shop windows. The shop was called Katie's Keepsakes, and the item that had caught her attention was a beautiful hand-made rag doll wearing a patchwork dress, its brown hair gathered in plaits at either side of its head and tied in little red bows. Adele would usually have pushed the pram onwards, but something about the doll made her stop, and for a moment she was oblivious to Ivy's increasingly fractious desire to free herself from the straps.

She was tempted to buy the doll for Ivy to take home with her, tucking it into her cot with her before she went to sleep that night, but she knew that doing so would mean having to explain to Callum that they had been out that morning. She might be able to keep the doll hidden for a while, but Ivy would slip up sooner or later and mention it. Though it was beautiful, it wasn't worth the risk of being caught out. Adele placed a hand to the window, her fingertips resting lightly against the glass. A moment later she noticed the shopkeeper watching her, and she hurried away, grateful when Ivy didn't kick up a fuss about going home empty-handed.

Three roads from the high street, she stopped on the pavement a few doors down from the house, tilting the pushchair's front wheels from the ground slightly as Ivy lunged forward to try to free herself from the buckles locking her in. Callum's car was parked outside. He was never usually home early on a Friday – if anything, she could count on it being the day he would be late home – and she knew that when she and Ivy got into the house, he would be there waiting for her, wondering where they had been. She wished she could turn around, take Ivy to the park or to a café for ice cream – take her anywhere – but as she glanced at her watch, she realised there was no escaping what waited indoors. The longer she was out, the worse his reaction was likely to be.

The house was a five-bedroom detached, with a double garage attached to the left and a large front garden that someone else was paid to tend to. The cars were always kept on the driveway, the garage converted into a gym where Callum spent much of his time in the evenings and at weekends. There were only four other houses on the street, which was part of an exclusive modern development less than ten years old. Adele imagined that for many people this chunk of elite suburbia represented success, the street name alone offering a status that only money could buy. But what lay behind closed doors was often unrecognisable from the facade on display for the eyes of the outside world.

Once they were inside, she took Ivy out of the pushchair and collapsed it, propping it in the corner of the hallway. Ivy rushed into the living room, and Adele followed her. Callum was there, his iPad resting on his lap and a bottle of beer clutched in his hand. She was tempted to point out that it was barely midday, but she said nothing. She wouldn't be thanked for expressing an opinion, in the same way she was never thanked for anything else.

'Dadda!' Ivy rushed to him, falling into his lap and wrapping her arms around his waist, and Adele felt a burning rush of jealousy race through her. She was relieved that Ivy's speech seemed a little slow, having yet to surpass 'mama', 'dadda' and 'doggy', but she knew she didn't have long before the little girl would be able to say more. Once Ivy's communication skills improved, their trips out would be limited. She was living on borrowed time.

Callum squeezed Ivy in an embrace and waited until she was distracted by one of her toys before he turned back to Adele and asked where she had been.

'There was no milk,' she stuttered.

He eyed her for too long, the look making her uncomfortable. 'So where is it then?'

'Where's what?'

'The milk.'

She didn't reply quickly enough. Her thoughts flitted to the rag doll in the shop window, grateful that she had resisted the temptation to buy it. He would probably have hidden it somewhere or binned it when Ivy wasn't looking, just to spite her. 'They'd run out of blue top. Ivy needs the blue top.'

Callum's eyes were cold. She assumed some women might find them attractive – she might even have thought so herself when they had met years earlier – but once you looked at them for longer than a glance, you could see the steeliness beyond the grey, the unforgiving nature of his stare when anyone attempted to cross him.

'I told you not to take her anywhere.'

'She needed milk,' Adele repeated, trying to keep her voice steady. 'I couldn't leave her here while I went to the shop, could I?'

Callum couldn't find out that she had taken Ivy to a playgroup. Fortunately, the church hall was far enough away from home to make it unlikely that anyone they knew would see her there. Callum had made his boundaries clear, set out the rules that she was to follow, and she knew she had to live by them if she was to move on from this place. He was trying to keep Ivy from her as much as he was able, though it was impossible for him to exercise the full control he desired. She was determined not to let him win, even if it meant swallowing her pride and doing as she was told, for the time being at least.

'Ivy, what do you want for your dinner?' he asked, getting up from his chair and putting his beer on the coffee table.

'I can do that.'

He thrust out a hand and Adele took a step back. 'I'm doing it,' he said without looking at her, and she watched as Ivy followed him into the kitchen like a puppy that had just heard the word 'treat'. She wondered what he would throw into the oven for her – something beige from the freezer, no doubt. Adele knew how to look after Ivy properly, but the silent power-struggle that played out in the house always saw her on the losing side, and there was nothing she could do about it.

She went upstairs to the bedroom and closed the door behind her, shutting herself into temporary solitude for a while. From the box in the wardrobe that had once been home to a job lot of instant noodles – one of the boxes that had been used to transport her life to this place – she took out the pink baby blanket and held it to her face, breathing in the new-skin smell that she imagined still clung to the fibres. She had meant to buy something nicer in which to store these keepsakes – one of those boxes with the lined insides that would keep everything smelling fresh and new – but as with so many other things, she had never got around to it. The memories deserved something better than this. They deserved something better than her.

She took out her phone and searched for the last number to have called her. Dani's. *Hi Dani*, she tapped out in a text message. *I hope you don't mind me saving your number, but I just wanted to say thanks again for earlier. I'm a nightmare with this phone! Anyway, Ivy loved playgroup and so did I. Maybe if you're free one week we could go for a coffee or something afterwards? Adele x*

She put the phone to one side and sat cross-legged on the carpet as she looked through the photographs from the box, needing them to remind herself of a time when everything was better, happier, and the future looked so different. It didn't seem long ago that things were unrecognisable, and yet it was somehow a lifetime away – someone else's life – and she felt herself caught between the future and the past, fearful of one and reluctant to let go of the other. That corner of the bedroom – that patch of carpet, that box – had become her safe place, somewhere she returned to when she found herself unable to make sense of the world. It never kept her protected for long, but she held onto it while she could, wilfully fooling her brain with the belief that if she just kept sitting there, she might be able to rewind time.

She stayed upstairs long enough for Ivy's dinner to have cooked and for Callum to have fed her. She had a message back from Dani – *Sounds great, would love to x* – and though it was short, it offered her hope. At some point – she wasn't sure what time it was – she heard footsteps on the stairs, the bathroom door, then Callum whistling, his exaggerated show of happiness an attempt to unsettle her and remind her who was in charge. He could have used the downstairs bathroom; he had only gone up there to remind her of his presence and to reinforce her place. He was making her feel suffocated, and she knew she would never be able to call this place her home. It was never meant to be that way, but for a time she had allowed herself to believe the possibility of it. She had no idea where she would go when all this came to an end, but she was certain of one thing: she had to get out of that house.

THREE

DANI

That evening, after reading Layla a story and settling her in her cot, Dani lay in bed and once again read the report about Eve's death, pausing after each sentence as though there might have been something she had missed the first time around, and the second, and the third. She had read it so many times already that she could probably have repeated it without looking at the screen, yet it still hadn't sunk in. She hadn't messaged Kelly Thompson back. It was difficult to know what to say. *Thanks for letting me know she's dead* didn't sound right. A bit abrupt, really, given the circumstances.

She went downstairs and put the kettle on. She made two cups of tea and took one through to the living room for her mother, who was sitting on the sofa watching television. Caroline was wearing a dressing gown that appeared to have come off worse in an encounter with Layla's dinner, the look added to by the smear of dark make-up under her left eye. For someone who took such diligent pride in the upkeep of her house, she was surprisingly relaxed about her own appearance.

Dani put the tea on the side table.

'Look at the state of that,' Caroline said, gesturing to the TV, where a middle-aged man with a balding head and a thick northern accent was grappling with a shortbread castle and a turret that refused to stay upright. 'Have you ever seen such a waste of time?

And ingredients, come to that. As if anyone's going to eat it now his sweaty mitts have been all over it.'

'Nice to have a hobby, though,' Dani mused as she sat in the chair opposite.

'Faffing about with pastry? I think I'd rather be bored.'

Dani bit her tongue. She had commented enough in the past on her mother's lack of interest in anything, and it had only ever led to arguments. Since Dani's dad had died, her mother had decided to shut herself off from the world. She seemed happy to spend all her time in the house, rarely going out and seeing people. It wasn't healthy, and the longer it went on, the more Dani worried about her.

They sat in silence and drank their tea, watching as the balding man's reign came to an end and he was eliminated from the competition along with his crumbling shortbread fortress. 'Right, I'm off to bed,' Caroline announced as soon as the programme's theme music kicked in, despite the fact that it was only just nine o'clock. 'Night.'

It occurred to Dani that in the forty minutes they'd spent together, she and her mother had spoken barely a handful of sentences to each other. This was nothing new, though that evening the silence had seemed somehow louder than ever before. She wondered what other mothers and daughters talked about. There was never much to say really – nothing exciting ever happened at work, and as Caroline saw Layla daily, she never needed updating about how she was doing. All the same, it seemed a bit of a waste, as though one of them – both, probably – should have been making more of an effort.

She waited until Caroline had brushed her teeth and was in her room before heading upstairs herself. Half an hour after turning off the light, though, she still hadn't found sleep. She felt the beginnings of a headache twitch at her temples, so she got up to fetch a glass of water. On her way back upstairs, a noise burst from the back bedroom. Layla was screaming again. It would have woken Dani if she hadn't already been up; it was loud enough to wake half the street.

When she went into the bedroom, Layla's blankets were shoved down the end of the cot and her little face was scrunched into a red ball. Dani climbed in with her. She'd done this before, though the first time she'd got herself stuck and had had to call for her mother to help her out. Since then she'd mastered a way to curl her body around Layla's so they both somehow had enough room. As soon as she felt Dani next to her, Layla stopped screaming and her little body shuddered with sobs. Dani didn't know what was causing these sudden disruptions to her sleep – someone at playgroup had mentioned night terrors, which she had never heard of before – but whatever it was, she hoped the phase passed as quickly as it had arrived.

She lay in the dark and tried not to think, which was far harder than it sounded. The more she tried not to think, the more thinking she did, until she trapped herself in a vicious circle that took her around and around. She felt the tiny cupboard that was Layla's bedroom close in on her, becoming even smaller. When Dani was little, her mother used to call this her dressing room – as though she was some sort of relation to the royal family or a character from *Downton Abbey* – but it was mostly the room she came to when she wanted to smoke and couldn't go outside because it was raining. For years the yellowing of the paint from the smoke fumes was visible in patches on the Artex ceiling, but Dani had redecorated when she was pregnant. Pastel pink for a baby girl, because she knew that Layla would be a girl even before the snooty cow of a sonographer confirmed it for her. Her daughter would be her new best friend, her little sidekick.

The sonographer wasn't the only person who looked down their nose at Dani. The problem was, she was young, but she looked younger, like someone still in sixth form. 'First-world problems,' her mother always said, then rolled her eyes as though Dani was being unreasonable by moaning about her looks, but the truth was they had never done her any favours, not in a world where you were treated with more respect by adults if you actually looked like a grown-up yourself. She knew what people thought when they met her. Young single mum, still living with her own mother, handful of okay-ish GCSEs, A levels she had never put to any use; only a trainee hairdresser – not even the proper thing. Not like Eve. She'd been going places.

And now she was nowhere.

Dani wondered what death felt like. She wondered if Eve had known she was about to die – she must have, she supposed – and whether it felt like a physical pain or more of a psychological one, a kind of emotional torture at everything she would be leaving behind and all the things she hadn't yet done and seen. The thought made her pull Layla a little closer to her. The child shifted beneath the arm that Dani had curled around her and made a tiny mewling sound like a kitten. Running a hand over Layla's soft dark hair, Dani closed her eyes and finally fell into a fitful sleep.

She didn't know what time it was when she woke – the blackout blinds in Layla's room made it any time of day or night – but her neck was stiff, her back aching. The mattress in the cot was too hard; she would have to save for a new one, but by the time she had enough money for it, Layla would likely have outgrown the cot and would need a toddler bed, so there didn't really seem much point.

The thought of money turned her mind to work. She started at 9 a.m., and Tracy, the salon owner, had booked in a couple of clients with her that morning. Dani was still on a probation period, and Tracy was waiting for her to mess up in some way, hoping for it even, so that getting rid of her would be easier and justified. Until recently, Dani had made the teas and coffees, washed hair and swept up other people's mess, but when she had accepted the job she had made it clear that she wanted to work her way up to stylist. It didn't look likely that would happen on Tracy's watch, though Dani had learned not to look too far into the future in a world that was prone to throwing up the unexpected.

Layla had woken and was staring at her silent and wide-eyed. Dani stared back, then pulled a face, and Layla started giggling, wriggling beneath the covers and climbing over Dani to try to get out of the cot. Dani pulled herself out first, then picked out an outfit from one of the drawers before taking Layla into her own bedroom. She had a collection of toys on top of her wardrobe that would be produced in stages during her morning ritual of shower, face, hair. It had taken her a while, but she had finally worked out a method that allowed her to get ready for work while Layla entertained herself. She passed her a flip-the-page book and the dog that talked and sang when you pressed its paws, then went to the bathroom and turned on the shower.

As she waited for the water to heat up, she stood outside her mother's bedroom door and pressed her ear to the wood. At that time of day, Caroline was either still sleeping or playing games on her phone, and Dani could always work out which because she never turned the sound down, so there was always this annoying jingly-jangly sound that she could hear through the wall.

She showered quickly – she hadn't enjoyed a relaxing shower or a soak in the bath since before giving birth – and when she got back to the bedroom, Layla's interest in the book and dog had waned and she had made her way dangerously close to Dani's make-up bag.

'I'll have that, thanks.' Dani swiped it from her reach, and Layla started to cry; moments later, Dani heard her mother's bedroom door open and a mumbled comment that was obviously intended to be heard. She grabbed another toy and thrust it in Layla's direction, but her daughter rejected it, choosing instead to throw herself onto the bed and continue her strop there.

She sighed. She needed to do her hair, but when she checked her phone, it was already 8.20. She never went to work without having done her hair properly first; she thought it equivalent to being an overweight dietician – if her own hair looked crap, why should anyone trust her to do a decent job with theirs? She wanted people to take her seriously, not think she was just some tea-making, minimum-wage skivvy unworthy of their attention.

'Dani!'

She swore beneath her breath and went out onto the landing. Caroline had left the stairgate open again, despite the number of times Dani had asked her to shut it behind her. She was just waiting for the day Layla took a tumble down the full flight, but no doubt her mother would find a way to make it somehow Dani's fault.

'What? I'm going to be late for work.'

Her mother was standing at the bottom of the stairs in her dressing gown, a sheet of paper in her hand. 'What the hell's this?' she asked, waving it about as though Dani could see the other side of it.

'I don't know, do I. What is it?'

'You'd better take a look.'

Dani sighed again. She could really have done without this, whatever *this* was. She probably wouldn't have time to eat anything now before she left the house.

She snatched the paper from her mother, impatient to get on, but as soon as she looked at it, she wished she hadn't been so hasty. She would have liked to be able to go back upstairs, get back into Layla's cot, flip a switch and start the morning all over again. The page was a flyer, printed on good-quality paper. On it, there was a photograph of her – the photo used as her Instagram profile picture. It had been taken before she was pregnant, on a night out with some of the girls she used to work with. Dani had never liked having her photograph taken – her nose always looked too big and too wonky and her skin shone no matter how much make-up she put on – but she had always quite liked this one. Maybe not so much any more.

Above the photo, printed in bold red lettering, was a single word: SLAG.

FOUR

ADELE

Adele and her sister, Steph, sat in the kitchen drinking tea and eating the lemon drizzle cake Adele had made the previous afternoon, while Ivy played out in the garden with her father. The doors that led from the kitchen opened out onto a large patio area, followed by a long lawn that to the little girl must have seemed the size of a football pitch. Not yet two, she already had a slide and a swing set, a Wendy house and a sandpit – a child's Christmas wish list provided in an instant.

This was the type of Saturday morning Adele had once longed for: a lazy breakfast in bed, the whip of a May breeze catching at the curtains, the sound of a child's laughter dancing in the spring air. Home baking and endless pots of tea. Later, a walk through the woods before heading home for dinner. These things had existed in her mind as an ideal before landing in her life as a reality, yet once they were with her, none of it looked as she had imagined.

Callum had barely spoken to her all morning, sidestepping her when he came into the kitchen to make himself a coffee and refusing a slice of cake when it was offered to him, as though she might have laced it with something debilitating and permanent. Every time he spoke to Ivy, it seemed he was yet again reinforcing everything Adele didn't have and would remain forever lacking.

'Come here, Daddy's girl. Let's go and play in the garden.'

Not meant for Ivy at all. A reminder to Adele that the child was his. She watched him guide her up the steps of the slide, his hand on her back to steady her, and she resented him more than ever. This was all a show, a performance of the doting father role; once Steph had gone, he would be back to his usual habits of scrolling on his phone and checking his hair in the nearest reflective item he could find.

'It's lovely,' Steph said, licking a smear of icing from the edge of her thumb. 'Even better than the caramel slices, if that's possible.'

Adele had read somewhere that baking was a form of therapy, and her sister had become her main taste-tester. It was true – it was relaxing and gave her something to focus on so she was able to keep her mind from other things, but Steph had joked that if she kept eating everything her sister made, she was going to end up the size of a house. Adele had bought some little gift boxes and some ribbon, boxing up cupcakes and brownies to give to the neighbours as an 'I'm new here' offering – and yet she saw the way Callum regarded her efforts, making snide remarks to suggest she was wasting her time.

'You're trying too hard,' he had told her. 'You look desperate.'

Of course he didn't say these things when anyone else was around to hear them, and he would never have said anything in front of Steph. He tried to keep what and who he really was hidden from her, but Adele felt sure it was only a matter of time before her sister saw him for what he really was.

She glanced again to the patio doors, through which they could see Callum and Ivy now chasing a ball around the garden. Ivy tried to kick it, stumbled into it, lost her balance and fell onto the grass. Callum followed, faking a tumble of his own, and the two of them lay laughing on the lawn, the sound dancing in through the open window like clocks swept in on a breeze from a blown dandelion. It should have been lovely, yet Adele couldn't smile at the scene in the way Steph did.

Was it possible for a person to be two conflicting things? Could someone really be a loving father and a disloyal husband? Could they truly be good *and* bad?

'You two okay now?' Steph asked.

Adele shrugged. She didn't want to say too much; didn't want to give Steph cause for concern. She was grateful for everything her sister had already done, trying to prop her up when she needed it most, but there was only so much help she was able to give. Steph hadn't always been there for her. There had been a time when she had been resentful of Adele, jealous of everything her sister had, but after a distanced period when they had communicated only when it was necessary, they had managed to build bridges. Time apart from one another had been good for their relationship, despite the circumstances.

'He can be hot-headed. He'll get over it.'

Though he hid his disdain for the most part, the previous week it had been obvious to everyone that Callum and Adele had argued. It had started over a set of keys, escalating from the trivial to the major in the way so many arguments seemed to. Callum hadn't been able to find his car keys; Adele had tidied them away, in the place that as far as she could tell was the intended location for keys. Why else have one of those wooden key hooks nailed to the wall in the hallway? Rather than respond like a normal person and thank her for tidying up after him, Callum reacted by telling her that she always interfered, that he couldn't breathe around her, which seemed ironic when that was exactly how he made her feel.

'How's the job hunting going?'

She'd known Steph would ask. It had been weeks since they'd last had the conversation, and she wondered whether Callum had put her sister up to it. Adele needed a job – she needed to get out of the house and be around other people more. She understood all that, but knowing it and actually doing it were two very different things, and she still didn't feel ready to throw herself back into the kind of environment in which all her flaws and inabilities would make themselves instantly known.

'I've applied for a few things,' she said, knowing that it sounded too vague and Steph was likely to probe further.

Steph raised her eyebrows, waiting for the details.

'There's a job going in the library in town. I've sent in an application form.'

'Well that's a good start,' she said, but her face said something different, something Adele found pitying and patronising. She had a degree, a background in nursing, but Steph tended to ignore the fact that she also had a big gap in her employment history and too many things she would have to explain away to any potential employer.

'I think I'd enjoy it,' she went on, forcing a cheery smile. 'I'd get to meet new people, possibly make friends… it could be just what I need.'

Steph smiled, but it looked insincere. It was okay for her, Adele thought; she had a solid career, a job as a producer with the BBC, and whenever a door had looked as though it was about to close on her, another had always made itself instantly apparent, flung wide open with a smiling face there to greet her and welcome her inside.

'Actually,' Adele added, 'I might have made a friend already.'

'Good. Who is it?'

'No one you know.'

'How did you meet her? I'm assuming it's a woman?'

'It is,' Adele said, picking at her cake. 'And I met her at church.'

Steph laughed. Its tinkle evaporated as she realised her sister wasn't joking. 'Sorry. It's just you've never been the church-going type.'

'Isn't it you who's always telling me to try something new?'

Adele was sure that when Steph had said as much, attending church had been as far from her mind as the idea of cliff diving, but there was something satisfying in watching the confusion that played out on her sister's face. She pushed the cake around her plate, aware that Steph's focus was resting on her.

'There's something up,' Steph said, tilting her head to study Adele's expression. 'Come on. You've been quiet for days. What is it?'

'I didn't realise I was usually loud.' Adele smiled. Steph had always been the exuberant one, confident and outspoken even as a young child. Adele was more withdrawn, the thinker of the two sisters. In recent years, people had used the fact against her, as though being quiet was an indication of being secretive, and that being secretive meant she couldn't be trusted.

Steph sighed. 'You don't always have to do that, you know. Pretend that everything's okay. I know when it's not.'

How wrong she was, Adele thought. No one could know, not really. There were plenty of times when even Adele herself hadn't realised the extent of just how not-okay things were for her, and by the time she *had* known, it had been too late to do anything about it. Steph would never understand how different Adele's life was to her own, and even if she could see, Adele suspected she would choose to remain blind to it.

'You don't have to be defined by what's happened,' Steph said, sounding like an amateur psychologist. She glanced at the door, and at Callum, who was still playing with Ivy in the garden. 'You can get through it. You're stronger than you realise.'

'Am I, though?'

There was a part of Adele that wanted to confide in Steph – to tell her everything she had been storing in her heart and in her head; all the secrets that, once out, would change everything forever – and yet she couldn't. There were certain things she had to deal with alone, and this would be another of them.

'What are you two plotting?' Callum asked, stamping his feet at the patio doors to shake off the grass stuck to his shoes. Behind him, Ivy was sitting on the patio slabs, tired from all the running around and now contentedly amusing herself with a Moses basket and a doll that required tucking beneath its blanket.

His tone was heavier than the question, and Adele heard through it, though Steph seemed oblivious to its intention to unsettle them.

'World domination,' Steph said with a wink. 'The Harper sisters take control… now there's a thought.'

Callum stood at the sink and filled a glass with cold water, his back turned to them. 'Once a Harper sister, always a Harper sister, is it?' He turned and caught Adele's eye, challenging her. He was threatened by the two of them together, and the thought filled her momentarily with something that felt a little like reassurance.

'Exactly,' she said flatly, holding his eye. Say something, she thought, willing him to contradict her. But he wouldn't. Not in front of Steph.

When he left the kitchen and went off to the garage, bored with playing with his daughter, Steph put a hand over Adele's. 'Whatever it is you're worrying about, stop. Things will get better, I promise.'

Adele at once admired and loathed her sister's optimism. It was naïve and built on weakened foundations, ones that would topple with the slightest nudge. Just yesterday, on the bus with Ivy, she had allowed herself to believe that things would get better, but the truth was, they had gone too far for that. She was trapped in her life, imprisoned by all the things she had allowed it to become. Revenge had come to consume her.

She couldn't forgive, and she wouldn't forget.

FIVE

DANI

Dani felt her stomach flip. 'Has this just been put through the door?' she asked, checking the pockets of the jacket that hung on the stair post, scrabbling about for the set of keys she had left somewhere. She found them and pushed past her mother, her shaky hands fumbling to fit the key into the lock.

'I don't know; it was there when I came down.'

There was no one on the street outside. Dani's heart was pounding so hard it was painful – the simmering anger beginning to rise to a bubble – and when one of the neighbours opposite opened his front door to throw something in the recycling bin, she turned and hurried back inside.

'What the hell is this about then?' Caroline asked.

'I don't know, do I.'

Dani went back upstairs and quickly applied some make-up, knowing she wouldn't have time to do her hair properly. Layla was unusually quiet, amusing herself with the flip-page book she had not long ago lost interest in, and Dani hoped that today might be one of the rare days she was able to leave the house without her daughter having a meltdown. On days when Layla didn't have nursery, Dani felt guilty about leaving her with Caroline. Her mother did nothing except shove her in front of the TV, but what choice did Dani have?

Back downstairs, she stuck a piece of bread in the toaster. While she put on her shoes and jacket, she wondered who was responsible for the flyer. It seemed a lot of trouble for someone to go to, a lot of expense, too – it was professionally printed, not just produced using someone's home computer. She glanced at the word again before ripping the flyer up and putting it in the recycling bin. There was only one person who would have done this, who would have used that word to describe her. She supposed she had always been waiting for something like this to happen; it was just a matter of time before the other woman came looking for her.

At the smell of burning, she swore and rushed back to the kitchen, where smoke was rising from the toaster. She pressed the button, shooting out a charred piece of bread that she threw into the sink, leaving it there for Caroline to deal with. She said nothing as she left the house, but made sure to slam the front door behind her, letting her mother know she had gone. Her stomach rumbled with hunger, but she didn't take any notice of it, not with everything else that was filling her head.

She hadn't even made it as far as the end of the street when she saw another flyer, its text and picture the same, taped to a lamp post. Her heart hammered in her chest – posting something through her door was one thing but taping it somewhere public for everyone to see crossed a whole different boundary. She ripped the flyer down, her fingernails scratching at the sticky tape as she checked her surroundings to make sure no one was watching her, then balled it in her fist and turned onto the main road. There was another. And another. There were suddenly too many people around, as though they had all been waiting for her to arrive. She knew she was being paranoid, and that probably no one was looking at her, but she couldn't get away from there fast enough. There was no time to take the others down, not without drawing attention to herself, so she started to run, and by the time she reached the salon, she was a sweaty mess, her already bedraggled hair clinging to the back of her neck, and her face red.

The salon was in the middle of the estate, which had the ironic name of Greenfields. There was no green field to be found for a mile, and even that was small and only existed as an extension of the playground. Half the shops in the row had closed over the past few years. The tattoo parlour was still going, and there was a Greggs and a dentist's surgery, but the three other premises had to-let boards above the signs showing the names of the former businesses. As she rushed into the salon, Dani managed to bump into the umbrella stand that stood by the door, the clattering of her entrance drawing the attention of her boss, who was sitting behind the reception desk talking to someone on her mobile.

Tracy looked at her as though she was sucking on something sour before ending her call. 'We need to talk.'

She ushered Dani to the back of the salon, to the storeroom where supplies were kept. The grimace she wore was impressive even for someone who spent most of her time looking as though she had just opened a tax bill.

'Have you seen these?' She pulled a handful of flyers from the shelving unit behind her. Dani's heart plummeted in her chest. Whoever had put those flyers about had kept themselves busy making sure nowhere was missed.

'I had to take six of them off the front window this morning.'

Dani felt her face burning and rage building in her chest. This was the last thing she needed when Tracy was already looking for an opportunity to get rid of her.

'What's it about, then?'

'I don't know,' she lied. Maybe it was only a half-lie. She had a suspicion but couldn't be sure, and the only way to know for certain would involve looking for the truth, something she didn't really want to do.

Tracy raised a cynical eyebrow. 'This isn't great for business.'

'I'm sorry,' Dani said, though apologising for something she wasn't directly responsible for nearly choked her.

'Try to keep your personal life at home.' And with that, Tracy turned and strutted back into the salon, tottering on her stupid heels like some matriarchal soap landlady. Dani wanted to shout something after her, to tell her that she could shove her job, but she needed the money, and anyway, she wasn't sure who else would have her.

She wondered what she was like, the other woman. She didn't know her name – she had never wanted to know anything about the wife that had been kept secret from her – she just knew she existed, like some mythical character who was real but not, unseen and therefore invisible. In a way, Dani pictured her a bit like Tracy. Impatient. Full of herself. Maybe that was why her husband had gone looking for something elsewhere, and Dani was the unlucky one he had landed his sights on. She felt instantly ashamed of the thought. Whoever was in the wrong in all this, it wasn't his wife, although thinking badly of her offered a momentary distraction from Dani's own guilt. Maybe she was nothing like Tracy. Maybe she was just nice, normal – the kind of woman Dani might get on with if she wasn't also the type to post flyers of her around her home town so that everyone knew just what she was. A roll of nausea twisted in her stomach. She hadn't known he was married, though that didn't change the facts of what had happened.

During her break, she took her phone to the toilet, where she locked herself in and ran an internet search for James. She didn't hold out much hope of finding him. Whenever curiosity had got the better of her before, nothing had come up in the search. She suspected he had lied about his name; after all, he had lied about everything else – where he lived, where he worked, being single. If she could find him, she would be able to find his wife. The irony had been that in finding out she had been lied to, she had learned nothing. At the time, she hadn't wanted to know any more; she had only wanted to be as far away from him as possible.

The truth had come from James's friend, and now Dani realised she couldn't even remember his name. In bed with the man she had begun to imagine a possible future with, she hadn't been anticipating someone else walking into the room. The man who really lived there, who clearly didn't appreciate James using his house as a base for a sordid affair. An argument between the two men had quickly escalated. Had James even mentioned his friend's name? She replayed the moment, hating every inch of the memory, yet this detail continued to elude her. Frustrated and no closer to answers, she returned to the salon to finish her shift.

After work she went to the tattoo parlour two doors down from the salon, hoping that Travis, the owner, would be there. She stood outside on her lunch break sometimes, usually the day after pay day, when she would treat herself to an end-of-the-month iced slice from Greggs, daydreaming while she looked at the images that had been inked onto customers' bodies. Budgeting for everything meant there were limited funds for luxuries; once Dani had paid Caroline her rent and food money, she had to make a couple of hundred pounds last her the rest of the month, and with Layla seeming to shift up a shoe size every few weeks, she had to find ways to make the money stretch. An iced slice was a treat; a tattoo was an extravagance she couldn't imagine ever being able to afford.

There was no one in the front of the shop, so she assumed that Travis was with a customer in the back room. She was sure he could see her; he had CCTV that showed him when someone entered the shop. The thought that he might be watching her made her self-conscious, and she distracted herself by looking at the montage of photographs pinned to the wall, a kaleidoscope of patterns, shapes and colour created by Travis's hands. For a moment that made her blush, she allowed herself to imagine what those hands might feel like on her skin.

The door to the back room opened and a customer stepped out, closely followed by Travis. He was wearing his trademark hooded sweater with the shop name printed on the left-hand side.

'All right, Dani,' he said, his smile suggesting he'd already known she was there. 'Be with you now.'

She waited as the customer passed him a handful of notes and waited for his change. Travis must have been somewhere in his thirties, but Dani wasn't sure which end; she guessed early, but experience had proved her useless at judging people's ages. She had always been attracted to older men, and she realised what a psychologist would make of it.

'Thanks, mate,' he said, waiting for the man to leave before turning to her. 'Dani. What can I do for you?'

His tattoo sleeve, awash with colour, caught her eye, and she looked away as though he might be able to read what she was thinking, as though her inappropriate thoughts were writing themselves across her forehead in permanent marker.

'Actually, I need to ask you a favour.'

'Depends what it is.'

'You've got CCTV, haven't you?'

'I have, yes.' His mouth twisted into an awkward smile, and she sensed what he was about to say. 'This about those pictures up on the salon window?'

She had hoped that Tracy had reached the salon before anyone else had arrived at work that morning, sparing her the embarrassment of having to explain the flyers away. 'Yeah. Look...'

'No one believes it. And those who do don't matter.'

Dani appreciated the kindness, but it made her feel even more uncomfortable than she already was.

'You want me to see if I can spot who put them up?'

'I mean, if you could just send me the footage, that'd be a massive help.'

He nodded. 'You'll have to give me a bit of time. Do you need to rush off?'

She shook her head.

'I've just stuck the kettle on if you fancy a coffee?'

'Thanks, that'd be lovely.'

He disappeared for a few minutes before returning with two mugs and his laptop. 'Who have you pissed off then?' he asked as he passed her a coffee.

'Ask me who I haven't, it'll be quicker,' she joked, masking her anxiety beneath a facade of nonchalance. She knew very well who she had upset, but she wasn't going to admit it to him. Her past was something she had tried to abandon.

She sipped her coffee as she waited for him to access the recordings.

'Seriously, though, you should report it to the police.'

'Yeah, I suppose so,' she said, though there was no way she was going to do that. She would deal with this herself, and anyway, she wasn't even convinced that what the woman had done was a crime. Mean, yes. Vindictive, definitely. Illegal… she wasn't so sure.

'Can I have your email address?'

'What?'

'Your email address. To send you the file.'

'Oh, yeah. Sorry.' She spelled the address out to him as he tapped it onto the keyboard.

'I never knew your surname was McNamara.'

'My grandfather was from Dublin.'

'Nice. You spent much time over there?'

'Never been.'

Travis stopped what he was doing and looked up from the laptop. 'No way? You should go. Nice people, great scenery, brilliant pubs.'

'Maybe one day.'

'There,' he said, pushing aside his laptop. 'Should come through any second now.'

Immediately there was a ping on Dani's phone, and she checked her emails.

'Got it. Thanks.'

'Do you want me to help you with this?'

'It's fine. Thanks, though.' She swallowed the last of the coffee before putting the mug down on his desk. In her hand, her phone pinged again. The message from an unknown number flashed up on the screen without her having to open it.

Enjoy getting your tattoo. I hope it's painful.

Without thinking, she hurried outside. The car park was busy, a few people loading bags into boots while other drivers waited for them to leave so they could take their spaces. She scanned the pavement for someone who might have been watching her. An elderly lady pushed a shopping trolley past Greggs, and a couple of teenage girls in school uniform were sitting on the low wall that divided the car park from the narrow grass border where the council had made a half-arsed attempt at growing flowers. They were looking down at a phone and laughing, and a wave of paranoia swept over Dani as she felt heat rise in her chest like a fever.

'Are you okay? You forgot this.'

Travis was standing behind her, holding the jacket she had left on the chair.

'Fine,' she said, taking it from him without making eye contact. 'Look… thanks for your help. I've got to go.'

SIX

ADELE

The rest of the weekend passed quietly, with Adele going about her daily chores as unassumingly as possible. On Sunday, Callum took Ivy to his mother's house. Adele tried to get out of the house whenever she could, and on the days that Ivy went to her grandmother's, she took long walks in the woodland that edged the village. The solitude of the place was punctuated at one point by a strip of the M4, and she had found a spot at which the two worlds existed in parallel: the humming, moving thread of motorway laced out in front of her; the still and soundless woodland behind.

Sitting in that special spot gave her plenty of time to think, though she had already done so much of that that thoughts had become her closest ally and her worst enemy. In a way, this place had come to mirror her existence: the quiet and the chaos; the moving and the inert. The before and after. Though she had accepted solitude as a lifestyle, she sometimes found herself wishing she had a friend, a real friend; someone she could talk to without fear of judgement or assumption. Sometimes it felt as though no one saw the world in the way she did, as though some shift in normal had occurred but no one had thought to notify her of it and now she lived there alone, isolated in the old world while the new one moved on and away from her.

Callum was becoming an obsession. She had never wanted it to happen, but the more she doubted him, the greater her fixation with his movements became. If he didn't already know that she was watching him, it would only be a matter of time. He was clever and calculating, and he hated anyone being a step ahead of him. He hated it especially when that person was Adele.

On Monday morning, he left the house in a hurry. She wasn't sure he had even eaten breakfast, and he had departed in such a state of urgency that he had left his phone in the bathroom, which seemed a strange place to have taken it – the kind of place he would go if he wanted to talk to someone privately or look at something he didn't want anyone else to see. She had heard him on the phone the previous night when he had thought everyone asleep. She had sat at the top of the stairs in her pyjamas and tried to listen to the conversation taking place behind the closed door of the living room, catching only snippets of a one-sided exchange.

'… can't wait any longer… need it now…'

A couple of years earlier, Callum had confessed to his infidelity under duress, in the way Adele imagined most affairs were admitted to. Of course, he never called it an affair: it was a 'one-off', which apparently was a much lesser marital offence and merited the expectation of a forgive-and-forget attitude akin to writing off a neglected anniversary. An email requesting that he leave a review of the Bristol hotel in which he had stayed on the night he had claimed to be in Swansea on a night out with work had popped up on his laptop, the evidence against him so damning that it had been impossible for him to do anything but tell the truth.

Adele saw through the subsequent excuses and lies, but she didn't have the energy to fight them alone. She spotted things he had hoped might go unnoticed: the stolen glances at his mobile, the telephone conversations at the bottom of the garden, the late evenings spent meeting deadlines. She knew he was doing it again, his ego overriding any judgement that might have tempted him to think twice. What could she do about it now? He had made it clear that she was powerless to change his behaviour, and there was part of her that was beginning to believe him.

She wondered if he had really gone to work that morning. People lied to their spouses every day, and there were plenty of cases in which wives had discovered that the man they loved and shared a home with had been living a different life with an entirely separate family, its existence concealed behind the pretence of a hectic work schedule. No one ever thought it would happen to them, which was presumably one of the reasons they didn't go in search of it.

Callum didn't have another family kept hidden away somewhere; he was too selfish for that. Working out and focusing on himself took up far too much of his time. A casual lover would be more his style, someone who had no expectations of him and didn't ask questions; someone he could pick up and put down as it suited him. Someone young and naïve. Someone happy to turn a blind eye. The thought sent a sliver of rage snaking through her. He was getting away with it. She was letting him.

In the bathroom, she slid his phone from the windowsill. It was unlocked. There had been a conversation about transparency, about not keeping anything hidden behind the shield of passwords and PINs, but she'd never for a moment thought he would stick to his promise. She went to the call log and looked for the last person he had rung. Diane. Her stomach flipped. She took no satisfaction in being right. Where were thoughts of Ivy in all this? One day she would be old enough to see things that for now she was blissfully oblivious to, and she would come to understand what went on in that house. What sort of man would she think her father? Did Ivy mean so little to him that he would risk everything for another cheap tart who would be gone from his life as quickly as she'd arrived?

With a shaking hand, she tapped the screen to call the number. She had to wait only a couple of rings before it was answered. It was impossible to tell anything about the woman from a single hello, but she imagined her to be young, attractive; probably brunette, which she assumed was his thing. Another one so soon? She felt her hand tightening around the phone, clutching it as though if she squeezed hard enough she might break the thing, crushing the other woman's existence with it.

'Callum?'

Adele moved the phone from her ear, cut the call. She stared at the screen, waiting to see whether Diane would ring back. She didn't. Had he told her he was married? Did she have any idea who she had got involved with? She went to the call log and deleted evidence of the outgoing call before returning the phone to the windowsill. There was always the possibility that this Diane would mention it to Callum when they next spoke, but she reassured herself with the thought that if there was nothing to prove the time of the call, there would be nothing to suggest any involvement on her part.

She started at a sound on the landing, turning as the bathroom door opened.

'Callum. I didn't hear you come back.'

He looked past her, seeing his mobile on the windowsill where he had left it. He had obviously remembered and returned for it.

'Everything okay?' she asked, forcing innocence into her voice.

'Where's Ivy?'

'Playing in her bedroom.'

He brushed past her as he reached for the phone, and she moved out of his way, not wanting to make contact. He sensed her back away, and in response he moved closer. His face was so close to hers that Adele could smell the toothpaste that lingered on his breath.

'Remember your place, Adele.'

He smiled, but the expression was devoid of any kindness. He pushed the phone into his pocket and moved away. When he turned back to her at the doorway, a silent message was delivered loud and clear so that she wouldn't mistake its meaning: he knew what she had been doing in there and what she was looking for.

She remained standing in the bathroom long after the front door had slammed behind him, alone and breathless with anger.

SEVEN

DANI

Dani spent the weekend with Layla, filling the time with normal things in an attempt to take her mind off the flyers that had been posted around town and the message she'd received while she had been talking to Travis. On Sunday morning they caught the bus into the city centre and went to the museum, where Layla made friends with a motorised woolly mammoth and cried when Dani had to carry her away from it to let other people get close. In typical Layla style, no distraction succeeded in abating the meltdown, and it was only when Dani found a melted and remoulded bar of chocolate stuffed at the bottom of the nappy bag that the tantrum subsided from window-shattering earthquake to minor tremor.

They had lunch in a café – a baked potato for Dani and fish fingers for Layla – and despite the normality of it all, Dani couldn't shake the feeling that they weren't alone. She found herself checking over her shoulder a couple of times in the museum, irrationally suspicious of people gazing idly at paintings and pulling faces at stuffed wildlife. At the bus stop, she distanced herself and Layla from the other passengers, uncomfortable at their closeness. She took a last glance behind her as they got on the bus to head home, as though a stalker would make him or herself known with a gesture to wave them off. She knew she was being irrational, and yet somehow her unease felt justified.

She had replied to the message she had been sent, and called the number, but both had gone ignored. She reminded herself that what had happened wasn't her fault. She hadn't known he was married, not until it was too late. Was his wife really responsible for the flyers and the text? If revenge was what she wanted, she was certainly doing a good job of unsettling her. Maybe she would finish there; perhaps this was just an attempt to make Dani feel uneasy, to remind her that her past was not quite as secret as she had hoped to keep it.

When Layla was asleep that evening, exhausted by the day's activities, Dani opened her emails and accessed the CCTV footage Travis had sent her. She had managed to delay looking at it until now, focusing on Layla as though she could pretend nothing and no one else existed, but she couldn't let go of the sense of injustice those flyers had inflicted upon her. If James's wife had set out to humiliate her, she had got what she'd wanted. Dani had never sought out the other woman online. Seeing her would have made it real. It would mean accepting that she was responsible for damaging a family, despite the fact that she'd had no idea she was doing so. When she'd found out she was pregnant, she had vowed never to look for the other woman, or to search for James again. They were nothing to her. She and Layla had all they needed. Now, she wished that she had seen her, just once, so she would know who she was looking for.

The camera was set up at the front of the building, with a clear view of anyone who passed the shop. She skipped through plenty of footage from Saturday morning, pausing the recording each time she caught a glimpse of life: a jogger out running while most people were still tucked up in bed, and a young woman who looked as though she was doing the walk of shame, a small handbag tucked under her arm and her legs exposed to the morning air. Then there was someone else, someone pushing a bike while carrying what looked like a large envelope.

She stopped the tape when he paused outside the tattoo parlour, and watched silently as he rested his bike against the locked shop door and taped something to the glass. Whoever he was, he was brazen enough to take a step back and tilt his head to one side as he appraised his handiwork. When Dani paused the recording, she got a good clear image of his face as he moved his focus to the designs on display in the window. He was about fifteen or sixteen, with dark hair and a pair of headphones hanging around his neck. He was wearing a grey hoodie, and jeans so tight they might have been painted on. She didn't recognise him.

She started at the sound of her bedroom door and flipped her laptop shut.

'Have you seen Dylan anywhere?'

'No.'

'Strange. He hasn't come back for his food.' Caroline glanced at the laptop. 'Is everything okay after yesterday?'

'Fine. Don't worry about it,' Dani said, eager to gloss over the subject of the flyers. 'Probably just a prank.' She hadn't told her mother about the text message. She didn't want to worry her, and she didn't want her to interfere. This was something she had to sort out for herself, and the less her mother knew the better.

Caroline looked sceptical. 'Who would think that's funny, though?'

'I don't know. But I said it's fine, Mum. Don't worry about it… I'm not.'

Her mother raised an eyebrow. 'You should go the police with it.'

'What for? They won't do anything.'

'You know best,' she said, holding up her hands in mock defence. With a tut she made no effort to conceal, she closed the door behind her.

Dani lifted the laptop lid and held her phone up to take a photo of the image, checking the quality of

She might be making a mistake, but she was already beyond caring what people might think of her, so she uploaded the image to her Facebook page, with a status that read, *Anyone recognise this kid? Please DM me.*

She wondered whether Travis had watched the footage. It mattered to Dani what he thought of her, and what would he think now, with her picture and that word plastered around the town for everyone to see and judge her by? She had thought for a moment that afternoon that he might ask her for her number or invite her out. It had been a naïve idea. Would he really be interested in her now, with the word 'slag' pinned to her like a badge of shame?

She turned the laptop off and shoved it under the bed, but as soon as one device was out of reach, another was in her hand, and she gave in to the temptation to look again at the article about Eve's death. Scrolling through and absorbing its details, she remembered the last conversation she had had with Eve, just before her family had made the move to Bath. Her father had been offered a business opportunity, whatever that meant. Dani had been so jealous that Eve was just able to up and leave while she herself was stuck in that place.

She had gone to their house. There were boxes and cases waiting on the driveway, but most of their things – the big stuff like the furniture – had already been taken in removal vans. There was something surreal about the scene, as though she had stepped onto a film set and was an onlooker to a life that had never touched her own; as though all that time she had spent in Eve's bedroom, listening to music and laughing at pointless crap on the internet, meant nothing now that she would never go in there again and they would never laugh as they once had. An entire chapter of their lives was coming to a sudden halt, as though the author penning their story hadn't known where to go with it and had just stamped a full stop, leaving their lives in limbo.

'You okay?' she had asked Eve.

Eve had nodded, but she wasn't really looking at Dani; she was looking through her, as though she couldn't wait to get away.

'I can't believe you're really leaving.'

Eve had turned and looked back at the house. Her mum had appeared in the doorway, smiling when she saw Dani, a sad smile that made her stomach do a flip.

'Hi, Mrs Gardiner.'

'Hi, Danielle.' She had looked at Dani apologetically. 'I'd invite you in, love, but everything's packed up – I can't even offer you a drink.' She glanced at her watch. 'We haven't got to leave for another hour. Why don't you two go and get a McDonald's or something?'

'I haven't finished packing,' Eve had said quickly.

'It's okay,' Dani had said. 'I've got to get back anyway.'

'We'll make up for it when we're up and running at the new place. You'll come and visit us, won't you?' Mrs Gardiner had said. Dani had glanced at Eve, who'd looked back at her, and neither of them needed to say anything, because they both knew that would never happen.

And now, as she remembered her last conversation with Eve, she realised it was also her last conversation with her mother. She wondered how Mrs Gardiner was – how Mr Gardiner was doing, and Eve's sister, Maddie, too – and felt a twist in her stomach at all the things that had been left unsaid.

She turned off the bedside lamp and pulled up the duvet. Closing her eyes, she allowed her thoughts to stray to Travis: where he might be and whether he was with someone else.

She was startled by a noise in the garden. 'Garden' was an exaggeration, when all it consisted of was a square of concrete just about big enough for a rotary washing line, and a fence with two panels missing. Gaps big enough for someone to squeeze if they were slim and determined enough. She lay still,

She heard the noise again, but when she went to the window, she couldn't see anything there. It was nothing, she told herself, closing the curtains. She was being neurotic.

Instead of getting back into bed, she went into Layla's room and sat beside her cot, holding her daughter's hand through the bars as she waited and listened for a noise that never repeated itself. She wished her dad was there. He would have known what to do, even if it was to fling himself through the back door wearing nothing but a pair of boxer shorts and brandishing a mop handle as a weapon against any potential intruders. The image made her laugh.

'Goodnight, Dad,' she whispered aloud, and in her head she heard him wish her goodnight back.

EIGHT

ADELE

The house was asleep, but she was not. Sleep eluded her most nights until well into the early hours, and even then it was endured in snatches, stolen from her as soon as it arrived. She was never sure which was preferable – being awake or being asleep. Awake, she had her thoughts for company, with their incessant echoes and relentless grip. Asleep, she was alone with her nightmares.

There was one that returned to her frequently. A little girl, blonde hair, blue eyes, was running towards her, arms outstretched. They were in a field, somewhere she didn't recognise; it was sprinkled with dazzling buttercups, a place so sunlit and beautiful it couldn't possibly have been real. The child ran fast, yet it seemed to take an age for her to get near, and the closer she got, the older she became. Her face changed, her limbs became longer and lither and she began to stumble as she approached. The smile stamped on her face dropped, replaced with an expression that was pained and frantic. Adele reached her arms out towards the girl, who was just metres away now, but before they could make contact, the child tripped and fell. Adele lunged to grab her, but the ground disappeared from beneath her and she was gone, and as Adele teetered at the edge of the abyss, she would wake, sweat-soaked and bone-cold.

To avoid the nightmare, she sometimes tried to stay awake. That night, the ache of her bruises was sufficient to keep her sleep, and she moved onto her side to ease the throbbing heat. It didn't work. The beating had been different this time, harder than before – or maybe she had just felt it differently, unable to switch off from the pain, allowing her brain to register the force of every blow.

She hid the bruises from Steph. Her sister could be lovely when she chose to be, but she was also naïve, and she saw what she wanted to see, existing in a world painted in pastel shades, one that smelled of roses and was lit by vanilla tea lights, Instagram-ready.

Unable to force a return to sleep, she went to the downstairs shower room, where she knew she wouldn't be heard. In the muted light of the mirror, the green and purple staining of her skin was a camouflage for the flesh that lay beneath. The damage was in all the hidden places: the stretch of stomach that was always concealed beneath her clothing; the base of her spine where her skin no longer saw the light of day. Each blow hurt a little less, as though her mind, now expecting them, had tuned itself to block the receptors that would make the pain known. It was afterwards that it hurt the most. The pain was delayed, like grief; it tiptoed around her before assaulting her when she least expected it.

She stripped off and shed her clothes, dropping them on the shower room floor. She turned on the water and waited for it to run hot, too hot, so that the small room was filled with steam and she was lost in a cloud of heat. If she stood under the flow for long enough, it began to feel as though she might be able to scald away the shame. It was her fault, all of it. She deserved this.

The house was big enough for her to move around downstairs unheard; she often snuck down during the dark hours to wash away the detritus of the day. It was paid for by her parents' money, though you would never have known it from the way Callum behaved. He had a sense of entitlement that was both obnoxious and unattractive, and he conveniently forgot when it suited him to do so just how much her family had done for him.

Once she had washed her hair twice and her skin was reddened by the temperature of the water, she turned off the shower, dried herself and got dressed. As she made her way back upstairs, she heard a child crying. It was a whimper at first, soft and vulnerable, but then it grew in intensity, insistent and pained.

Adele made her way to Ivy's bedroom. She eased the door open gently, careful not to disturb her, and when she stepped into the darkened room, the sound came to an abrupt stop. She could make out the shape of Ivy's little body beneath the blanket. She was fast asleep – the sobs nothing more than Adele's imagination – the tiny purr of her snores the only sound to break the silence of the night. She had managed to end up at the wrong end of her cot, her head angled awkwardly and one foot hanging between the wooden bars. Adele moved her carefully, readjusting her on the sheet, and the little girl exhaled softly, relieved at being righted.

Adele sat down on the carpet at the side of the cot and watched the child's little chest rise and fall. Ivy was a beautiful girl. She had blonde hair and long lashes – the kind of eyelashes women paid a fortune for – and when she smiled, she had a look about her as though she was far wiser than her years and had been on this earth longer than anyone realised. As though she had been here before. In the darkness, the thought made Adele shiver. Part of Ivy's beauty was her innocence, and Adele felt a sadness for the times that were yet to come, when her childhood would be lost and she would be exposed to all the unkindness and brutality that the world was capable of. *You can't keep them protected forever,* her mother had once told her. And she was right.

What kind of girl would Ivy be when she was older? It was inevitable that she would be influenced by her father, though Adele hoped that in her case nature might triumph over nurture and she would prove to be better than the start she'd been given. She did not believe that a beginning must determine an end. Take Steph and her as an example. Plenty of people had said it: same parents, same upbringing – two such different women. How could one be one way, and one be another?

She knew that the following morning she would wish sleep had been her friend that night, yet she found herself unable to move from Ivy's side. With her arm between the bars of the cot, she smoothed the child's hair with her fingers and murmured a lullaby, one she hadn't sung in such a long time that she had to drag the words from a corner of her memory. She was tempted to climb into the cot with her, to hold Ivy's warm sleeping body against her own and stay with her until she woke. Instead, she rose and left, returning to the cold bed where she would lie sleepless until sunrise, imagining a day when she might take the little girl away from this place.

NINE

DANI

Playgroup had barely been running for twenty minutes when Layla decided to kick off. The art supplies were out and the place was already a mess, colouring sheets and crayons swiped by chubby arms from the table to the floor. Dani saw the tantrum coming before it erupted – she saw the boy take the crayon as Layla was reaching for it, and she knew Layla wouldn't back down until she got it back, regardless of the countless other crayons available in front of her. It wasn't the first time the two children had clashed. For some reason, tears and tantrums escalated whenever they were within a foot of each other, almost as though Layla sensed the unpleasantness that the boy's mother directed towards her own. Amy Davies seemed to have taken the role of head of the 'other' mothers and had been dismissive of Dani since the first time she had taken Layla there.

There was a part of Dani that was quietly proud of Layla's determination. She herself had always been the kid who sat at the back and didn't get involved – she was happy just to blend into the background if it meant she didn't have to be the focus of anyone's attention. By the time she reached her teens and had started to realise just how unfair life could be, she was annoyed with herself for not doing more. Blending into the background meant allowing herself to become an easy target for bullies, and until she met Eve, that was exactly what she was – the brunt of other people's jokes.

She hoped Layla wouldn't be like she had been, and yet watching her now – seeing her little face scrunch itself into a ball of reddened fury – she had to hope, too, that her passionate character wouldn't morph into a tendency towards anger.

'No!' Layla shouted as the boy shoved her, and before Dani could reach them to intervene, her daughter had grabbed his arm and pulled him onto the floor with her. The boy's landing was mostly cushioned by Layla, but he started wailing like a wounded cat, and Amy came rushing over, glaring at Dani as though it were she who had just assaulted her precious offspring.

'Come on,' she said, almost stepping over Layla as she scooped up her son. 'You're okay.' She glared at Dani. 'You should make her say sorry.'

'Perhaps your boy should say sorry for pushing her.'

Amy tutted and turned away, and as she carried her son across the room, Dani heard her mutter something inaudible to one of the other mothers.

In competition with the boy's cries, Layla started screaming. There was nothing wrong with her, she wasn't hurt, but this had become her recent go-to reaction when she couldn't get her own way or was unhappy about something – she screamed until she turned purple and sounded as though she was going to be sick. Not here, Dani thought. Not now, Layla. Please. But the screaming intensified, and the whole far side of the hall – *that* side, Amy's snooty middle-class sidekicks who liked to think themselves superior – stared in Dani's direction, eyebrows raised as though they had been pulled by strings, as Layla threw herself on the floor and continued to work herself up into a state of hysterics.

Amy looked straight at Dani and her lips tilted into a smirk, and Dani could have happily crossed the room and tipped her tea over her silly smug head. Instead, she swept Layla up from the floor and left the room. She couldn't go home – their coats and her bag were still under the seats in the hall – so she went to the toilets to hide, hoping that by the time Layla had calmed down, something else would have happened to distract from their drama.

Layla continued to scream and wriggled with such force that Dani almost dropped her as she put her down. She stared at her daughter silently and wondered where the hell she had gone wrong. Maybe it was just her, or maybe this was her comeuppance. Perhaps she deserved for her life to always be difficult. She was a slag, wasn't she, just as someone had chosen to remind her. Layla deserved better.

Before she could do anything to stop them, frustrated tears rolled from her eyes. She sat down on the tiled floor and rested her back against the wall, crying along with her daughter, feeling useless – a failure. Guilt churned in her stomach like an illness, and she supposed that was what this was; the constant rolling nausea was like living with a disease, one that couldn't be eased with treatment and had no cure. When she shut her eyes, Eve was looking back at her, beautiful and accusing. She opened her eyes and looked at Layla to try to banish the vision. Her daughter was still wailing, relentless in her belief that everything was against her, and for a moment Dani sympathised, believing she knew how Layla felt.

She wiped a hand hurriedly across her face at the sound of the door, trying to hide her tears. Layla was temporarily silenced, but when she saw Adele, the crying flared back up, though thankfully with the volume turned down.

'Where am I going wrong with her?' Dani asked as she stood. As soon as the words left her, she felt embarrassed at having spoken them to someone who was little more than a stranger. Adele would think she couldn't cope with her own child. She certainly wouldn't want Ivy mixing with Layla after this morning.

Adele put a hand on her arm. 'Trust me, it's not you. It's her age. They all have phases – she'll grow out of it.'

Dani stepped away, unsettled by Adele's closeness, and turned on the cold tap, splashing water on her face to cool the redness of her cheeks. Great, she thought. She would have to go back into that room to get her things with everyone able to see she had been crying. They would think her weak, unable to cope; they would think she was a bad mother. She shouldn't have cared what those women thought, yet she did.

'Half the kids in there are the same age,' she reminded Adele. 'You don't see any of them losing it like Layla does.'

At the mention of her name, Layla snapped into silence again, and looked up at her mother intently, as though listening for what else might be said about her. Her mouth was turned down into a pout, and if Dani hadn't been so tired and fed up with everything, she might have found the expression funny. It was so exaggerated that Layla almost looked not real, as though her features had been moulded out of Play-Doh.

'Maybe not here,' Adele said, 'but you don't know what they're like at home, do you?'

Dani would rather Layla had saved her tantrums for the privacy of the house, somewhere she didn't have to deal with looks and judgement from other people. 'It had to be that kid, though, didn't it?'

'What do you mean?'

'His mother already looks down her nose at me. I think it's because I don't own a four-by-four and Layla's pram came from a supermarket.' Dani rolled her eyes.

'Oh. She's one of those.'

Dani smiled. 'She is definitely "one of those".'

'Don't worry about her,' Adele told her. 'And you're not doing anything wrong. You give it a year and you'll see – she'll be a different girl. She's obviously a bright kid, anyone can see that. There's a big brain in that head; maybe she's just frustrated by everything she can't communicate.'

Dani knew how that felt, but she said nothing. It felt nice to talk to Adele, even though she barely knew the woman. In just a few minutes she had offered Dani more reassurance than Caroline had in the two years since Layla had been born. It would be nice for her own mother to be a bit more understanding, she thought, and instantly felt guilty for it, as though she had somehow betrayed Caroline.

Even though she suspected Adele was lying to make her feel better, her words seemed like the right kind of lie – the sort of well-intended mistruth her mother could never bring herself to use to soften the blow of what she really wanted to say. Dani remembered the moment her mother found out she was pregnant – how her face hadn't been able to hide her thoughts. 'You bloody fool,' she'd mumbled, and then she'd sighed, shaking her head, and stepped out into the back yard to light a cigarette. You regret me, Dani thought, and the idea of it stuck like chewing gum, refusing to be scraped away no matter how cold it grew.

She wanted to talk to someone about the flyers and her suspicions, but she didn't feel able to tell her mother. It would involve admitting the truth about the relationship she'd had with Layla's father, and she could only imagine how Caroline might react. As far as Caroline knew, Layla was the result of a one-night stand. Dani was aware what her mother thought of her for it, but at the time, letting her think that had seemed a better idea than admitting she had been seduced by the false promises of a man who was probably nearer Caroline's age than Dani's.

'Come on,' Adele said, touching Dani's arm again. 'Let's get another cup of tea.'

Dani reached for Layla's hand, grateful when she accepted it without argument or fuss. They went back into the hall and she avoided making eye contact with anyone as they returned to their corner.

'You okay?' Elaine asked.

'You know what she's like,' Dani said, feeling embarrassed by Layla's behaviour despite the fact that Elaine had seen it before.

'Children are hard work. *All* of them.' Adele smiled, and Dani was grateful for the kindness. She wondered whether this was why she tended to gravitate towards older women. She had done the same as a child with Eve, who even at just twelve years old was advanced in a way the rest of the girls weren't, with the kind of maturity the others envied but her mother had probably hated. Dani understood it now. No one wanted their kids to grow up too quickly. Once the innocence was gone, it was gone forever.

'I doubt that,' she said, pulling her thoughts from Eve. 'I mean, look at Ivy.' She nodded at Adele's daughter, who was sitting on a play mat tucking a doll into a Moses basket.

'She has her moments, believe me.'

Dani smiled, disbelieving, and Elaine managed to divert the conversation onto another subject. The rest of the session passed without further incident.

Dani took Layla home and made her lunch while she played with some building blocks on the kitchen floor. She checked her phone, read the message from Kelly Thompson again, then found Eve's mum on Facebook. It had been a week since she had learned of Eve's death, yet she still hadn't been able to bring herself to message Mrs Gardiner, not knowing the right words to say; not really knowing whether the right words existed. She had blocked her from her mind in the same way she had blocked out Eve for the past few years, a fight for self-preservation from the guilt that gripped her whenever the thought of her friend settled for too long.

Eve's mother hadn't changed – her profile picture showed her immaculately dressed as Dani remembered her, and she wore the smile that had always seemed to be her default expression. Dani wondered where that smile was now, and how much Eve's death might have already changed her.

She went to Messenger and began to type:

Hi Mrs Gardiner. I just wanted to say how sorry I am to hear about Eve. I can't imagine what you're all going through. I know we hadn't seen each other in a long time, but you know how close Eve and I once were, and I wish things had been different.

She stopped, read over the message, deleted the last few words.

And then she didn't know what to say. *I'm sorry for your loss? Take care? Best wishes?* Everything sounded meaningless; nothing would bring her daughter back. Nothing would disguise the fact that no matter how great Dani claimed their friendship had been, they hadn't seen each other in four years.

Her phone vibrated. It was a message from Adele. *Just thought I'd check you're okay after this morning. Layla is lovely – you're doing a brilliant job x*

The message made her smile, yet at the same time she felt like crying. She didn't feel as though she was doing a brilliant job. Most of the time she didn't even feel she was doing a satisfactory job. Barely scraping by would be the description she would use.

Before she had a chance to begin a reply, the phone vibrated with another message from Adele, this time a parenting meme: a cartoon woman launching a nappy-clad cartoon baby into the air, with the caption *My therapist said I should declutter.*

Haha, Dani typed in response. *I can definitely relate to this!*

Just remember, came Adele's reply, *everyone is winging it. Everyone x*

Perhaps she was right. Maybe Dani gave herself too much of a hard time, but it was impossible not to compare Layla to the children who sat quietly and played without damaging anything or anyone, and it was impossible not to compare herself to the mums who seemed to get everything right. None of the other mothers from the playgroup got photos of themselves stuck on flyers around the town. Where had everything gone so wrong?

The phone vibrated again, this time with an email. It was from an address she didn't recognise, with the subject line *Temper, Temper*. There was a link to a newspaper website, and when she clicked it open, she felt her stomach turn. She remembered this article. It was only a useless local paper – one of those free things everyone got through their letter boxes but hardly anyone bothered to read – but it had been enough to bring shame on her and on Caroline, who hadn't spoken to her for most of the following week.

She closed the article. She didn't need to read it; she knew what it said. The headline – *Young Woman in Bar Brawl* – was exaggerated and misleading, but that didn't change the facts.

There was nothing else written in the body of the email, but when she looked at the recipients, she realised she wasn't the only person who'd been sent it. There was a list of about twenty addresses, none of which she recognised. Why did someone want these people to know about this incident? Hadn't she been humiliated enough already? She fought back angry tears. Of course she hadn't, she thought; at least, not as far as whoever was doing this was concerned. The flyers, now this… It was clear to Dani that she was intent on destroying her.

TEN

ADELE

On Tuesday, Adele met with Tim. As always, their meeting took place in his office, a sparsely furnished room with low seating and soft lighting, the walls painted an institutional grey. All evidence of paperwork was kept concealed within a large cupboard with multiple doors always kept closed, and other than the faded rug at their feet, the only thing to offer any colour was the world map fixed to the wall above the seating area. Adele sat with Australia floating over her head, the less-than-subtle suggestion that she could go anywhere she wanted her life to take her hanging there silently, a promise of greens and blues. Of course, it wasn't true. It was a nice idea – an optimistic notion that she was sure for some offered a reassuring sense of hope – but the practicalities of endless possibilities weren't quite so simplistic.

'Our last meeting,' Tim said, his palms outstretched as though he was taking part in some sort of religious ceremony. 'The end of an era.' He smiled and crossed one leg over the other. 'How are you feeling about it?'

Adele nodded and faked a smile. 'Good. I mean, I'm grateful for everything you've done for me, I really am, but…' She stopped and bit her lip. She was going to say that she didn't need him any more, but that probably wasn't true. Coming to this office and just talking had kept her tethered to something that had felt secure, even on the days when she had left feeling as though she hadn't really said much. It wasn't what she had expected from their sessions. Tim was nothing like her. He professed to understand her life – and there had been times when he had been convincing – but he would never know why she was the way she was, not really. She had talked to him to an extent, but there were still so many things she couldn't bring herself to tell him, things she had never told anyone and would take to her grave.

'But my work here is done?'

She smiled. 'Exactly.'

'There are a couple of things I need you to sign for me. That okay?'

He went to the cupboard, pulled out a file and returned with a handful of documents. 'Take your time. Shall I get us a coffee?'

'Thanks.'

He left the room, leaving Adele to read the documents. She scanned them, the words barely registering in her brain, and signed at the starred places without thinking too much about the emptiness that lay ahead of her. Their visits had given her some structure, a safe place in which she had been able to speak her mind without editing her words before they left her mouth. She liked Tim. He was a rarity, someone who managed somehow to listen without judgement.

'How are things going with the job hunting?' he asked when he returned with two mugs of coffee.

'Okay. I mean, I've applied for a few things, so we'll wait and see.'

'Keep going. Something will come up. It'll be a good thing for you. What are you doing to keep yourself busy?'

'Spending time with Ivy. Walking. Baking.'

'Are you eating properly?' he asked, one eyebrow raised.

'Yes,' she lied.

'And the drink?'

She shook her head. This was one thing she didn't have to lie about. 'Not a drop, I swear.'

'You've done amazingly well, you really have. If you ever feel uncertain about things, just remind yourself how far you've come. No one can take that away from you. *You* did it – no one else.'

Adele sipped her coffee. 'Why are you so nice? You don't have to be.'

'No one has to be. I just find life is generally easier when you are.'

'There aren't many people like you, though.'

'I've been told before that I'm an exception to the rule,' Tim said with a smile. 'If that's true, it's a shame. Anyway, this isn't about me. Is there anything you want to talk about?'

There was a lot Adele wanted to talk about, but the limited time they had remaining would never be long enough, and the things she held silent in her head would have altered every perception he had developed of her. He might have thought she was happier than she had once been, that her mind was healthier, but he was wrong. He didn't need to know that, though. She didn't know why it mattered to her what Tim thought of her, but she wanted to leave the room as she had entered it, an apparent positive case, something he could add to his success rate.

'I might have made a friend,' she said.

'Good. Are we talking male friend, female friend?'

'Female. She's a lot younger than I am, but we seem to have a lot in common.'

'Age isn't a determining factor in how well we get on with someone, though, is it. Have you talked to her about any of this?'

'God, no. Bit soon for that.'

Tim smiled, but the look was tinged with sadness. 'One day you'll find yourself able to talk without feeling the sense of shame you do now. It won't mean you've forgotten or tried to cancel it from your past; it'll just mean that you've reached acceptance. And I know you still feel that shame, Adele. It means you're a good person.'

'Am I?'

'Don't do that. Don't question yourself. There are plenty of other people ready to do that for you – you don't need to do it as well. My dad used to say something that has always stuck with me. "The hardest person to forgive is yourself." Sound familiar?'

'Wise man, your dad. Must be where you get it from.'

He gathered up the documents she had signed. 'Always made me wonder what he'd done, though. Nobody's faultless or without sin, are they?'

'Except you, maybe?' Adele said, handing back his pen.

Tim laughed. 'Well, yeah… you've got me there.' He stood. 'I'm probably not supposed to do this,' he said, 'but come here.' She stood, and he gave her a hug. 'A fresh start now, okay?' He walked her out of the office and to the front door. 'I'm not going to say good luck. You don't need it. Just take care.'

Adele thanked him and left, knowing as she walked away from the building that everything that he thought he knew about her was a lie, and that it was just a matter of time before she let him down.

The carpet scratched her face. She felt her cheekbone press against the floorboards beneath, and she closed her eyes, waiting for the first blow to land upon her back. When it came, it sent pain ripping through her body, a searing flame so intense it seemed to burn through to her blood. She sucked in air between her teeth, bracing herself for the next impact, and when it came, she curled in on herself, tightening her body against the attack. Every nerve ending tingled, every sense was heightened rather than numbed, and as the beating intensified – each blow delivered quicker and with more force than the last – she felt an old pain die and a new one take its place.

'No more. Please. Stop.'

She had been counting the seconds that passed, trying to focus on the numbers to distract her from the pain, but she had lost count and there was no escaping it. There was a metallic tang on the tip of her tongue, and she realised she had bitten her bottom lip hard enough to draw blood from the dry, cracked skin.

'Please.'

The final blow cracked into the small of her back, forcing her ribs harder against the floor. She pushed a hand to her side and pressed her palm against the bottom of her ribcage, but the slightest pressure made her wince with pain.

The room fell silent until the still air was punctuated by the sound of her weeping. She never usually cried, and she was ashamed of her tears, their existence seeming to symbolise her weakness. She waited before pulling herself up, having to clamp her teeth together to stop herself from screaming with the burning agony of the beating.

She dragged her body towards the bathroom and gripped the door frame to steady herself. Closing the door, she doubled forward, staggering against the sink. When she looked in the mirror, she barely recognised the person who stared back at her. Her eyes were two hollows, dark and lifeless. Her hair was sweaty and matted, stuck to the sides of her neck. She felt something warm and wet on the small of her back, and when she ran her palm across her skin, it was stained red. Her complexion was sallow, and she had grown so thin that she seemed barely there, skin following bone along the contours of her skull.

She looked down, not wanting to look at herself any longer.

There was a knock at the door.

'Adele. Adele, let me in.'

She slid to the tiled floor and pulled her knees up to her chest, banging the back of her head against the wall with a repetitive thud. She had been told it regularly enough, and it was what she had come to believe. This was how things were meant to be. This was what she deserved.

ELEVEN

DANI

The photograph arrived on Thursday lunchtime while she was making a cup of tea for Mrs Bracknell, a regular client who came in once a month to get her roots done. She didn't notice the number at first, though the fact that it wasn't attached to a name stored in her contacts should have set alarm bells ringing. Dylan was sitting on what might have been patio slabs, though the photograph was taken so close to him that much of the background couldn't be seen. There was a splash of colour behind him, a red and orange blur of what might have been a flower bed, but when she enlarged the photo, she could see something else, something that dangled by the cat's side and sloped off out of the photo. It was a dog's lead. Dylan was tethered, being held somewhere.

Who the hell is this? she messaged, her fingers shaking. *Bring the cat back.*

She didn't expect to get anything back, but before the kettle had boiled, her phone had pinged again.

You should really learn to say please.

Go to hell, she wrote, but she deleted it before the temptation to press send overruled her common sense. She didn't know what this person was capable of, and she feared that worse was to come.

The flyers… the email… now Dylan. He was just an innocent animal. Not like her.

She made Mrs Bracknell's tea, having to return to the back of the salon for the forgotten spoonful of sugar, then busied herself with sweeping the floor. When the colour on the client's hair had been given long enough to set in, Dani ushered her over to the sink area. She couldn't stop thinking about poor Dylan. He might have looked okay in the photograph, but he must have been scared being tied up like that. He had been with Caroline since he was a kitten, and he was old and fragile now, used to his home comforts. The previous summer, he had been injured when another cat attacked him, his paw left bloodied and needing stitches. He hadn't been himself for months afterwards, and Dani wasn't sure how much more his poor heart would handle.

She held the water over Mrs Bracknell's head and began to work her fingers through the woman's wet hair. She wondered what her mother was doing, and how much television Layla would have watched since she had been picked up from nursery. She knew Caroline was upset about Dylan's disappearance, but she would use it as an excuse now, blaming the cat's absence for her spending all day in her dressing gown and not leaving the house.

Mrs Bracknell said something, but Dani didn't hear her. She was distracted by thoughts of Dylan, of where he might be and who he might be with. How was she going to get him home unharmed? Whatever that woman wanted with her – or whatever she wished upon her – using the cat for revenge seemed a callous and cowardly way to make Dani pay.

'You're burning me!'

She was brought back to the room by Mrs Bracknell flinging herself forward in the chair to escape the heat of the water. She saw steam rising from the shower head she held in her hand, then the red skin at the woman's temple. Her own palm was crimson, but she hadn't noticed the heat that now coursed through her fingers.

'What's going on?' Tracy appeared, scissors in hand, to find out what the noise was about. Mrs Bracknell stood up and turned with her hand pressed to her head. 'I told her it was too hot, but she didn't listen. She wasn't paying attention at all.'

Tracy shot Dani a glare. 'I am so sorry, Mrs Bracknell,' she said, gesturing to another chair. 'Here, let me take a look.'

The woman sat down, and Tracy gently touched her forehead. 'What were you thinking?' she mouthed at Dani before ordering her to go and get a cool cloth.

'I'm so sorry, Mrs Bracknell,' Dani said when she returned with the cloth and passed it to Tracy.

'Go and wait out the back, please, Dani. I'll finish seeing to Mrs Bracknell.'

Dani lowered her head and went into the back room. She felt thirteen again, as if she was in trouble at school, and she was angry with herself for allowing that photograph to throw her off balance and steal her concentration. If she lost her job, it would be her own fault. She was already in Tracy's bad books, and the woman didn't need any excuse to let her go.

She studied her hand, the scalded palm and the lines that curved in white slivers through it. Blood, she thought, looking at her crimson skin. There was blood on her hands. She retrieved her phone and returned to the photo of Dylan. Sadness tightened its grip on her chest. She had made mistakes, so many of them, and she had always known that one day they might come back to haunt her. But it wasn't Dylan's fault. It wasn't her mother's. No one else deserved to suffer because of the things she had done.

'What are you playing at, Dani?'

She looked up to see Tracy standing in the doorway, her hands on her hips and her thin mouth clamped with disapproval.

'I'm sorry. I don't know what happened.'

'You never seem to know what happened. It always seems to be someone else's fault.'

Dani said nothing. Perhaps Tracy was right.

'You're lucky Mrs Bracknell wasn't scalded.'

'She's okay?'

Tracy nodded. 'You may well have lost us a client, though.'

'I'm sorry.'

She rolled her eyes. 'I want you to go home now, please.'

'Please,' Dani began. 'I need this job, I can't—'

'Dani, I just don't think it's a good idea for you to stay today. Get your things. I'll be in touch.'

'What does that mean?'

Tracy narrowed her eyes, and Dani took the hint. If she wanted any chance at keeping her job, she needed to stop talking herself out of it. She put her phone into her pocket and went to get her jacket.

'I'm sorry,' she muttered to Mrs Bracknell as she left the salon, but if the client heard the mumbled apology, she chose to ignore it.

She had just passed the tattoo parlour when she heard Travis calling her name.

'Jesus,' she said, turning. 'Are you following me as well now?'

His face dropped at her bluntness, and she immediately regretted her reaction. 'I'm sorry,' she said, raising her hands in apology. 'It's been a long morning.'

He smiled. 'Want to talk about it?' He dipped his head towards the door of the shop, inviting her in. She followed, even though she didn't really want to talk. She didn't want to go home either, though. Getting back early would mean having to explain to her mother what had happened.

'No customers?'

'Next one's booked in at two thirty,' he said, dropping onto the sofa in the waiting room. 'So what's up?'

'Nothing. Honestly, I'm fine.' She sat down next to him.

'You're a bad liar.'

'Is that a bad thing or a good thing?'

There was a moment's silence. Travis watched her with unwavering attention, and for an awkward moment Dani felt as though she might cry. It felt good to have someone really look at her, as though he was actually seeing her.

'I've just burned an old woman's head. Someone's been watching me – they texted me while I was here with you the other day – and it's probably the same person who put up those flyers, but now the cat's gone missing too and my mother is really worried about him, and I'm saying all this and I don't know why because I sound like some sort of crazy person.' It was a good time to stop talking, so she did.

Travis's lip was slightly curled, as though he was waiting for the punchline. 'What did you burn the woman with?'

She sighed. 'My fiery wit.'

He laughed. 'Is she going to sue you?'

'She can try if she likes.'

He paused.

'Was the CCTV any good to you?'

'I don't know yet.'

'If there's anything I can do…'

'I know,' Dani said. 'Thanks.'

She studied his mouth, thinking there *was* something he could do, though it probably wasn't what he had in mind. A flush of shame rushed through her, but she just wanted to forget it all: Layla's father, his wife, the flyers, Dylan. Eve.

He gave her a look she was sure she hadn't misread. She reached for him and put a hand to the back of his head, winding her fingers into his hair and pulling him closer. She had never noticed how unusual his eyes were before, but this close she could see the flecks of green amid the hazel, and all she wanted was for him to close them and kiss her. When he did, it was better than she had imagined it.

She hadn't kissed a man since the last time she had been with Layla's father, swearing off men and vowing that she would grow old with cats and celibacy. It didn't mean she hadn't thought about sex – she had thought about it every time she had been near Travis – but she had liked the idea that perhaps she would never need anyone. Maybe she didn't need this, she thought as her hand moved beneath his T-shirt, but she wanted it, wanted him, more than she had ever wanted anyone.

She pressed a hand flat to his stomach. His body was hard, more toned than he looked; if he worked out, he wasn't the type who made a show of the fact. His tongue moved against hers and his hands roamed beneath her shirt, and when the coldness of his fingers made her body tremble, he pulled away from her.

'I'm sorry,' he said, his touch leaving her.

'What for?'

'I just… I shouldn't have done that. I shouldn't have taken advantage.'

Dani laughed nervously. 'You didn't.' She watched his face change. 'What do you mean?'

'You've obviously got a lot going on, and—'

'Oh,' Dani said, with a humourless laugh. The thought had struck her like an invisible blow. This was exactly what he would expect from her. She might as well have been wearing a sign with the word 'slag' in blazing neon lights. 'This is about those flyers, isn't it?'

'What?'

She stood, desperate to be away from there and from him.

'Dani, I don't know what you think I—'

'Forget it,' she said, and left the shop, letting the door bang shut behind her.

She wiped away a tear as she hurried home, hoping she wouldn't see anyone she knew before she got back to the house. She had been so stupid. What would he think of her now, just throwing herself at him like that? If she was trying to prove right whoever was trying to ruin her reputation, she was going the best way about doing it.

When she got home, there was an envelope addressed to her mother waiting on the mat inside the front door. Caroline was in the yard taking washing off the line. Dani flicked on the kettle and made two cups of tea, taking one out to her with the envelope. She wondered whether, if things had been different between them, she might have confided in her mother about Travis and what had just happened. She knew those kind of mother/daughter relationships existed, but she wasn't even close enough to Caroline to tell her about the email. She didn't want to tell her about Dylan either, but she didn't think she had a choice.

'Everything all right?' her mother asked as she took the envelope from her, the words muffled by the peg between her teeth.

'Fine. Where's Layla?'

'Having a nap. I tried to keep her awake, but she just dropped off.' Caroline took the peg from her mouth and clipped it onto the line. 'She said something today about a mushroom at nursery.' She slid a nail into the corner of the envelope and ripped it open. 'I think she was saying mushroom anyway. I hope she hasn't been eating anything she's picked in that garden they've got... There could be God-knows-what growing in there.' She reached into the envelope and pulled out a photograph. 'What the—'

Dani didn't need to look at the photograph to know what it was. She had been going to tell her mother – she was just waiting for the right moment – but the woman had beaten her to it. Caroline was looking at her questioningly, as though this was all her fault. Maybe it was. She glanced away, shielding herself from the sight of her mother's imminent tears.

The photo was another close-up, but this time Dylan was locked in some sort of cage. It wasn't much bigger than he was, with barely room for him to turn. He must be so scared, she thought, and a knot twisted in her gut, bringing bile clawing to the back of her throat.

TWELVE

ADELE

That Friday, Dani arrived at playgroup dressed in her usual outfit of leggings, oversized sweater and trainers, her choice of footwear giving her the look of someone who was permanently ready to make a dash for it if needed. It made Adele question what she was expecting. Or who. Her hair, usually loose and curled into the type of wave that looked effortless but had probably taken the best part of an hour to achieve (presumably the reason she always seemed to be late), was pulled into a long ponytail that hung limply down her back. She looked flustered as she shoved open the door with her shoulder, her rain jacket glistening with the spray of an early June downpour.

Layla's hair was dishevelled, and Adele watched as Dani dragged her fingers through it – a last-ditch attempt to make her presentable. The little girl winced as her mother's hand caught in a tangle of knots, and Dani responded by gripping her daughter's shoulder to keep her still, muttering something inaudible in her ear.

Though Dani clearly wasn't the most patient of people, it was obvious that Layla adored her. She played well with Josh – and now Ivy, too – but she was never far from her mother's side, constantly seeking her presence by climbing up onto her lap or sitting on the floor with a hand on her leg. The three children had quickly formed a little friendship group. It was lovely to see. Adele thought Ivy spent too little time around other children her own age, and she already seemed to be thriving after just a few weeks of attending the playgroup.

'What's your email address?' Dani asked Elaine.

'Jonesandjones1980@echat.co.uk. The year me and Trevor got married. Why?'

'I just…' Dani drifted into silence. 'When did you last check it?'

'God, I can't remember. I'm useless with it.'

'Did they ask you for it when you started bringing Josh to the playgroup?'

'I don't know. They might have.'

'I gave mine,' Adele told her. 'They said they use it to update people about events.'

Dani turned to look at the women on the other side of the room. When she looked back, her eyes were filled with tears. 'Have you received anything? Something about me?'

'What's the problem, love?' Elaine asked.

Adele shifted uncomfortably. 'I did get something, but look, it doesn't matter, okay? It's your business, and whoever sent it was out of order.'

'Sent what?' Elaine asked.

Dani shot Adele a look that begged her not to say any more. Adele had become her confidante, and she had underestimated just how comforting gaining Dani's trust would prove to be.

Dani stood hurriedly, having to peel Layla from her leg to get up from her chair. 'Look,' she said, pointing to the craft table, where one of the volunteers was emptying crayons and glue sticks from a plastic ice-cream tub. 'Do you want to do some colouring with Josh?'

Elaine glanced at Adele as Layla raced off to get herself a seat at the table and Ivy followed her. Adele headed after them, not fully trusting Ivy with anything that might be jabbed into an eye or used to graffiti a wall. She put a hand on Dani's shoulder and leaned towards her. 'It doesn't matter what anyone thinks,' she said, but Dani ignored the comment, apparently intent on putting on a brave face.

'Come on,' she said to Layla with false cheer in her voice. 'You can sit here.'

It wasn't long before Layla managed to get herself into another altercation with the boy from the previous week. Her screams of frustration filled the room, pulling Dani from her ongoing conversation with Elaine. She rushed over, but not quickly enough to stop the row from escalating. Layla and the boy were grappling with the ice-cream tub, its remaining contents leaping out as the two children swung back and forth as though enacting a particularly aggressive version of 'Row, Row, Row Your Boat'.

'Layla!'

But she was too late; before she could intervene, Layla had claimed victory, removing the tub from the boy's grip with one final yank. Losing his balance, the boy staggered back and fell, catching his head on the back of one of the plastic chairs as he tumbled to the floor. Instantly the room was filled with wailing, and the noise had a ripple effect, sweeping through the children like a Mexican wave. Dani was about to reprimand Layla, the little girl's flushed face fixed in an imminent bout of temper, but her attention was diverted by the woman who rushed to the boy's aid. She muttered something beneath her breath, something Adele didn't hear but Dani obviously did. The young woman's reaction was fuelled by a fiery temper Adele hadn't seen before but had guessed was there, simmering just beneath the surface.

'Say it to my face this time!'

'Whoa!' Adele grabbed her by the sleeve and pulled her away; Dani dropped her raised arm, realising with a look of bewilderment what she had been about to do.

The women fell into an uncomfortable silence, the apparent focus of Dani's anger standing with her mouth in a perfect O, seemingly oblivious to whatever had triggered the outburst. Most of the children were still playing, offering no attention to the drama that had escalated at the centre of the room. Unfortunately, there was one child who had noticed what was going on: Layla, still standing at the craft table, now staring wide-eyed at her mother as though she didn't recognise her. Adele didn't think that Dani, now simmering down from her moment of rage, had noticed Layla's reaction; she wondered how she might respond if she were to see the effect her outburst had had on her daughter.

'Come on,' Dani snapped, stepping towards Layla and grabbing her by the hand. 'We're going.'

Layla started crying and tried to wriggle from her grip, but Dani tightened her hold as she retrieved their jackets and bag.

Elaine looked at Adele with a what-do-we-do-now expression. Adele had no idea what had prompted Dani's reaction to the other woman, though she could guess it was something relating to that email, and she knew that if she hadn't stopped her, things would have become physical.

'We can't have that sort of behaviour here,' she heard one of the volunteers say.

'Use your eyes,' Dani retorted, still grappling with a crying Layla. 'We're going.'

Elaine followed her from the room, and Adele did the same, not wanting to become the new focus of attention for the group of women gathered around the little boy, who was now milking his invisible injury. Josh and Ivy continued to play together at the plastic kitchen in the corner, and Adele kept an eye on them through the glass pane in the door as she stood with Elaine in the hallway.

'Dani, love. Wait a minute.'

'I wouldn't have hurt her,' Dani said, turning to Elaine, sounding as though she was trying to convince herself as much as anyone else, her voice betraying a lack of faith in her own words. Adele suspected she didn't know what she was capable of. Had she scared herself, or did she regret that she hadn't been allowed the chance to find out?

'Don't leave like this,' Elaine said. 'Let me go and talk to them, sort this out.'

Dani began to object, but Elaine ignored her and went back into the room.

'I wouldn't have hurt her,' Dani repeated, and this time there was no doubt that the words were for herself and not for Adele.

'I don't know what just happened in there,' Adele told her, 'but if you want to chat, you've got my number. Just give me a call, okay?'

Dani grappled her daughter into a chokehold and battled through the door with her wriggling body. Adele watched as she crossed the main road and headed into the estate, wondering whether Dani would call her, or if it would be left to her to make the next move.

THIRTEEN

DANI

Dani was rereading the email she had received from Travis two days earlier.

> *I'm sorry I upset you, but I think you misunderstood me. I really like you, but I know you're going through a lot at the moment and I didn't want to put any pressure on you. I'm here when you're ready. Travis x*

She hadn't replied. She wanted to, but she was embarrassed at the way she had just run off, and she didn't want the complication of having to explain to him exactly what was going on. She had mentioned the missing cat to him during her rambling outburst at the tattoo parlour but going into detail now about the photograph of Dylan that had been sent to her mother would surely scare him off completely. He would wonder just what sort of family he was getting himself involved with, and the thought of losing someone else from her life – a person who had barely stepped into it – was one Dani didn't want to consider.

Tracy had let her return to the salon, though she was on a final warning. She needed to keep her head down and avoid drawing any further attention to herself, so she had made a point of taking a longer route home after work to avoid having to walk past the tattoo parlour. Her sometimes impulsive nature had got her into trouble before, and she couldn't stop thinking about what had happened at playgroup the previous day. No one else seemed to have heard what Amy Davies had said to her, which was exactly the way the woman had intended it. Still, Dani knew she shouldn't have reacted the way she did. What if Adele hadn't stopped her? Would she have hurt Amy? All the way home she was stalked by the implications of what might have happened and what it would have made her, and by the time she got back to the house, she felt exhausted from regret.

She was standing in the kitchen reading his email for the twentieth time when a message notification popped up on her phone screen. Tension made her body rigid any time her mobile sounded now; she was still reeling from Dylan's disappearance and the email about her arrest. She realised that the only way she was going to get this person to stop was by confronting her. But who was it? She still felt it had to be James's wife, but what if she was wrong? In a way, the thought of her tormentor being a complete unknown was even more terrifying.

When she opened the message, her stomach churned at the sight of Mrs Gardiner's name. She hadn't expected to hear back from her.

> *Thanks for your message, Dani. Sorry I've been slow to reply – the days all feel the same at the moment. None of us can comprehend what has happened. It doesn't feel real yet – I don't know that it ever will. I hope you're well. Take care of that lovely little girl of yours – life is so short and precious.*

She must have looked at Dani's profile to have found out about Layla, unless she had already known, perhaps from Eve. Had they talked about her, pitying Dani her sad, simple life? Eve had never contacted her when Layla was born. Perhaps she hadn't been sure whether Dani would want congratulations. Mrs Gardiner had had high hopes for her daughter's future career, and Dani wondered then what else she must have imagined for Eve. Travel? Marriage? A family? All those dreams turned to dust.

She would never have admitted it to anyone – she barely wanted to acknowledge the fact herself – but when she had first seen those two blue lines on that white stick, Dani had thought her life was over. An entire future – one she had barely planned for and had been as yet unable to imagine – had collapsed in front of her, and she had felt as though she was drowning in air, the past and the future colliding in a tsunami that crashed down upon her in an unstoppable wave. When she looked at Layla now, she felt guilt for that first reaction and for those sleepless nights that had followed. *You can't imagine life without her now, can you?* so many people had said to her, but the truth was that Dani *could* imagine it. That life was different, calmer, more organised, and when Layla was at her most challenging, there were moments when Dani fantasised about it in the same way other people daydreamed about bucket-list destinations they would never visit.

She went into the living room, where Layla was banging a toy drum with the remote control for the TV. She considered taking it off her, but the promise of the inevitable tantrum that would follow prompted her to let her continue. Instead, she sat behind her on the rug and leaned towards her to breathe in the smell of her shampooed hair, and when she placed her hands on her daughter's shoulders to kiss the top of her head, Layla for once stayed still enough to let her. She was going to be better, Dani thought. She was going to be less hot-headed; she was going to learn to ignore what people said.

When she closed her eyes, the thump of the remote against the top of the drum thudded out like an erratic heartbeat, and she felt a burning guilt for all the moments she had allowed herself to imagine a different life, when no ticked-off bucket list could have given her what she had there in that room, right in front of her.

The banging stopped abruptly; something else had caught Layla's attention. She got up and ran across the living room to retrieve a plastic mobile phone she had spotted abandoned beneath the TV unit, and as she sat pressing buttons and making pretend calls, Dani's thoughts were moved to her own phone. She went back to the kitchen to get it and found Adele's number. Despite what Adele had claimed, finding out that Dani had been arrested for assault must have altered her opinion of her.

I'm sorry about what happened yesterday, Dani wrote. *I shouldn't have reacted the way I did. Thanks for stepping in x*

After getting home from playgroup, Dani had checked the list of email recipients again. Elaine was one of them. The thought that everyone there now knew about her past brought a shame Dani couldn't escape. She didn't want to go back to the church hall, especially after what had happened yesterday, and yet the stubborn part of her didn't want to let a woman like Amy Davies win. She didn't want to let James's wife win. And yet could James's wife have managed to track down contact details of all the people from the playgroup? How was that even possible?

A moment later, her mobile vibrated.

No need to apologise. Try not to worry about that email – it'll all be forgotten soon enough. You okay? X

Layla's temper filled the room in a burst of sudden noise. She had already moved on from the plastic phone and was now grappling with the toy box in the corner, trying to prise a pair of fairy wings from beneath a wooden farmhouse.

'Layla, wait.'

Dani dropped her phone on the sofa and went to her daughter's aid, but the meltdown had escalated at record speed and Layla's face was already red with fury.

'Stop,' Dani said, 'you're going to—'

Layla gave a final yank at the wings and fell back as they ripped in half. A spray of glitter landed on the laminate beside her, and her temper rose to a full-blooded scream when she saw her fairy wings torn in two.

'For God's sake, Layla, I told you to stop it.'

Dani picked up both parts of the wings, but the fine mesh was ruined, and they were beyond repair. Layla was now lying on her back, fat tears rolling down her cheeks as she screamed herself into a stupor. Dani sat on the floor beside her, resigning herself to defeat.

'Why did you do that?'

The question was pointless; Layla was too young to answer it, and even had she not been, she was by now too inconsolable to do anything but cry. There had been days when Dani would have shouted at her, then felt guilty for her reaction. Today, though, she reached for her. She was expecting to be met with resistance, but for once Layla allowed herself to be held, her little body limp in her mother's lap as she sobbed. At last she fell asleep there, her eyes red and her cheeks wet, and when the room had finally fallen into silence, Dani carried her to the sofa.

She retrieved her phone and returned to Adele's text.

I was until Layla just decided to have another meltdown, she wrote in response. *I love the bones of her, but her tantrums are off the scale. I'll be grey before I'm 25 at this rate! X*

A moment later, Adele replied.

Just as well you're a hairdresser then! Don't worry about it – we're all grey. Do you want to bring Layla over for a playdate with Ivy one day? X

She did, if purely for selfish reasons. With communication between her and Caroline reduced to what was for dinner and where Layla had left her shoes, Dani had no one to talk to other than the pensioners whose curls she swept up from the salon floor, and a two-year-old whose vocabulary was yet to extend much beyond her own name and the words 'snack' and 'ball'. Adele had been kind to her, and she hadn't judged her despite the terrible things she now knew. It would be good for Layla to spend time with another child of a similar age, if only to show her that descending into bouts of hysterics whenever she didn't get what she wanted wasn't the way other children behaved on a daily basis.

It was the thought of a possible tantrum in someone else's house that made Dani write, *It's a lovely offer, thanks, but I don't want to risk it. Layla is a bit too unpredictable at the moment x* She could barely contain the meltdowns in her own home; the prospect of Layla losing her cool at Adele's didn't hold much appeal.

Ivy would love it, came the reply. *Don't think it's just your child – it really isn't. Wait until you see Ivy in full flow! We have a quiet day on Monday if you don't have other plans. Have a think about it x*

Dani replied that she would, then stuffed her phone behind a cushion and cuddled Layla closer to her.

FOURTEEN

ADELE

Arranging the playdate was easy. Child's play. Dani had resisted at first, deterred by the possibility of a tantrum from Layla. Adele didn't blame her for feeling reluctant. Had Layla been her child, she might have felt the same. She had attempted to reassure her with the promise that all toddlers were unpredictable, but the truth was that Layla's emotions were extreme, her temper already volatile at such a tender age. Perhaps she had inherited the trait from her mother.

Preparing the house for their arrival had taken some consideration. Adele had kept Ivy amused with far more television and snacks than she would usually have permitted while she moved from room to room rearranging things. It was while doing this that she realised how many family photographs there were. The largest and most obvious was the portrait that greeted people in the hallway. It was a posed photograph, the three of them sitting on the lawn beneath the oak tree at the bottom of the garden. Ivy stole the limelight, centre stage in her pastel-lemon summer dress, her head tilted to the sky mid-giggle. They looked happy, an aspirational family unit; beautiful people put together for a clothing catalogue. Wife, husband, child. Picture perfect. All of it a lie.

Dani turned up at ten past eleven, late as ever. Her R-registration Fiat Panda looked out of place amid the neighbours' Audis and

Mercedes, and as Adele watched from the window while Dani got Layla from her car seat, she witnessed the awe and discomfort in the younger woman's expression.

'Sorry we're late,' Dani said, as Adele welcomed them into the house. 'I thought we'd taken a wrong turn.' She barely looked at Adele, her attention focused on taking in the details of the house. 'This is like one of those homes you see on TV. Layla! Shoes!'

She grabbed her daughter by the hood of her rain jacket as she made a bid for freedom, and Layla squirmed as Dani pulled off her trainers.

'Ivy's just through there,' Adele told the little girl, pointing to the living room. 'Would you like to go and play with her?'

They watched as Layla trotted into the room.

'Relax,' Adele said. 'She'll be fine. Coffee?'

Dani followed her down the hallway and into the kitchen. 'Oh my God, look at that garden.' She stood at the patio doors while Adele set about making the coffee. 'Ivy must love it out there, all that space to play in.' The words were tinged with something other than admiration: not quite envy, but almost a sadness.

'You'd think, wouldn't you, but she only ever plays in that corner.' Adele pointed to the side of the house. 'Children don't really want much. Not at that age, anyway. That's reserved for the adults. Would you like some cake?'

Dani nodded. 'Thanks.'

Adele went to the living room to call the girls, who came rushing into the kitchen at the promise of a sweet treat.

'Do you work?' Dani asked, trying to make the question sound casual. She must have wondered what Adele did to be able to afford to live there.

'I'm a nurse. Well, I was. I haven't worked for a while.' She passed Dani a slice of chocolate cake before handing a bowl to each of the girls.

'I don't blame you. It's hard going when you've got a kid. You see these women with, like, three or four children and they've got a career as well, and you wonder how they all get out of the house in the morning.'

'Nanny?'

Dani smiled. 'Yeah, probably.' She took a bite of cake. 'Did you make this?' she asked through half a mouthful. 'It's lovely.' She wiped the corner of her mouth with a thumb. 'So what does your husband do?'

Adele hesitated. The silence was filled by a loud clatter as Layla's bowl fell to the tiled floor.

'Oh God, Layla!'

Dani jumped up from her seat and knelt to collect the spray of chocolate sponge that had gone everywhere. Realising her cake was now inedible, Layla started to cry.

Adele reached for the little girl's hand. 'Come with me and we'll get you another piece of cake. Don't worry about that,' she said to Dani. 'I'll get the dustpan and brush out.'

Dani was red-faced and flustered, but Adele was grateful for the interjection that Layla's clumsy hands had provided. It had saved her having to answer Dani's question.

Once the cake had been eaten, the four of them went into the living room, where the girls played with Ivy's kitchen, moving wooden fruit and vegetables from the washing machine to the sink and back again.

'Is everything okay?' Adele asked. 'You know… after Friday?'

Dani felt herself wince at the reference, embarrassed by what had happened at playgroup. 'I'm sorry. I shouldn't have reacted the way I did. No one heard what Amy said, though, did they? "Like mother, like daughter." I mean, that snide cow next to her probably heard her say it, but she wasn't going to back me up, was she?'

'She was out of order.'

'People can say what they want about me, I don't care, but leave Layla out of it.'

'You think she was referring to that email?'

'Must have been. I mean, you got the email, and it was sent to Elaine's address too, so I imagine everyone at playgroup has seen it.'

'You don't have to tell me about it.'

The comment was like a flame to a gas leak, and as the story came spilling out, Adele realised Dani had been waiting for someone to confide in. She was glad it was her. She needed Dani to trust her, and it seemed now that she had done enough to convince the younger woman she was worthy of her secrets.

'I was arrested for assault a couple of years back.' Dani lowered her voice, as though either child would know what she was talking about. 'Sounds bad, doesn't it? It was bad.' She shifted on the sofa and sipped her second coffee. 'I'd just found out that Layla's dad had lied to me, and I went on a night out with a couple of girls from school, just to let off some steam. I drank too much – stupid really, as though drinking was going to help me forget what had happened – but anyway, while I was on my way to the toilets, this man I'd noticed staring at me while I was on the dance floor put a hand up my skirt. Everything happened so quickly. I shoved him – that was all I meant to do, just to get him off me – but he must have been so drunk that he lost his balance easily, and he fell back and hit his head on the corner of a fruit machine. It knocked him out cold. He was awake by the time the ambulance and the police arrived, though, and he told them that I'd lashed out at him from nowhere, that I was just some drunk who attacked him. There was no CCTV footage. There were no witnesses to him groping me. No one believed me.'

'I'm so sorry. What an ar—' Adele stopped herself and put a finger to her lips, censoring herself for the sake of the children. 'Sounds as though you were in the wrong place at the wrong time.'

'That's not what the police thought.'

'Were you charged?'

Dani nodded. 'Sixty hours' community service and a fine. Oh... and a criminal record that any potential employer gets to see.' Her focus rested on the floor between her feet. 'Anyway, that's what Amy meant when she made that comment.' She looked over at the girls, who were playing quietly. '"Temper, temper",' she added, quoting the email. Her face was flushed, as though she was embarrassed now at having revealed so much, and she changed the subject. 'What brought you to our playgroup, anyway? It took me twenty-five minutes to get here... there must be groups closer to home.'

Adele had prepared for this question. 'There are, but to be honest, they're not really my thing. They're not about the children, more about the mothers. Everyone's in competition with each other – who's got the most expensive pram, whose baby started to walk earliest. They've got them signed up for private school before they've left the womb.'

Dani smiled. 'Sounds a bit like some of the ones at our group. They like to think they're middle class, but they're no different to the rest of us.'

'Anyway, I'm glad we ventured further afield. We wouldn't have met you and Layla otherwise, would we? Look... do you fancy doing something one evening, just you and me? It's lovely with the kids, but it's nice to have a break, isn't it?'

There was a moment's hesitation from Dani before she said, 'Yeah. That sounds good.'

Adele glanced at her watch. She had already told Dani she needed to be somewhere for one o'clock. 'We'll have to make tracks soon. Ivy always goes to her nan's for dinner on a Monday. What about tomorrow?'

'Tomorrow?'

'Tomorrow evening? I mean, if it's too soon, we can leave it until the weekend, but I thought a weekday might be easier for getting a babysitter.'

She watched Dani as she deliberated. 'Yeah, okay.'

'Shall I come over your way? I could book a restaurant.'

Another hesitation. She was being too keen, too pushy.

'Sorry,' she said with a smile. 'Listen to me. I'm so desperate for a bit of child-free time, I'm planning your week for you. It's just been nice to chat with someone I don't already live with. Ignore me. I mean, why would a gorgeous young thing like you want to be seen out with an old lady like me?'

It worked. 'Don't be daft,' Dani said, guilted into compliance. 'I'll have to check with Mum that she'll have Layla for me, but it should be fine, she never goes anywhere.'

'Great.' Adele stood. 'Ivy, are you going to give Layla a cuddle?'

They watched as the two little girls eyed each other uncertainly, before Ivy relented and threw her arms around Layla's shoulders.

'I'll book somewhere and send you the details,' Adele said.

'Thanks. And thanks for today. It's been lovely.'

She saw them to the door, and she and Ivy waved as Dani drove away. Once they were gone, she rearranged the things she had moved earlier, clearing away any evidence that she had had company.

As Ivy played in her bedroom, Adele used her phone to book a table at a restaurant just a couple of miles from where Dani lived, before sending her the link and saying she'd see her there at seven the following evening. All she needed to do now was plan the lie she would use to excuse herself from the house.

FIFTEEN

DANI

She was due to leave the house in little under an hour's time when Caroline walked into the kitchen, her hair piled on her head in an intricate nest of curls and Kirby grips and her feet pushed into a pair of heels Dani had never seen before.

'I thought you were looking after Layla tonight?'

'You'll have to rearrange for another night,' her mother said.

In all the years since her dad had left, Dani could count on one hand the number of times her mother had gone out for something other than shopping or a medical appointment. Of course, her dad hadn't left – not through choice, at least. His life – all their lives as they had known them until then – had come crashing to an end when he fell from some scaffolding and broke his neck one windy February afternoon, but Dani often told herself the story that he had just gone one day, opting for another life with another family they had known nothing about rather than sticking with the one he had. At least that way she could imagine him somewhere, living in some parallel existence, rather than having to think of him being gone forever. His ashes had sat in a cardboard tube – it was never too late to 'think green', apparently – at the back of her mother's wardrobe for eighteen months before she had finally emptied them at the top of Pen y Fan – a mountain that, as far as Dani knew, her father had never even driven past, let alone climbed.

'Where are you going?'

'Bingo.'

Dani fought back a smirk. 'Bingo? What are you… eighty?
Who with?'

'Julie and the girls.'

'Julie?'

'Yes, Polly Parrot… Julie. That okay with you?'

'Carer Julie, the one you said smells like TCP all the time and
is an opinionated cow? That Julie?'

Her mother said nothing, but Dani saw her eyes roll. She took
a deep breath, reminding herself not to be too hard on her. They
were both still upset about Dylan, shaken and disturbed by the
photograph that had been sent to Caroline. She had been to the
police about it and was told they would look into it, whatever that
meant. If this was her way of trying to distract herself for a few
hours then she deserved it.

'You said you'd have Layla for me, that's all. It doesn't matter,
though.'

'She's your daughter, Dani. I've done my time.'

Dani bit her lip and reached for her phone to call Adele. 'Have
a good night,' she said as Caroline left the room, though she was
still smarting from her mother's choice of words. The way she spoke
sometimes, it was as though Dani had been a prison sentence rather
than a daughter. Dani vowed never to speak of Layla in the same
way, though she wondered whether she inadvertently already had.
Parents messed their kids up, then their kids went on to do the
same to their own.

'I'm so sorry,' she said when Adele answered. 'I know this is short
notice, but I can't make tonight. There's no one to look after Layla.'

'Oh no, that's a shame. Okay.'

'Have you already left? Where are you?'

'On the bus. I jumped on an earlier one to save being late.'

'Okay, um… I'm really sorry.'

'I could come to yours?'

It was exactly what Dani had hoped Adele wouldn't suggest. The truth was, she was a bit embarrassed by where they lived. Their end of the estate had a reputation, and the house itself was nothing to look at, still managing a state of chaos even with her mother's daily vacuuming habit – a routine that hadn't subsided even in Dylan's absence. It appeared even more shabby now that she had seen Adele's place, but with Layla in bed and Caroline out for the evening, Dani didn't fancy the prospect of being on her own.

'What about the restaurant?'

'I'll call them now to cancel.'

'Are you sure you don't mind? I'll text you the address.'

Adele arrived twenty minutes later, while Caroline was still there. She lingered in the hallway, clearly hovering in the hope of meeting Dani's new friend.

'Shall I leave my shoes here?' Adele asked.

'Don't worry about that, love,' Caroline said, beckoning her into the hallway. 'Dani never does.'

They headed through into the kitchen, Dani mouthing a silent apology at Adele.

'Wine?' Caroline offered, opening the fridge.

'No thanks. I don't drink.'

Dani wondered why Adele was teetotal, but it seemed rude to ask.

'I'll put the kettle on,' she said, embarrassed by her mother's uncharacteristic hospitality.

As she made tea, she asked how Ivy was doing and where she was, and Adele told her that she was at home with her father. They played with Layla for a while before Dani took her upstairs to put her to bed. Caroline was still there when she came back down and managed to bring up the subject of both the flyers and the missing cat, watching Dani from the corner of her eye as though she held her personally responsible. She didn't need to make her feel any worse, not when Dani realised that whatever had happened, she had indirectly caused it.

'I am so sorry about my mother,' she said once Caroline had left.

'Don't be daft, she seems lovely.' Adele took a sip of tea. 'She's obviously upset about Dylan.' When Dani said nothing, Adele asked, 'Is everything okay?'

'Yeah, fine.' It wasn't, though. She was shaken by everything that was going on. First the flyers, then the email, not to mention poor Dylan. Who hated her that much? James's wife had motive, but the more she thought about it, the less likely it seemed. For her to access the email addresses of everyone in the playgroup, she must have been to the church. That was unlikely, which would mean someone else was responsible. Someone from the group. Was Amy Davies spiteful enough to have sent that email? If so, was she also responsible for the flyers?

Dani thought of Dylan, tied up and trapped somewhere, and the image brought tears to her eyes. Surely Amy couldn't have done that as well. It would have been easy for her to get hold of the playgroup members' records; the church volunteers ran everything as though it was 1993, with just a file at the desk that held everyone's registration details. All she would have needed to do was wait until the volunteers were all in the kitchen making tea, then go to the file and photograph the relevant pages. But Dylan? That was just cruel. Sick.

'You're still thinking about that email?'

'I just wonder what Layla's going to think when she grows up and finds out her mother's got a criminal record.'

'She's not going to think anything. She'll know you and she'll love you. It won't matter.'

'I wonder if Elaine has seen it yet.'

'It's not going to matter to her either.'

It might, Dani thought. Elaine might think it had been deceitful of her to keep it a secret. Perhaps she wouldn't have wanted Josh mixing with Layla had she known.

'Stop torturing yourself with it. We all do things we regret.'

Dani raised her eyebrows. 'Not to that extent. I mean, what's your biggest regret? I bet it's nothing on that scale.'

Adele fell silent for a moment. 'I had a friend who died. It happened suddenly – he had a massive heart attack, killed him outright. We hadn't spoken for years. After he'd gone, all I could think about were the things I wished I'd said to him. It doesn't go away, does it? It just stays there and grows bigger.'

Dani felt a knot tighten in her chest. Eve. She hadn't thought of her in a couple of days, not since hearing back from her mother. Now, the absence of thought felt like a betrayal.

'Are you okay?' Adele asked.

'Sorry, not really. I actually found out recently that one of my friends from school had died.'

'God. I'm sorry. What happened?'

'She drowned.'

Dani remembered school swimming lessons, how Eve would almost always have a note to get her out of having to take part. When she did go in the pool, she would stay down the shallow end. They had been to the beach together on several occasions, but Eve made a point of never going near the sea, not even close enough to get her toes wet. She was scared of the water, she always had been; she didn't want to learn to swim, and so she never did.

Adele said nothing, but then Dani supposed there wasn't much that could be said.

'The thing is…'

She trailed into silence because she didn't really know how to say what she was feeling. She knew how it felt to grieve for someone who had died, but she had lost Eve long before her death. She had mourned their friendship for a while, in the same way someone might mourn a death. All the might-have-beens and the things she would never know. But now, it almost felt as though she didn't have the right to feel sad about Eve being gone, not when they hadn't seen each other in four years.

'The thing is what?'

Dani sighed, trying to expel the tension that had risen to her temples. 'I just… I feel guilty, that's all.'

'Guilty about what?'

She hesitated over an answer. 'We didn't see each other for a long time. We fell out. It was ages ago now, but sometimes it feels like it was just a couple of months back, you know?'

Adele sipped her tea. Dani didn't know why, what it was about her, but she felt able to talk to her, as though perhaps she wouldn't judge her and maybe she might understand. If she hadn't judged her for the assault conviction, she wondered what else she might excuse.

'Can I ask what you fell out over?'

'Just girl stuff.' Dani took a mouthful of her own tea. She felt suddenly hot, her skin itching beneath her sweater, and her head was thumping, as though the tea was laced with something stronger than wine.

Adele was watching her sympathetically.

'A boy?'

Dani shook her head. 'It was nothing really,' she lied again. 'We just sort of lost touch, you know… like people do.'

'Guilt will eat you up. Trust me, I know. Our circumstances sound similar, you know – my friend and I had fallen out as well. I think we could have put things right, given the opportunity, but it never arose. And then it was too late.'

'I'm so sorry,' Dani said, not really knowing what else to say.

Adele looked as though she was going to say something else, as though she might offer more about this person who had died, this friend she had lost, but instead she turned to reach over the end of the sofa to where her bag was sitting on the floor. She took out her phone and swiped the screen, and Dani found herself distracted by her back, which was exposed by the T-shirt that had ridden up above her waist.

'Sorry,' Adele said, dropping the phone back into the bag. 'Just wanted to check Ivy's okay.'

'Is she?' Dani looked away; she didn't want it to be obvious that she'd been staring.

'Well, no text, so I'm assuming so.'

She couldn't keep her mind off the bruises she had just seen on Adele's back. A trick of the light, perhaps? No. They covered her skin, green and purple and mottled, and Dani felt sure her face must have betrayed the fact that she had seen them.

'Those flyers,' Adele said, tilting her head as though trying to wake Dani from a daydream. 'Do you know who's responsible?'

'I've got an idea.'

Adele waited, eyebrows raised, and Dani longed for her story to just fall from her mouth so she could get rid of the nasty taste it had left there for so long.

'Layla's father was married. I didn't know,' she added quickly when she saw the involuntary twitch of Adele's cheek that revealed what she had feared – that Adele would hate her for what she'd done. 'We met at a petrol station – how stupid does that sound? I had Mum's car, and she never fills it up – I swear she waits for me to use it first so I'll have to do it. Anyway, I went in to pay, and when I got to the counter, I realised I'd left my purse at home. It was so embarrassing. A queue started building up behind me, which was typical, and I was getting really flustered. That was when the man behind me offered to pay.'

'Layla's father?'

Dani nodded. 'I didn't want to accept, but I didn't really have much choice. I said I'd pay him straight back, so we swapped numbers and I went home and got my purse.'

'And then…?'

'And then when I met up with him to give him the money, we chatted a bit and he seemed nice and he asked me out for a drink, and like an idiot I said yes. I mean, he was good-looking and everything, but to be honest, I was probably a bit bored, and it just seemed like a good idea. He wasn't wearing a wedding ring, I swear. I know how bad it makes me look, but I never knew he had a wife and when I found out about her, that was it, it was over.'

Adele wore a wedding ring, though she never really talked about her husband. Dani didn't like to pry too much – some people liked their privacy and it seemed cheeky to ask when she wasn't volunteering the information. Plus, Dani was enjoying being the one to do the talking. It felt nice to have someone just listen.

'How did you find out?'

'We used to go to his house, you know, to be alone.' She stopped, picked at her nail and laughed – not a happy laugh, but the kind that laughed at itself, as though it knew what an idiot she was. 'Turns out it wasn't even his house – it was a friend's. He had a spare key. We were together one afternoon when his friend came in and found us in his bed. I mean, you can imagine what I thought when this strange bloke walked in. I thought we were being robbed or something. Anyway, his friend went mental when he found us there. Told me there and then that he was married.' She shook her head, still angry with herself for being so naïve and only seeing what she had wanted to. 'He lied about everything. And then three weeks later, I found out I was pregnant.'

It had happened the week after she'd been charged with assault. She had worried herself sick with the thought of having been drunk while not knowing there was the stem of a little life growing inside her, and convinced herself that she had killed the baby, picturing the sonographer at her scan turning solemnly to her as she caught a glimpse of the lifeless shadow on the screen in front of her.

Then there was the thought of being a young single mother with a criminal record, of her child growing up and discovering what sort of mother it had and resenting her for not being better. It had seemed so unfair that the men who had ruined her life – the one who had groped her, the one who had neglected to mention the wife he had back at home, the one who had been stupid enough to climb scaffolding while the sky was filled with a storm – had all escaped having to face repercussions for their misdemeanours. Well, all except her dad, although he hadn't had much to face. It was the people left behind who suffered.

Adele looked down at her tea. 'He knows about Layla, though?'

The hesitation lingered too long, and Dani was sure that Adele saw her answer before she gave it. She knew it made her look calculating, and she had heard it all before – all the 'he has a right to know' and 'a child should know its father' speeches. Her mother had said the same thing, though Dani thought she just said it because she knew it was exactly what Dani didn't want to hear.

'He didn't want me in his life. I don't want him in mine.'

Perhaps she was being selfish. She tried to read Adele's face for signs she might think the same, but the other woman was a blank page.

'Do you think he'd want Layla in his life, though? If he knew about her?'

'Probably not,' Dani answered, too quickly, because the question felt as though Adele was having a dig, and she felt it in her side as though she had physically assaulted her.

'I'm sorry. I didn't mean…'

'It's fine. You don't need to apologise.' Dani sighed. 'I'm doing my best, you know. I thought I'd be enough for her, but sometimes I'm not so sure. Sometimes I feel like I'm failing her, like I'm just not good enough. Is that normal? Do you ever feel like that?'

Adele gave her a sad smile. 'All the time.'

There was a moment of awkward silence in which Dani regretted having said so much. 'Anyway,' she said, keen to ease the tension. 'How long have you been living round here? You've never said where you're from.'

SIXTEEN

ADELE

Adele was saved from answering the question by Dani's mobile ringing, and from the look on Dani's face, she was similarly grateful for the reprieve it offered them. Adele watched her take the call, and the look quickly morphed from relief to frustration.

'I don't understand,' she said. 'She never... No, I know that, I just...' She turned her back to Adele as though it would stop her from hearing what was said. 'I can't. Layla's in bed. Julie, I...' She sighed loudly. 'I'll call you back in five, okay?'

'Everything okay?'

'My mother's drunk,' Dani said, throwing her hands up in a gesture of exasperation. 'Typical. She would pick tonight.'

'What do you mean?'

'She hardly ever drinks. She doesn't go out much.'

'Is she okay?'

Dani shrugged. 'She's upset about the cat. That's probably why she's done this.'

'Is someone going to bring her home?'

'They've all had too much to drink. Julie asked if I'd go and get her, but the car's there, and I can't leave Layla, can I?'

'I'd offer you a lift, but I don't drive. Sorry. Can't they just call your mother a taxi? You could pick up the car tomorrow.'

'I don't really want to leave it there overnight. She'll probably have parked it down by the industrial estate, and it'll have a ticket on it by the morning. Either that or it'll have no tyres left. There are always gangs of kids hanging about down there.' Dani looked at her phone as though its screen might somehow throw up a solution to her dilemma.

'Why don't I stay here with Layla,' Adele offered. 'How far away is your mum? You could get a taxi there and drive back.'

Dani hesitated on a response, clearly tempted by the offer.

'Do you need money for a taxi?'

'No, no. I mean, thanks, but it's okay.' Dani swiped a thumb across her phone and tapped in the passcode. 'Are you sure about this? I'll just let Julie know. I won't be more than half an hour.'

'It's fine.'

She called Julie back, told her she was on her way, then rang for a taxi. 'Layla won't wake up,' she told Adele. 'She never does until after midnight. I really appreciate this.'

The taxi arrived less than ten minutes later, and once Dani was gone, Adele went upstairs to use the bathroom. There were three bedrooms, and she could tell which was Layla's by the glow of a night light escaping through the gap in the door, casting a soft puddle of orange on the landing carpet. She should have gone back downstairs, but instead she lingered, holding her breath, trying to listen for the sound of the child's breathing. The door creaked when she pushed it; she waited a moment to hear if the sound had disturbed her, but Layla didn't move.

The room was tiny, the furniture cheap and chipped, and when Adele rested her hands on Layla's cot, the bars were loose. The wardrobe needed a lick of paint to hide the damage that appeared to have been done possibly during transit. It might have been purchased at a charity shop, or perhaps donated second-hand, with the faint shadow of old stickers still visible on the doors. Either way, Dani had clearly made an effort to make the room appear nicer than it was, putting animal transfers on the walls and lining up Layla's soft toys on the windowsill.

Layla was sleeping on her back, her arms up at the sides of her head in the way a much younger baby would sleep. Her blanket was kicked to the foot of the cot and her hair covered her face, and when Adele leaned into the cot and breathed in, she inhaled the scent of apple shampoo. She remembered the smell from years ago, the kind of cheap supermarket own-brand shampoo her mother used to buy, and the memory of it pulled her to a forgotten place, somewhere cast aside in her mind's locked drawer and abandoned until then with all the other memories she had chosen to neglect. She felt sadness tighten in her chest like indigestion, and she placed a hand on Layla's face, using her palm to brush her hair from her cheeks, little circles of flushed rosy red that were hot to the touch. Layla's breath escaped her in a tiny soft snore and she snuffled with the movement above her, and Adele felt she could have happily stayed there until Dani arrived back home, just listening to the child's breathing and watching the rise and fall of her sleeping body.

She kissed her fingertips and placed them on Layla's warm little forehead before leaving the bedroom and pulling the door closed behind her. At the top of the stairs, she hesitated, temptation holding her there until it pulled her into the room next to Layla's.

Though Dani was a young woman in her twenties, her bedroom was still a teenage girl's: a tangle of headphones and an array of make-up pencils and nail varnish pots sat on the messy dressing table, and behind the bed there were dots of chipped paintwork where posters had been stuck. The drawer of her bedside table had been left open, a box of tampons shoved in beside a couple of bottles of perfume and a selection of chargers. The wardrobe was also open, though there were probably more clothes thrown over the end of the bed than there were on the hangers. Adele sat on the mattress and smoothed a hand over the sheet. It felt strange being there, and she knew it was wrong, but she felt closer to the truth somehow, as though just being there allowed her a glimpse of all the things she had yet to see.

Her fingers gripped the side of the bed as a hot rush of anger pulsed through her veins; when she stood, dizziness pulled her sideways, and she steadied herself with a hand against the wall. She took a deep breath and counted to ten – in through the nose and out through the mouth – and thoughts of Tim flashed into her head, of what he would advise her to do if he could see her now. She opened her eyes and refocused.

On one of the shelves, wedged between a stack of magazines and a box decorated with butterflies, something caught her eye. A set of Russian nesting dolls, yellows and reds, the colours faded, the veneer scratched and damaged. She took them down and turned them in her hands, feeling the surprising weight of them. She hadn't seen such a set in a long time, and this one looked as though it was probably older than Dani. When she left the bedroom, she took the dolls downstairs with her.

She was in the living room when she heard a key in the front door, and she realised how long she had been upstairs. She went into the hallway as Dani helped her mother into the house.

'Layla okay?'

She nodded. 'All fine.'

She helped Dani guide Caroline up the stairs, waiting on the landing as she settled her into bed.

'You okay?' she asked when Dani came back out of the bedroom.

'It'll all be forgotten about by the morning,' Dani said with a roll of her eyes. 'As though nothing happened.'

'Maybe for the best. We all need to let our hair down sometimes.'

'Thanks for staying with Layla. I've asked the taxi driver to wait outside for you. I hope that was okay?'

'Great. Thanks.' Adele moved towards her, saw Dani flinch at the imminent contact, yet when she put her arms around her to give her a hug, Dani let her. 'Try not to worry about anything.'

Dani followed her downstairs and watched at the door as Adele got into the back of the taxi. Once the car had left the street, Adele took her phone from her bag and tapped out a text. Amid all the distractions, she had forgotten her manners.

Thanks for a lovely evening. Let's do it again soon x

SEVENTEEN

DANI

On Wednesday morning, Dani woke with a headache and a sore throat. She was sure there was nothing wrong with her, but she had worked herself up over what happened at playgroup the previous week, and she knew she had let Layla down by reacting the way she had. Thoughts of her tormentor had plagued her through the night. As soon as she resolved on one thing, she changed her mind again. Amy did it. Amy didn't do it. What if James's wife had somehow managed to gain access to that email list? She had more motive than anyone at the playgroup, particularly if she was also responsible for the flyers. If the aim was to destroy Dani's reputation, the email was a great way of aiding the desecration. And without knowing anything about the woman, Dani had no idea whether she was capable of abducting an innocent animal. She was going to have to confront her, if only to rule her out.

Then there was Eve. Since her conversation with Adele, she couldn't stop thinking about her, about her death and everything that had been left unsaid between them. Though she hadn't seen her in years and had had no intention of ever meeting up with her again, she couldn't accept that there was now no chance of them ever doing so. Confiding in Adele had seemed a good idea at the time, but in the cold light of morning, Dani realised it had made no difference. She couldn't tell her the whole truth about what had happened between her and Eve, and now she had to bear the burden alone.

On top of everything else, she had her mother to worry about. Caroline's behaviour the previous evening had been completely out of character. When Dani had gone to collect her, she had found her outside the bingo hall with Julie, who was propping her up, the pair of them puffing on cigarettes and looking like a couple of drunken aunties on a hen night. Julie had hiccups, which managed to make her even more annoying than usual, and trying to get any sense out of her about what had happened to Caroline was like trying to get Layla to tidy up after herself. The car was parked two streets away, just a few doors down from the boarded-up block of factory units where all the kids still hung about at night, and as they headed there, two teenage boys on bikes went past, one of them throwing an empty Coke can at them and shouting something inaudible as he passed. Dani shouted something back, and when her mother tripped over her own feet, it took all her willpower not to drop her on the pavement.

In the car on the way home, Caroline sat with her forehead pressed against the window, speaking in incoherent mumbles.

'Dylan's dead, isn't he?' she slurred.

'What have you been drinking?'

'Cider and black,' she said, 'cider' sounding more like 'slider'. 'But I only had two.'

Adele helped her to get her mother upstairs when they got back. Caroline was asleep by the time Dani lifted her legs up onto the bed. She went in to check on her a while later, then found herself unable to get back to sleep. She was not a bad person, she told herself repeatedly as the darkness of the early hours stood beside her bed like the Grim Reaper. She hadn't known that Layla's father was married; if she had, then perhaps this punishment would have been justly deserved. But this wasn't fair. Yet as every nerve in her body tingled with doubt, she wondered if in fact it was true. She *was* a bad person. Was this how things were rebalanced? There were other bad things she had done; things she had never been punished for. Maybe this was how she would pay.

Somewhere in the night, caught up in her wakefulness, she retrieved her phone from where she had left it downstairs.

It had been nearly three years since she had last looked at any of Eve's social media. Watching Eve's life move forward had kept a hand gripped over the throat of her own, and once she had eased those fingers from around her neck it felt as though she could start to breathe again. Sometimes the idea of returning to those pages to see what Eve was doing and where life had taken her was tempting, but she always managed to stop herself. She would remember what Eve had done – what she had made Dani responsible for – and then keeping her away would be easy, as though Dani had never needed her friendship at all.

Now, Eve was a distraction from all the other things that haunted her, so she clicked into Facebook and typed her name into the search bar. Fifteen mutual friends; they must all be people they'd been at school with.

She scrolled through the comments that had been left in the aftermath of Eve's death, pausing at the ones left by people they both knew.

Can't believe you're gone, hun. Beautiful girl with the angels now xx

Hayley Maitland. Never used to bother with Eve at school; in fact, might even have actively disliked her. This kind of falseness was one of the reasons Dani barely looked at her social media any more, though she had not quite got to the point of deleting her profiles. Sometimes she felt the need to have some sort of presence online to remind herself that she was just twenty-two and not middle-aged already.

There had been a lot of things written on Eve's wall, as though posting those messages wasn't completely pointless – the recipient couldn't see any of them, could she? – and Dani wondered whether maybe she was the one whose thought processes were wrong, but the comments seemed almost offensive somehow, as though it was acceptable to start taking an interest in someone's life once they had ceased to exist.

Further down the page, there was a post from Eve's sister, Maddie.

> *Some of you may already know, but on 11 May 2019, we lost my little sister, Eve. Those of you who knew her know what an amazing person she was – smart, funny, beautiful. Thank you to the people who have sent cards and flowers to my parents' house – it means a lot to know how much Eve meant to everyone, and your words have brought us some comfort at this awful time. Life will never be the same and we will miss Eve every day.*

There was a litany of tributes in the comments section beneath.

> *Can't believe she's gone! Crazy to think I spoke to her not long ago!*

Crazy. It seemed likely that many people spoke to someone in the hours or days before their death, but for some reason what might have been the briefest of exchanges always became a point of relevance, as though the person regretted not having had the foresight to know that the other would be deceased before the week was over. And what would they have said differently, had they known? Nothing, Dani suspected. What could you say?

I can't stop crying. She was so beautiful.

The hyperbole irritated her. Dani was certain Molly Lancaster could in fact stop crying, and she wasn't sure Molly had even spoken to Eve while they were at school. Why the focus on her appearance, as though her death might have been less tragic if she'd had a face peppered with acne or been the owner of a monobrow? What was it with these people? And why were they all so desperate to be a part of someone else's tragedy?

Dani kept reading, her frustration building, but eventually her phone slipped from her hand and her heavy eyes surrendered to the lure of sleep. When she woke, hours later, the morning sun pushing through the gaps in the curtains, her mobile was still on the bed beside her. There was a message waiting for her on Facebook Messenger, from the brother of someone Dani had been at college with.

This hasn't come from me, but the boy in your post is Corey Sinclair. He lives on the Greenfields estate – he's one of Robbie Sinclair's boys.

She was aware of the family; the Sinclairs had a reputation on the estate for causing trouble, though Dani had never had reason to mix with them. She knew one of the older daughters – her son went to the same nursery as Layla – but there had never been reason for their paths to cross, not until now.

She searched for the name on Instagram and within minutes had found who she was looking for. The teenager in the profile picture was obviously the same boy as the one on Travis's CCTV footage. She scrolled his page and studied the photographs he had posted, most taken with a bike close at hand. She knew the skate park where he seemed to spend much of his time, where the previous summer a teenage girl had died after taking drugs that she had bought from a dealer now serving time for manslaughter. She hoped Layla would never be so reckless, but the thought that she wouldn't be able to keep her protected from the world forever served as a reminder of how fleeting her control over her daughter would be.

She put the phone on her bedside table and closed her eyes. The name Corey Sinclair circled her brain like a taunt. Now all she had to do was pay him a visit.

EIGHTEEN

ADELE

On Wednesday morning, Adele hired a car. She hadn't driven in a while and the brakes took some getting used to, the car shuddering every time her foot made the slightest contact with the pedal, but after half an hour's practice on a nearby industrial estate she felt confident enough to get back out on the main roads. As she drove to the car showroom at which Callum worked, her thoughts lingered on Dani and what had happened at her house. She had never expected the girl to confide in her to the extent she had, and gaining her trust filled her with an unprecedented confidence.

On the passenger seat beside her lay the Russian doll, smuggled into her bag while a distracted Dani fretted about her mother's drunken state. The doll's red and yellow exterior was aged and worn, and as she ran a fingertip along a hairline fracture in the veneer, she wondered how many hands had touched its surface and cracked open its middle to see what lay inside. Inanimate objects often carried a silent history, their stories kept mute inside their owners. Exactly how much did Dani keep inside her, and what weight did she carry? Did Callum bear the weight of the things he had done, or did his ego keep him elevated, floating above everything he was guilty of?

Dani was more stressed out by everything than Adele had realised, and she felt a thrill at being the only person she seemed to have spoken to about her worries. There was a friction between her and Caroline that kept Dani from confiding in her fully, and it occurred to Adele not for the first time that she was taking the role of mother. It was a role she had never meant to take, and yet there was something satisfying in being needed and in being the keeper of Dani's darkest secrets.

There was the other thing that had happened at the house, too. Adele had caught the look on Dani's face when she had reached to her bag, and she knew Dani had seen the bruises that covered her lower back. Her expression had been a mixture of shock and concern, and for a moment Adele had found herself feeling sorry for her. She had reprimanded herself for being so careless, though in hindsight, it seemed that maybe it wasn't such a bad thing. Hadn't she wanted to be seen, to be noticed, for so long now? Dani would surely wonder how she had come by the bruises, and what else she might be trying to keep hidden. Would she fear for her safety enough to try to do something to help her?

Her thoughts were cut short as she reached the car showroom and parked up opposite an impressive display of Porsches, the kind of car Callum aspired to afford but would never quite make enough to purchase. If he wanted one, he was going to have to pay for it in the way he seemed to fund most of his life purchases: with someone else's money.

He had worked for Porsche for over a decade but had never risen to the position he had aimed for. He had been refused a promotion five years earlier and had never got over his resentment of his boss, which Adele believed contributed to his hostility towards everyone else, as though the world was to blame for his failings. He could have moved to another company, but opting for a 'devil you know' attitude had kept him anchored with the familiar, and he had no one to blame for his failures but himself.

She scanned the car park and realised his car wasn't there. She drove around the side streets for a while, thinking perhaps it had been busy there that morning and he had parked in a different area, but when she couldn't see the car anywhere, she went back to the building and parked up outside. If he wasn't at work, then where was he? She tried his phone, thinking she could use an excuse about misplacing something for having to contact him in the middle of the day like this, but it went straight through to voicemail. A part of her was relieved at his absence. She hadn't had a proper plan, and he was only likely to be suspicious.

Another part of her was angry. He was lying again.

She got out of the car, locked it and went into the building. At reception, a dark-haired woman of a similar age to her was talking on a phone. She smiled at Adele and gestured for her to take a seat. As she waited, she scanned the magazine on the coffee table, a glossy publication featuring happy couples with gleaming teeth standing alongside shiny cars with immaculate paintwork. It was all a bit vacuous really. A lifestyle bought and paid for. An aspiration dictated by a marketing team.

'Do you have an appointment?' the receptionist asked. She smiled widely, flashing teeth as blinding as those in the magazine, and Adele wondered whether Callum's looks had been part of his interview success when he had been offered the job here all those years ago. He was nearing forty now; those looks would begin to fade given time. Like the cars he sold, the shine would diminish, his performance outdone by something newer and more appealing, and what would become of him then, when he was less desirable to potential buyers?

'Is Callum here?'

The woman smiled again, as though part of her job description was to grin inanely at anyone who walked through the showroom doors. If so, she was excelling in her role.

'Callum's not in today, I'm afraid. Can I take a message for him?'

Adele shook her head. 'No thanks. I'll catch up with him later.' She felt the woman's eyes on her as she left the building.

Instead of heading back to the hire car, Adele rounded the corner and waited at the side of the showroom, taking deep breaths as she allowed her racing thoughts to settle. She took out her phone and made a call. He might have thought he had got away with it before, but she would not let him do this again.

NINETEEN

DANI

It was Friday, which usually meant playgroup, but that morning it meant staying in their pyjamas with no urgency to be anywhere. Though no one had told her she wasn't to go back there, Dani knew she couldn't face those other mothers at playgroup, not after what had happened the week before. Of course, there were a couple of places she needed to go, but she couldn't pay either Corey or James's friend a visit while she had Layla with her, so for now she had to wait. Dani hated lazy mornings; the more time Layla was allowed to idle, the more difficult it inevitably was to get her to do anything or go anywhere.

She had finally replied to Travis's message.

> *You're right – there's a lot going on at the moment. I'm sorry I ran off like that. It wasn't your fault x*

She hoped for a reply, as though Travis might have spent the last week just waiting for her with his phone in his hand, but when one didn't come, she put her phone into her bag, resisting the urge to check it every thirty seconds.

After throwing a screaming fit over a lost Peppa Pig camper van, Layla ate a piece of toast and lay sprawled on the rug watching TV. When the doorbell rang, her focus remained fixed on the cartoon as Dani went into the hallway, grateful for a moment's respite from her daughter's unpredictable mood. Elaine and Adele were on the doorstep, Josh and Ivy standing between them.

'Surprise,' said Elaine, and she held up a striped bag with a picnic blanket hooked at the side of it. 'We thought we'd take the kids to the park – it's supposed to warm up in a bit.' She looked Dani up and down and pulled a face. 'I'm not being seen anywhere with you looking like that, though.'

'You're missing playgroup.'

'Not the same without you there, love. Now come on, get yourself dressed.'

Dani stepped aside to let them in, though having them there made her feel uncomfortable. Her mother was in the shower, and she hoped she wouldn't come downstairs before they had left. She showed them to the living room, and they sat on the sofa while Layla played with Josh and Ivy on the rug and Dani went upstairs to make herself a little more presentable.

They walked the short distance to the park and spent an hour pushing the kids on the swings and the roundabout. The sun inched from behind the scattered clouds and they laid the picnic blanket out on the grass beside the tennis court, the kids succumbing to the idea of sitting still for two minutes once a packet of biscuits had been produced from Elaine's bag with the flair of a magician whipping a rabbit from his hat.

'This was all her idea,' Elaine told Dani, gesturing to Adele.

'It's lovely. Thanks.'

'Are you coming back to play group next week? Don't let that lot win, love.'

'I don't know. I'm not sure I want to.'

Ignoring her, Elaine offered around a plastic punnet of strawberries, and Dani took one, picking absent-mindedly at its leaves. In her pocket, her phone beeped. She took it out to look at it, thinking it was a message, but instead she found a news update. She felt her skin prickle, and though every part of her told her not to look at it then and there, she clicked it open.

Murder Investigation Following 'Accident'

She scrolled through the article, though she didn't really need to. The headline told her everything there was to know, yet the reality of it sat outside her, an uninvited guest at the gathering.

The death of Eve Gardiner, whose body was recovered from the River Avon last month in what was initially believed to have been a case of accidental drowning, is now being investigated as a possible murder. Following a post-mortem, Somerset Police have issued a statement saying there is reason to believe Miss Gardiner, 22, was involved in an altercation on the night she died.

'Everything okay, love?'

'Fine,' Dani said, hurriedly returning her phone to her pocket. She smiled and bit into the strawberry, hoping her stomach wouldn't reject it. The word 'murder' reverberated at the front of her brain, making her feel dizzy. It couldn't be true. And how did her phone know to throw up news relating to Eve? Her rational mind realised her recent search history would dictate the contents of her home page, yet it felt as though she was constantly being watched.

Adele picked up Ivy and pulled a face. 'Good timing,' she said, casting a look of mock disgust at the child's padded backside. 'Is there somewhere I can change her?'

'Just do it there,' Elaine said, pointing at the grass, but Adele looked horrified at the suggestion.

'Not while you're eating.'

'Good point.'

Dani directed her to the disabled toilet at the back of the nearby bowls club and watched as Adele carried Ivy away in one arm, her bag under the other. She tried to push what she had just read to the far corner of her mind, but the headline reverberated, thoughts of what might have happened to Eve before she died circling her like predators. Was it a random attack for a purse or a phone, or had Eve been targeted for another reason?

She forced her thoughts back to the present. 'I'm guessing you've checked your emails by now?' she said.

Elaine waved a hand in the air, dismissing the question. 'We're having a nice day. Stop worrying about things you don't need to fret about.'

'I need your advice.'

'What about?'

'Adele. She came over to the house on Tuesday night, and...' Dani pictured what she'd seen, trying to convince herself it could have been something else – a pattern on a vest top under Adele's T-shirt; an intricate spattering of shadows thrown by the lamp in the living room. But she knew what she had seen, and she knew what it was. 'Her back is covered in bruises.'

Elaine pulled a face. 'What do you mean?'

'She leaned over to pick something up from the floor, and her top rose up and she's got all, like, purple bruising on the bottom of her back. Here.' She gestured to her own lower back, putting a hand about where she guessed her kidneys were.

'Are you sure?'

'Definite. And it wasn't just one bruise, it was like most of her back was covered. I could barely make out any skin.'

'You reckon someone's been hurting her?'

'You don't get that kind of bruising from a fall. More like a beating.'

It occurred to Dani that whatever was going on in Adele's private life might have explained why she was so keen to meet up on Tuesday. She seemed lonely. Maybe she didn't get out of the house much. But if she had wanted to confide in Dani about the bruises and how she had got them, she'd had an opportunity to do so that evening. Yet she hadn't mentioned them. Perhaps fear had kept her silent; if that was the case, it was obvious what conclusion Dani was going to come to.

Elaine's mouth twisted with concern. As though reading Dani's mind, she asked, 'You think her husband's done it?'

'I'm not saying anything.' She didn't want to make an accusation without proof; she knew how much damage a rumour could do; how much destruction loose words could cause.

'She never really mentions him, though, does she? Makes you wonder.'

They were pulled from the ensuing silence when Josh and Layla started arguing over the last pink wafer biscuit.

'You're obviously worried about her,' Elaine said as she snatched the biscuit from the paper plate and snapped it in half without looking at either child. 'What do you want to do?'

'I don't know. I mean, have you noticed how she dresses? She's always covered up, isn't she, even when the weather's nice.'

Elaine passed half a biscuit to Josh and the other half to Layla, and Dani prompted her daughter to say thank you. 'Mention it, love. You obviously feel you should, or you wouldn't be asking me about it. Just tell her the truth – that you noticed it when she leaned over, and you just wanted to check she's all right.'

'What if she gets defensive about it?'

The truth was, she didn't want to probe into Adele's private life if there was a chance it might make things worse for her. If her husband was responsible for the bruises and found out that she had exposed his abuse, what further suffering might lie ahead for her? Maybe Dani was jumping to conclusions. She barely knew anything about Adele. She knew she had a daughter and that she used to be a nurse, but other than that, she was a bit of a mystery. She was embarrassed at having revealed so much of herself to Adele, though at the time she had felt compelled to do so. However the woman had come by her injuries, the last thing she needed was a share in Dani's problems. She didn't want to put Adele at any further risk, but she realised that if she did nothing and something happened to her, she would live to regret it, and she already lived with too much guilt.

Elaine shrugged. 'Chance you've got to take, I suppose. At least you won't have it on your conscience.'

'She might have seen me looking, I'm not sure. She pulled her top down pretty quickly, anyway.'

'There we are then. Maybe it's not what you're thinking. She might have had a fall or some sort of treatment maybe. We don't know.'

But she could tell that Elaine was as sceptical about it as she was. There was really only one explanation as to how someone would end up with bruises like the ones she'd seen. If her husband was responsible, it was no wonder Adele never spoke of him.

TWENTY

ADELE

On Saturday, Adele followed Callum. He said he was meeting a friend to play golf, but she could no longer believe anything that left his mouth. Ivy was playing with Steph, and as soon as Callum left the house, Adele found the keys to the hire car and made an excuse about needing to pop to the bank before it closed.

She thought she had lost him within a few roads of their house, but when she spotted his car turning left at the traffic lights at the top of the high street, she followed him from the village and kept him in sight as he made his way to the M4.

He was only on the motorway until the next junction, so it wasn't difficult for her to keep up with him. If he'd spotted her, he showed no signs of it, and as he made his way towards Cardiff Bay, her suspicions were confirmed. She shifted in the driver's seat and tried to take the pressure off her back. The bruising was starting to fade, and the pain had been replaced with an ache she carried around with her all day, unable to escape it even in the rare moments of sleep she managed to claim during the night.

She turned left as Callum did, heading towards a side street lined with marked parking areas. He pulled over, so she stopped a few spaces behind him and watched as he got out of the car and locked it. He had even dressed as though he was going to play golf, the ridiculous pair of trousers making him look like a cartoon character from an episode of *Charlie Chalk*. She assumed he was meeting up with Diane – unless there were others. It occurred to her that whoever she was, the other woman must have a tolerance for crap dress sense and lies, because how else would he get away with meeting her in a public place wearing those trousers?

She got out of her own car, locked it and began to follow him. It was already warm, expected to hit twenty-five degrees that afternoon, and as she hurried to keep him in sight, she wished she hadn't put on jeans that morning. Callum headed back to the main road, crossed at the pedestrian crossing, then walked towards the heart of the Bay's bar and restaurant area. It was already busy: youthful couples walking hand in hand, families with young children in prams, gangs of teenagers gathered by the railings where the boats took off for Penarth. For a moment she thought she had lost him, before spotting him taking money out of a cashpoint.

She watched him tuck the cash into his wallet and return it to his trouser pocket before he veered left and headed towards one of the buildings. A tapas bar. He looked around before he went in, as though checking no one was watching, which Adele imagined was a default gesture for someone used to living a life in which looking over his shoulder had become a necessary pastime. She felt sweat pool at the neck of her T-shirt, and her stomach fluttered with the possibilities of what she suspected she might be about to witness.

There was a gift shop at the other side of the street, and she lingered there as though browsing the contents of the window, able to turn to the side to watch them. The woman was older than she had expected; older than she had sounded on the phone. She guessed mid to late forties, though she might have been in her fifties, dressed smartly in fitted trousers and a collared blouse as though she had just come from an office. Adele wondered whether this was part of the thrill, the sneaking off from work and meeting on neutral territory, somewhere private enough to be alone but sufficiently exposed to allow the possibility of being caught. Was this what Callum was hoping for, that being caught might offer him an opportunity out of the marriage?

They kept their distance as they greeted one another, presumably cautious of any physical show of affection that might draw attention. He gestured to a table and held out an arm, a show of hypocritical chivalrousness that filled Adele with anger. They sat opposite one another near the window, a choice Adele considered either obnoxiously arrogant or dangerously relaxed. Within moments, a member of staff had come over to take their order, and once she was gone, the woman took something from her bag that she placed on the table between them.

Nauseous from the heat and from not having eaten anything that morning, Adele crossed the road and lingered outside a vegan café, feigning interest in a two-course lunchtime offer. Callum's attention hadn't left the woman and whatever they were looking at, so Adele continued in her role as spectator, confident that he wouldn't spot her. She wondered whether they would order the same thing; whether Diane was one of those insipid women who would wait for a partner to order before self-consciously muttering, 'I'll have the same, thanks.'

How many of the women he had involved himself with had known that he was married? There would be those who had been oblivious, those who knew but didn't care, the ones who suspected but had never brought themselves to ask, then those who had given him an ultimatum. Yet there had not been one who had thought to tell his wife what he was up to.

Her phone vibrated in her pocket. Dani.

Just checking in to see how you're doing. Thanks again for yesterday – I really enjoyed it x

She messaged back.

All good here, thanks. Glad you enjoyed! Let's arrange another catch-up soon x

She accessed the camera on her phone and returned her focus to Callum. He was leaning across the table now, speaking conspiratorially to the woman, and she moved a couple of shops nearer, close enough that she would be able to zoom in on the two of them together. She hurriedly took a couple of photos before heading back to the car, her heart racing with the sense that when the truth came out, Callum might finally be made to pay for what he had done.

TWENTY-ONE

DANI

Corey Sinclair turned out to be as easy to find as Dani had suspected he might be, courtesy of his Instagram profile and his apparent second home of the skate park. Dani sat in her car at the side of the road and waited. She realised that time spent waiting there was time that could have been spent going to see James's friend, but the more she thought about going to that house again, the more she talked herself out of it. Given the choice, she decided that even a showdown with one of the Sinclair family seemed preferable to facing up to the ghosts of her past.

The skate park was quiet, though every time she did see a new face appear, it looked the same as the last, every teenage boy who frequented the place a copy of the previous arrival, with the same clothing and the same hairstyle. As she waited, she checked her phone. She had received a message from Travis the previous evening, one she had still not replied to.

You have nothing to apologise for. Let me take you for a drink one night? X

She didn't know how to respond. She had always hoped he would ask her out, yet now that he had, all she could think about were the ways in which she might mess things up.

She was mid reply when she saw Corey Sinclair with a group of boys of a similar age, all on bikes or with skateboards. They chatted for a while before dispersing, and when Corey left the park, she followed him. He stopped at an off-licence on the main route from the estate into Cardiff, and she parked and waited for him outside. He was wearing an ill-fitting tracksuit and had a pair of oversized headphones hanging around his neck, the same ones he had been wearing when he had been picked up on Travis's CCTV.

'Corey.'

He turned and narrowed his eyes defensively, managing to question who she was and what she wanted with him without opening his mouth.

'Recognise me?' she asked. 'Or this?' She waved one of the flyers in front of him, but he didn't need to look too closely to know who she was.

'Fuck off,' he mumbled. He made a grab for his bike, but she got there first, resting against the seat so the only way he would be able to leave with it was to manhandle her off.

'You can try it if you want,' she said, reading his thoughts as he considered a possible next move, 'but it didn't end well for the last person.'

If she hadn't been so tired and so angry, she might have been able to laugh at herself. Here she was, standing outside an off-licence making clichéd action-movie threats to a teenager who happened to belong to one of the most notorious families on the estate, while indirectly bragging about her own criminal record. All this so she could avoid returning to the house where her daughter had been conceived in circumstances that she had naïvely believed at the time to be some sort of love. It would have been funny if it wasn't so tragic.

'Someone paid you to put these up, didn't they? Who was she?'

He reacted at the 'she', a flicker of the eyes as he realised that she already knew something at least, and that she wasn't going to move until he gave her answers.

'Fuck off,' he said again, although this time there was less conviction in the words, and he looked around him, clearly worried that someone might notice their exchange.

She shrugged. 'Your choice.' She whipped the scissors from her pocket – a pair she had taken from the salon – and raised her arm above the bike's back wheel before swinging it down towards the tyre.

'Whoa!' Corey lunged forward and grabbed her arm, stopping the scissors before they touched the bike. Then he looked at his hand on her and his face contorted into a confused mix of anger and panic at the thought of what she might do next. No doubt he wouldn't be the first member of his family to be accused of violence.

He pulled his hand away and stepped back. 'What are you, mental or something?'

He might be right, she thought. All she knew was that the woman who had put him up to this was doing her best to ruin her life, and even if she didn't succeed in that, she was already winning by making Dani feel as though she was losing her mind.

'Just tell me who it was.'

Dani guessed he had been paid – why else would the kid waste his time like that? – and she was curious to know how much he had been given to stick those flyers up around the estate. If she only learned one thing, however, she would rather it was a name.

'I don't know,' he said. 'I've never seen her before.'

'Yeah, right. She just approached you and asked you to do it, did she?'

'Actually, yeah. I was in the skate park and this woman comes up to me and offers me money, so I was hardly going to turn it down, was I?'

'Clearly not.' She glanced at the scissors still in her hand and then back at his tyre. The unspoken threat was enough. 'Who was she?'

'That bike probably cost more than your house,' he said, eyes narrowed.

'Stolen, is it?'

'My sisters will come looking for you, you crazy bitch.'

'Oh no,' Dani said, raising a hand to her mouth in mock horror. 'I'm terrified.' In truth, the prospect of coming face to face with any of the other members of the Sinclair family was one she didn't welcome. She raised the scissors again, but this time rather than bringing them down towards the tyre, she held them in front of her, brandishing them towards Corey.

'I don't know who she was, all right,' he said, stepping back. 'She was just normal. Thirties, I suppose. I dunno. Brown hair.'

The description covered a million women. Had he just described James's wife, or was it one of the mothers from the playgroup?

She stepped away from the bike and Corey moved quickly to retrieve it.

'Bitch!' he called as he cycled away, his confidence returned once he was safely out of reach.

Dani sighed. She was no closer to the truth than she had been when she left the house, and all that coming here had done was confirm what she already knew.

She took her phone from her pocket, remembering that she had never finished replying to Travis.

I'd like that. Thanks x

Before she could talk herself out of it, she pressed send.

She went back to the car, frustrated that her encounter with Corey had led her nowhere. She had hoped that by seeing him she might avoid what she now knew she was going to have to do next. She tapped an address into the search engine on her phone. An image of a street appeared at the top of the screen. She recognised it instantly. Just seeing the place made her feel sick. She had been there a few times, though back then it had never occurred to her that these visits were always spontaneous and always short. Her naïvety was painful to look back upon, but she wouldn't be made a fool of twice.

It took her twenty minutes to reach the address. As she got out of the car, her hands shook. She glanced up at the front bedroom, where Layla had been conceived. It all seemed so cheap and sordid now, yet at the time she had been stupid enough to believe James had had feelings for her.

She rang the doorbell and waited. She would remember his friend, she was sure of it; she was terrible with names, but she didn't forget faces. He was tall and broad-shouldered, with dark hair that had looked as though it needed cutting. He had been wearing a shirt and trousers when he'd walked in on them that day, as though he'd just come back from work. He must have been away and had been foolish enough to trust his friend with a key.

She held her breath when she saw a shadow behind the frosted glass. Everything she had planned to say escaped her, and when a woman answered the door, neither of them spoke for a moment. The woman looked at her expectantly, obviously waiting for her to say something.

'Hi,' Dani said awkwardly.

The woman was young – not much older than Dani – and there was a pram parked behind her, a trail of plastic toys snaking along the hallway.

'Um, sorry… I'm looking for my cousin. He used to live here. Have you been here long?'

'Moved in about six months ago.' There was a crash from one of the back rooms, followed by the sound of a baby wailing. 'Jackson! Excuse me a minute.'

The woman rushed to retrieve the baby and reprimand the toddler who followed at her heels when she returned. 'What's his name?'

'Sorry?'

'Your cousin. What's his name?'

Dani was a useless liar. She felt her face flush as the woman eyed her cynically. Glancing into the house, she wondered whether this woman had a husband or a partner, someone to help her with the chaos of being a parent. 'I lied,' she blurted. 'I'm sorry. I just… I'm looking for my daughter's father. The man who used to live here knows him.' She described James's friend, and the woman nodded.

'We bought the house off him. Paul something… sorry, I can't remember.' Her face softened slightly at the sight of Dani's disappointment, pity replacing the scepticism. 'He worked for a bank, I remember that. He'd just been promoted – he couldn't wait to drop it into conversation.'

'Thanks anyway. Sorry for disturbing you.'

The woman closed the door, the baby on her hip wriggling to be put down, and Dani went back to the car. She drove two streets away before stopping and returning to her phone.

It took over half an hour and a search of five different banks before finding him, but she knew his face as soon as she saw his photograph, and with it the humiliation of that afternoon came rolling back like a wave. She opened Facebook and typed his full name into the search bar, finding his profile within moments. It was open, and therefore so was access to his friends list. All 1,047 of them.

She sat back and began scrolling, taking in each and every face. After sitting there for what felt an age, she reached the end of the list, with James nowhere to be seen. She would know his face when she saw him: it wasn't something she would ever forget. Had he kept a low profile to keep his secrets from his wife? she wondered.

Whatever his real name was, he had done a good job at keeping his true identity hidden.

Exasperated, she returned to his profile and scanned the comments made on his recent statuses. She was about to give up and close the app when one of the photographs caught her attention. It was a group of men standing at the side of a football pitch, all dressed in kit. They had their arms around each other's shoulders, posing for what was a celebratory photo. Paul was standing in the middle, grinning inanely and brandishing a bottle of champagne like a Formula One racing driver.

Top fundraiser, the caption said. *See you all next year.*

Dani's eyes moved along the line of men, until she stopped at the second from the end. Her heart jolted in her chest at the sight of him – but more than his face, at the football shirt he was wearing. Paul's shirt featured the logo of the bank he worked for, but James's showed something different. She zoomed in on the company logo emblazoned on his chest. Finally, she had found him.

TWENTY-TWO

ADELE

Adele watched Dani leave the salon and turn right. She had expected her to go in the other direction – she thought Dani would need to head her way to get home – so she had to hurry to follow her, managing to cut across her path at the far corner of the car park.

'Dani! Dani!' She waved an arm, realising as she did so that she must be looking too desperate.

Dani turned, seemingly thrown off balance at seeing her there. All thoughts of making this encounter seem casual had been sent off course by her unexpected choice of route home, and Adele took a deep breath, trying to calm her throbbing heart and cool the hot sweat that was building at the back of her neck.

'Adele. What are you doing here?'

'I've just come from the dentist,' she said, which wasn't a lie – she may not have had an appointment there, but she had gone inside the building. She gestured back to the row of shops. 'Is this where you work?'

'Reluctantly, yes. Ignore me – it's been one of those days.' Dani looked awkward, as though there was something she wanted to say but wasn't sure how she should approach the topic. 'Thanks for Friday.'

'You don't have to keep thanking me. It was lovely. Ivy really enjoyed herself too.'

'Look.' Dani shifted her weight from one leg to the other and looked over Adele's shoulder, unable to meet her eye. 'There's something I want to ask you about. The other night when you were at mine, I… well… I saw the bruises on your back. I don't want to be nosy or anything, but… well, I just wanted to check you're okay.'

The pain of the last beating was already fading, and the previous night Adele had slept better than she had in a long time. Being productive helped to disguise the constant ache that dragged at her weary bones, making her appear to be someone she wasn't. She reminded herself that what she was doing was the right thing. Though she was about to lie to Dani, it would be the first untruth she had told her.

'Stupid,' she said, with a self-deprecating tut, 'but it's the result of a DIY mishap. Fell off a ladder. Could have killed myself.'

Dani's face altered, some imperceptible shift that was only invisible to someone looking for it, though she did her best to remain impassive at Adele's apparently innocent words.

'Are you okay?' Adele asked.

'I'm fine,' Dani said quickly. 'I just… What were you doing up a ladder?'

'Painting a ceiling. I'm no Michelangelo, clearly.' Adele laughed, the sound tinkly and carefree, a spoon upon a glass to precede a wedding speech. But the lie sat leaden between them.

'Anyway,' she said, offering a moment's respite from the awkwardness that had settled. 'What about you? Have you done anything about those flyers?'

'Actually, I have.' Dani reached into her bag and scrabbled about for her phone before tapping in her passcode. She swiped the screen and went to her photo gallery, then held the phone up. 'This kid,' she said. 'Apparently "some woman" paid him to post the flyers up around town.'

Adele took the phone from her and studied the picture, a still from CCTV footage, presumably from the tattoo parlour. Dani was smarter than she pretended to be.

'Some woman?' She handed back the phone.

'Yeah, exactly.'

'You still think it's her? The wife?'

'I did, but then there was that email and now I'm not sure.'

'If it is the wife, why now, though? Layla's two now. It's taken her a while to get around to revenge, if that's what she sees this as.'

'I don't know. Maybe she's only just found out. Perhaps he finally felt some guilt and told her about us.'

Adele laughed, and Dani seemed affronted by the response, as though she was ridiculing her naïvety. Whatever she said, there must have been a part of Dani that had wondered whether her lover was the single man he had claimed to be. Perhaps she had known but had hoped he'd leave his wife for her, and when he chose not to, she felt too foolish to admit her fault. Maybe she had been excited by the possible danger of it all, and now she was paying the price for her selfishness.

'What do you think I should do?'

'I don't know. I mean, I know what I'd do, but…'

'Go on. What would you do?'

'Confront her,' Adele said, checking Dani's face for the flicker of a response. 'She could have lost you your job. How much further do you think she'll take things?'

Dani fell silent as she digested the suggestion. 'I've found him. Layla's dad. I know where he works, at least.'

'Go with your gut,' Adele advised her.

After Dani was gone, Adele delayed going home. She stayed near the salon for a while, watching the owner chat to someone on the phone on the other side of the glass. Someone left the tattoo parlour – a tall pale man with skin the colour of weak tea and a sleeve of tattoos illuminated in a burst of reds and oranges, like flames licking at his skin – and Adele wondered if this was who Dani seemed so interested in. As far as Adele had been able to tell, Dani didn't have any tattoos, and she had made no mention of getting one any time soon, so she could only assume that when she went there, she did so to see him. Was the man her type? Did she even have a type, or did she take whatever she could get?

She waited for him to return before going into the tattoo parlour, where she studied the array of artwork pinned to the walls.

'Hi there.' He came out from the back room, needle in hand. She glanced through the open door, at the customer who lay in the chair, mid tattoo. 'I'm with someone at the moment, but we'll be finished in about half an hour if you want to come back then.'

Adele smiled and gestured to the sofa. 'I'll wait, if that's okay?'

'Great. There's some magazines in the rack.' He pointed to the corner beside the sofa before returning to his client and closing the door.

Adele resumed her study of the images on the wall, her attention caught by a photograph of a butterfly tattoo inked on a woman's shoulder. It was only a small tattoo, an inch or so wide, but it lay there as though it had landed on her skin, delicate and fleeting.

She sat on the sofa and waited for the tattooist to return.

'Are you looking to have something done today, or did you just want to talk over an idea?' he asked once his client had left.

Adele stood and crossed the room to point at the butterfly tattoo. 'This is pretty. Could you do something like this for me? But with a bit more colour.'

'Now?'

She glanced at the clock on the far wall. 'Were you planning to close up?'

He shrugged. 'It's fine, I'm in no rush.'

'No girlfriend to get home to?'

His eyes narrowed slightly, his mouth tilting at the question. Did he think she was flirting with him? she wondered.

'Where would you like it?' he asked, not answering her.

She lifted her hair, touched the back of her neck and smiled. 'Just here, please.'

TWENTY-THREE

DANI

On Tuesday, Dani had the day off work. She took Layla to nursery, went to the supermarket to pick up a few things, then headed back home to prepare a surprise picnic lunch. She would take Layla to the park after picking her up and treat her to an ice cream once they'd had their sandwiches. She wanted to keep things as normal as possible for her, though she wasn't sure what normal was any more.

It had occurred to her that in just over a year, Layla would be at nursery every morning, and the following September she would be in school all day every day. There had been times when the thought of this might have offered some reassurance, the promise of a break and five minutes to herself, but now that the reality of it was getting closer, she was already mourning the time that she and Layla had together, just the two of them. As she buttered bread and grated cheese, she felt a sadness grip at her heart. Layla was only on loan to her, and Dani was living on borrowed time before she would have to give her away to the world. She wiped a stray tear from the corner of her eye, grateful that there was no one there to witness it.

Her mother had stayed in bed even later than usual that morning. She was still understandably upset about Dylan, but Dani knew there was more to it than that. Caroline was worried about her, about what she might have got herself involved in. Dani fretted about the days when she wouldn't be able to keep her daughter protected, but Caroline was already living them. Her mother hadn't left the house in days, and even the vacuuming had been abandoned.

As she busied herself with preparing the picnic, she resisted the temptation to check her phone. Travis hadn't replied to her message, and the longer it went without a response, the more convinced she became that he had changed his mind.

Being near her phone now also meant an inevitable temptation to look again at the photograph of James that she had screenshot from Paul's profile. She didn't want to look at him, though she knew she was going to have to face him in person at some point. She was going to have to face his wife.

She was searching the cupboard next to the fridge for a Tupperware box when there was a knock at the door. She waited for the sound of her mother on the staircase, but when Caroline didn't shift herself from her room, Dani sighed, abandoned her search and went out into the hallway.

When she opened the front door, she was greeted by a bouquet of flowers sitting on the doorstep. She checked the street, but there was no one to be seen. The flowers were a beautiful mix of yellow roses and white chrysanthemums, and when she saw a card with her name printed on it, she smiled to herself as she picked up the box and took it into the house.

No one had ever bought her flowers. She had never even had a proper boyfriend before, not one that had meant anything. Romance was something that seemed archaic and outdated, yet as she took the flowers into the kitchen, she felt herself warmed by the kind of feeling she could happily allow herself to grow used to. Maybe Travis did want her, she thought. Maybe she wasn't such a disaster, after all.

The flowers were wrapped in lemon-coloured tissue paper and a sheet of plastic, and after sitting them on the kitchen worktop near the sink, Dani reached into the box to lift them out. Pain ripped through her right hand, and she recoiled with shock. When she looked at her bloodied palm, she saw a series of cuts patterning the skin. The flesh hung back from a couple of the wounds, and bright red blood pumped from the incisions, making her legs feel weak. She had never dealt well with the sight of blood, feeling nauseous at just a scraped knee whenever Layla had fallen, and the sight of it dripping onto the kitchen tiles made her feel faint.

'Mum! Mum!' When there was no response, she called again. 'Caroline!'

She grabbed a tea towel and wrapped it around her hand, wincing at the stinging pain that travelled the length of her arm.

She heard her mother clatter down the stairs, mumbling something as she made her way to the kitchen. 'What's all the noise about?'

Caroline looked terrible, as though she had barely slept, around her eyes the reddened telltale signs of crying. Neither Dani nor her mother ever cried. They were both more likely to resort to anger than tears, and the sight unsettled Dani more than the blood had.

'Who are the flowers from?' Caroline asked, noticing the bouquet near the sink.

'Plasters. Can you get me some plasters?'

'What's the matter?' She reached for Dani's hand.

'Mum!' Dani pulled away. 'Can you just get me the plasters, please?'

She tightened the tea towel as her mum left the room, and with her left hand grabbed the top of the plastic wrapped around the flowers. With a few wiggles, the bouquet came loose from the box, and when she pulled it out, she could see dozens of tiny razor blades embedded into the individual stems. Something had fallen onto the floor, and when she stooped down, she saw it was a card. She picked it up and managed to open it with one hand.

Consider this a polite warning.

Caroline came back into the kitchen with a box of plasters. 'Let me look,' she said, and unwrapped the tea towel. 'What the bloody hell happened?' She glanced at the flowers and then at the card in Dani's hand. 'Dani!'

Backed into a corner, Dani had little choice but to tell her mother about her visit to Corey Sinclair. It meant mentioning Travis and the CCTV footage, though she omitted the detail about the text she had received while she'd been in the tattoo parlour with him. She also left out the details of Layla's father and the wife she hadn't known about. Though she planned to, she still hadn't been to confront him. Trepidation and fear of further humiliation kept stalling her.

'Sinclair? As in *the* Sinclairs?' Caroline eyed her questioningly. 'Great. There'll be dog shit through the letter box next. Or maybe a parcel bomb, who knows. They're responsible for those flyers then?'

'I don't know. I mean, yes, Corey obviously posted them up around town, but it's someone else who's likely to be behind it.'

'Who?'

Dani said nothing. Caroline's face dropped as a thought occurred to her. 'Did those bastards take Dylan as well?'

'No, Mum,' Dani said, pulling her hand away. 'It wasn't the Sinclairs, I'm sure of that.'

'Then who was it, Dani?'

She felt her jaw tighten as she fought back tears. Her mother cared more about that cat than she did about her, and she couldn't even spare her feelings by trying to hide the fact. 'I don't know, all right?'

'That needs stitches,' Caroline said, gesturing to her hand. 'I'll take you to the hospital and then we're going to report this to the police.'

'Are you mad? And then what?'

'And if we don't report it, then what?'

'They're just trying to scare me off,' Dani said, getting a fresh tea towel from the drawer. 'We won't hear any more from them.'

'How do you know?'

'I just do, okay?'

'Like you know who took Dylan?'

Dani said nothing.

'Whatever the hell is going on,' Caroline said, 'I don't want this trouble coming to my house. If you think you can handle it, then do it, Danielle, but do it quickly before someone gets seriously hurt. Come on.' She looked at the clock. 'I'll get dressed and we'll pick up Layla, then I'll take you to A&E.'

TWENTY-FOUR

ADELE

Adele suspected that Dani saw her as a mother figure, a replacement for the one she already had but seemed unable to confide in. For whatever reason, Dani and Caroline clearly weren't very close. Dani had never said it, but it became more obvious with all the things she didn't say, and when Adele had seen the way she behaved towards her mother the week before, suspicion of her contempt was stamped with certainty. Living with resentment was difficult. Living in the same house as it was impossible. Adele knew that better than anyone.

They stood side by side at the swings, Dani pushing Layla as Adele pushed Ivy. The clouds that had lingered earlier that morning had been nudged aside by a broad sweep of blue sky, and the girls were an image of summer in their dresses and sandals. Despite the temperature, Dani was wearing black, as she always seemed to. It appeared to reflect her mood, a signal to others that they should keep their distance, as though she was in a constant state of mourning.

'I invited Elaine,' Adele said, 'but she couldn't make it. Josh stayed home today – he isn't very well.'

'That's a shame,' Dani said. Adele knew she would text Elaine later to ask whether everything was okay. It didn't matter. Things needed to unravel at some point, and Adele wanted to be the person to unpick the first loose thread.

Ivy started to whine and wriggle, so she pulled her from the swing and set her on her feet. Ivy headed towards the roundabout and Adele followed dutifully, knowing that Layla would soon want to join her new little friend. As she pushed Ivy in circles, she looked back over at Dani. The young woman was distracted by her phone, oblivious to Layla, who was reaching with arms outstretched to be lifted from the swing. When she finally took notice of her daughter, she looked glassy-eyed and distant.

'Everything okay?' Adele asked as they joined them, but Dani nodded without speaking and then changed the subject, asking whether Ivy was allowed an ice cream. When Adele reached into her bag for her purse, Dani insisted that she would pay.

'What happened to your hand?'

A series of marks patterned Dani's palm, and when Adele focused on them, she could see there were stitches.

'I tripped over while carrying a cheese grater. You couldn't make it up, could you?'

Except Dani had made it up, Adele thought, in the same way that she herself had invented her painting accident. She wondered whether all the lies in Dani's life had been uttered so easily and with such carelessness.

'I won't be long.' Dani left Layla in Adele's charge while she went to the ice-cream van parked near the entrance to the park.

'Layla.' Adele beckoned the little girl to her and pointed to the trees that lined the outer edge of the playground. 'You see over there? There's a unicorn that lives there.'

The child looked at her sceptically, cynicism mixed with awe at the possibility.

'Really,' Adele said, widening her eyes. 'She's a bit shy, so only special people get to see her. Would you like to see the unicorn?'

Layla nodded, her head turned to the trees, eager not to miss anything.

Adele checked on Ivy, who was sitting on the floor trying to pull off one of her shoes. 'Here's what we'll do. I'll keep a lookout for it, and when I see it, I'll do this.' She put her hand over her eyes and looked at Layla between her fingers. The little girl laughed. 'It's a game, okay? So when I do that' – she repeated the action – 'it means the unicorn is there and you've got to go and find her. Understand?'

Layla stared at her for a moment before nodding, but Adele wasn't convinced her understanding was mature enough to follow the instructions she had been given. The child turned back to the trees, still searching for the magic that had been promised, but Adele shook her head.

'It's our secret, okay? And not yet. Only when I do this.' She put her hand to her face again, peeping between her fingers. 'Look! Mummy's got ice cream!'

At the sight of Dani, Layla made a run for her, and Ivy – now wearing only one shoe – gave wobbly chase behind her. They sat on a bench together, Dani and Adele armed with wet wipes to mop up the sticky mess of ice cream and strawberry sauce, and when the girls had finished, they ran to play on the roundabout.

'Oh great. Look who it is.' Dani turned her head and rolled her eyes, and when Adele looked behind her, she saw Amy Davies from the playgroup – the mother of the boy Layla had pushed over. The same woman Dani had come close to attacking. Amy's son was climbing up a rope ladder with another, older, boy Adele assumed was his brother. Amy was with one of the other women from the group, her toddler asleep in the pushchair beside her. They were both looking over, making no attempt to hide their interest in Dani.

'Just ignore them,' Adele advised. 'They won't say anything.'

But she was wrong. When the girls ran back to the swings and Adele and Dani took up their respective places to push them, Amy neared, ushering her son in their direction as an excuse to approach them.

'Haven't seen you at playgroup recently,' she said, her eyes boring into Dani defiantly, a fake smile stretching her lips.

Adele looked at Dani and shook her head, reminding her not to react.

'Must have been that email,' Amy continued. 'I'm sure it didn't come as too much of a shock to anyone. I mean, they all saw your true colours a couple of weeks ago, didn't they?'

Dani's head snapped to her left. 'It was you?'

'What was me?' Amy replied, her voice thick with feigned innocence. 'Come on, Joseph, let's go and play somewhere safer.'

'Were those flyers you as well?' Dani stepped towards her but made sure to keep a distance.

'Careful,' Amy said lightly, goading her. 'Don't want to let that temper of yours get the better of you.'

'Have you taken my mother's cat?'

She pulled a face. 'Your mother's cat?' And then she laughed.

'Dani,' Adele said quietly. 'Don't rise to it.'

'Come on, Joseph,' Amy said again. 'Good luck with the cat,' she added.

The two of them watched as she headed back to her friend. When Adele looked at Dani, the young woman's face had crumpled with something that might have been shock or anger but was instead confusion, as though everything she had thought had been tipped up and shaken beyond recognition.

'Come on,' Adele said, lifting Ivy out of the swing. She did the same to Layla, and as she did so, she motioned their secret gesture to her. Layla's attention moved straight to the trees that edged the park.

'Why would she do that?' Dani asked quietly, more a question to herself than to Adele. 'I know that lot look down at me, but why would she go to all that trouble?'

Adele stooped to tidy Ivy's hair, covering her ears in the process. 'Some women are just bitches.'

'Is that what people think, that their kids aren't safe around me? "Let's go and play somewhere safer."'

Dani's attention was still on Amy and her friend. Adele had heard their laughter dance carefree across the playground, and for a surprising moment she felt sorry for Dani. She pushed the feeling away and turned to Ivy.

'Ivy, come and look at this.' She caught the girl by the hand, stealing her attention by showing her an intricate spider's web that had been spun in silvery circles on the climbing frame.

'Where's Layla?' Dani asked.

Adele glanced past her and saw a flash of pink cotton amid the trees. Layla couldn't go far beyond them – the park was bordered by high railings, and the nearest exit was so far along that one of them would see her before she had a chance to reach the gate.

'Layla!'

Dani hurried to one of the other climbing frames, searching for her daughter in the boat-shaped hidey-hole beneath it. Adele made a pretence of looking for her by the toilet block, keeping an eye on Ivy, who was still sitting on the bench drinking from her bottle.

'Layla!'

It took just moments for Dani's voice to change, its pitch and tone higher. The panic was audible, enough to give Adele what she needed – the sense that soon Dani would understand exactly how Adele had been made to feel: that gut-churning, heart-stopping sensation of an entire world being ripped from beneath her feet. It would be momentary, of course, but the taste would linger for long afterwards.

'Adele, where's Layla? Where's she gone?'

'She can't have got far. You go that way,' Adele told her, gesturing in the direction of the ice-cream van. 'I'll take Ivy and look over there.'

There were only a few other people in the park – a pair of teenage boys playing football, and a young couple holding the hands of a toddler who looked as though he had only recently started to walk. As Dani rushed back up the path to the top of the park, the couple's attention was drawn by her shouting Layla's name; they exchanged glances, words, and then looked around as though they might be able to help. Adele was sure their grip on their son's little hands must have tightened, grateful that it was someone else's child who was missing.

'Come on,' she said, scooping Ivy up into her arms. 'Let's go and find Layla.'

They headed towards the far end of the playground, making their way across the grass. She would find her waiting behind one of the trees, maybe looking up into its branches, still hoping for a flash of white wings or a sparkling horn among the leaves.

'Layla!'

She called her name, expecting her little face to emerge, but when she reached the trees, Layla wasn't there. She started to feel sickness swell in her stomach. She couldn't see her. Layla had gone.

Every moment that passed seemed to stretch into an awful void of empty time, and all the things that came next clattered through her brain – police, search parties… questions. She'd never meant to harm Dani's child. She would never hurt a child. She hadn't even believed that her plan to distract her would work. She just wanted Dani to suffer as she had made her suffer.

'Layla!'

She heard Dani's voice from the other side of the park, frantic and terrified.

And then she saw her. Layla was on the pavement, on the wrong side of the railings.

'Layla! Layla!'

Adele ran. Layla didn't seem to have heard her, or if she had, she was choosing to ignore her, distracted by something on the other side of the road. She heard another voice shouting – Dani's – but

Adele was closer, and as she neared the gate, she saw clearly what was going to happen. There was a dog. Its lead was tied to a railing outside the newsagent's across the street, and it was barking at Layla as though beckoning her.

'Layla, stop!'

But she was too late. Layla had stepped into the road.

As Adele raced towards her, she saw a flash of white to the right before she heard the screech of brakes and the scream that came from somewhere behind her. She braced herself for the pain, but nothing came. When she opened her eyes, she found herself lying on concrete, a small figure in pink on the ground ahead of her. There was silence for a moment, and then a flood of sound: a woman screaming, someone shouting for help, a child crying.

'Are you okay?' a voice was asking her. 'Where are you hurt?'

A man crouched beside her and placed a hand on her arm. She wasn't hurt, but she couldn't open her mouth to say so, the shock of the moment stunning her into temporary silence. 'Layla,' was all she could manage.

The little girl was surrounded by people – bystanders who had rushed to help, the shopkeeper, who had a phone held to his ear, and the dog owner, whose pet had fallen silent amid the sudden rush of activity. Among them was Dani, though she couldn't be seen amid the huddle.

'She just came from nowhere,' the man said, and she heard the fear and relief in his voice as the possibilities, the what-ifs reared up in front of him.

Adele pushed herself up.

'No, don't move!' he instructed.

'I'm fine.'

'You might have broken something.'

'Honestly, I'm fine. Here.' Adele reached out a hand and the man took it, helping her to her feet.

'Are you sure you're okay, love? God, I hate to think what might have happened if you hadn't been there. The kid just came from nowhere.'

'Is Layla all right?' Adele asked. She could see a single little leg poking between the adults surrounding her. The sight stalled her heart, the air held back from her lungs in a chokehold.

The leg left the floor as Layla was lifted from the concrete, and Dani emerged from the huddle, her daughter clinging to her as she sobbed into her mother's hair. Relief hit Adele with such force that it left her body as a guttural groan, and she felt the man's hand on her arm again.

'Is she okay?' he asked Dani. 'I'm so sorry, she just ran out in front of me.'

'She's fine. She's got a few grazes, but that's it. I'll take her to get her checked over, just in case.' Dani shifted Layla further up her shoulder and put her other arm around Adele. 'Thank you,' she said, the words spluttered through relieved sobs. 'Thank you so, so much.'

Adele felt Dani's chest shudder against her own as she cried, and she put a hand to Layla's hair, smoothing it against the back of her head. She tried to shut out the words, forcing the sound of Dani's gratitude to some far corner of her brain that had become home to all the other things she didn't deserve to be owner of. She was guilty of many things, but whatever else she was, she wasn't a hero.

TWENTY-FIVE

DANI

For days afterwards, Dani wouldn't let Layla out of her sight. What had happened at the park kept repeating in her head, and she viewed each replay differently, changing what she had done so that her daughter had never had a chance to be out on the road by herself. If only she hadn't looked away. If only she hadn't allowed herself to be distracted by that awful woman from the playgroup.

Maybe the other mothers had been right all along. Maybe it wasn't safe to be around her. She couldn't even protect her own child. The worst thing imaginable might have happened – and would have done had Adele not been there. She had saved Layla's life. She had run out onto the road without looking at what was coming, apparently seeing nothing but Layla, and for Dani, time had stopped in that moment: her daughter in the middle of the road, Adele just feet behind her; the white van to the right, its tyres screeching as the driver slammed on the brakes.

Adele had shoved Layla in the back, flinging her to the kerbside like a soft toy thrown from a pushchair by a toddler mid tantrum. She might have tried to make a grab for her, but had lost her footing and stumbled, and the van had swerved just a foot or so away from her, leaving everyone who was witness to it open-mouthed at the near horror of what might have happened. The fact that both Layla and Adele had walked away unharmed was little short of a miracle, though had it not been for Adele's quick reactions, the outcome would have been far different.

Sitting in Layla's room that evening and watching her daughter as she slept, Dani fought against the thought of returning home without her, the cot empty, never to be slept in again. The idea scraped at her insides, leaving her hollow. The pain that lingered from the cuts to her palm was nothing compared with the thought of something happening to her daughter. She promised herself she would be better. She would be more patient with Layla, calmer, kinder.

She glanced at her phone on the carpet beside her, turned to silent so as not to disturb Layla. She'd had an email from Travis.

> *Sorry I didn't get back to you. My brother's been in hospital.*
> *I'll explain when I see you x*

She wondered whether Travis had been at the hospital that afternoon, when she had taken Layla to get her checked over. The doctor had confirmed what she had suspected – that Layla was lucky to have escaped the incident with nothing more than scrapes and bruises. Dani had tried to get Adele to go with them, but she had refused, insisting that she was fine. Amid the confusion of the aftermath, she and Ivy had somehow managed to slope away without a goodbye, and though Dani had tried to call her and left messages on her voicemail, they hadn't yet been replied to.

She thought about sending Adele something – flowers, or a keepsake that would show her gratitude – but she couldn't decide upon a gift that seemed appropriate. She wondered whether she herself would have been brave enough to do the same had it been Ivy who had stepped into the road and she who had spotted her first. She hoped she would have been, that some maternal instinct would have pushed her into action without thought of the consequences, but she wasn't so sure that all the qualities ascribed to mothers came naturally to her. It seemed to her that unless she was disconnected in some way – some part of her brain wired incorrectly – a maternal instinct was something that grew over time rather than something that was born and instant.

She looked at her sleeping daughter, watching the gentle rise and fall of her chest. Layla was getting too big for the cot. Stretched out, she would soon be the length of it, and it seemed that in no time at all, her baby had morphed into a little girl. The grandmothers at the playgroup were right: Layla would be grown before Dani realised it was happening. She felt a sadness grip her, threatening to draw tears, and stood and lifted Layla out of the cot, wanting to feel the warmth of her sleeping body against her own. Returning to the carpet, she sat with her daughter slumped against her chest, wondering what dreams might fill the child's head.

The thought of playgroup took her back to Amy Davies. Whenever she thought about the woman, a burning anger took hold in her chest, but each time it quickly subsided, replaced by a sadness that was stronger. For whatever reason, Amy had never liked her. They were different in so many ways, but Dani never thought Amy would be venomous enough to destroy her reputation. And then there were the flowers. That was another level of severity altogether. She might have slit her wrist had she reached into the bouquet at a different angle. She had assumed they had come from the Sinclairs, but what if they hadn't? Amy was unpleasant, but Dani didn't think she was evil, and it occurred to her that whoever had sent those flowers must surely be teetering on the edge of psychopathy.

There was also the fact that Corey had described the woman who had given him the flyers as a brunette. Amy had blonde hair. James's wife was brunette, though – if the woman she had seen in his Facebook photos really was his wife.

After an hour or so, Dani gently settled Layla back in her cot, then went downstairs. Caroline was curled on the sofa in her dressing gown, a cup of tea on the coffee table.

'Do you want one?'

'No thanks.'

'You okay?'

Dani nodded, but before she could stop herself, she started crying. Her mother gestured to the sofa beside her, and she sank against the cushions, embarrassed at the unfamiliar show of emotion.

'She's okay,' Caroline said, reading her thoughts. 'You've got to stop worrying now.'

'It was my fault, Mum. I wasn't watching her.'

'No one can keep an eye on their kids twenty-four-seven, and anyone who says they do is a liar. You've got to stop giving yourself a hard time.'

Dani watched her mother pick up her cup, noticing the surface of the tea ripple in her shaking hand. 'Are you okay?'

'You've got to get this sorted out. Whoever's responsible for those flyers… whoever took Dylan…' Caroline paused, unable to bring herself to say anything more about the cat. Neither of them wanted to think about where he might be or what might have happened to him. Instead she took Dani's hand in hers and traced her fingertip along the stitches. 'I don't know what the hell's going on, because you won't talk to me, but just get it sorted out before anything else happens. I still think we should go to the police about those flowers, but—'

'Mum, please,' Dani said, cutting her short. 'I said I'll sort it and I will, I promise.'

But her mother's words lingered. *Before anything else happens.* Dani had considered the possibility of where all this might lead, though she didn't want to dwell on it for too long. She felt certain that despite her run-in with Corey, the Sinclair family hadn't sent those flowers. It just didn't seem their style. If she stayed away from them, they would leave her alone, but she didn't think the same rule applied to the real perpetrator. Amy Davies had looked genuinely confused by the question about the missing cat, so if she hadn't taken Dylan, it seemed logical that it must have been James's wife who was responsible. Maybe she wasn't as nice as she looked in her photograph.

She broke the silence. 'Why do we never talk about him?'

'Who?'

'Dad. It's as though he never existed.'

He had been on Dani's mind a lot recently. She had wondered what he would have made of all this. Would he too be mourning the cat? He hadn't known Dylan; Caroline had got the animal after her husband had died, as something to focus her affections on. She'd seemed unable to send them in Dani's direction.

Caroline's jaw tightened. 'What do you want to talk about?'

'Anything, Mum. The way he always had one and a half sugars in his tea, and if there was too much or too little he'd know from the first sip. That time on holiday in Tenby when he thought it'd be a good idea to walk over to Caldey Island and we got cut off by the tide and had to be rescued by the coastguard. That Christmas he knocked the oven off and we ended up having egg and chips.'

It hadn't been done in so long that talking about him felt alien. The memories were so sharp they cut her more painfully than any razor blade. Beside her, Caroline clutched her cup of tea. 'We can talk about him whenever you want.'

'But we don't. You never want to.'

'I don't want to upset you.'

'It upsets me that we *don't* talk about him.'

Caroline put her cup down and crossed one leg over the other. 'Do you remember what happened when I got the photo albums out?'

Dani remembered, though she didn't like to admit it. A couple of months after the accident, Caroline had come into the living room with a pile of old albums. The television was on, but Dani wasn't really watching it. Words had been exchanged; Dani couldn't recall them, but she remembered taking one of the albums and throwing it across the room, knocking a picture frame from the mantelpiece, its glass smashing at her mother's feet.

'You were so angry, Dani, all the time. You seem to have forgotten it, and that's fine, but it's like you've managed to blank out everything that came after your dad died. You wouldn't talk to me… for a long time you wouldn't even look at me. Everything I said or did was wrong. I used to think you blamed me for his death.'

'I didn't.'

'Maybe not, but it felt like it. You idolised your father. He was everything to you, and when he went… I wasn't enough, was I? I'm not saying it's your fault,' she added, cutting her daughter short before she could do the same to her. 'Nothing I did was going to be enough. I wasn't him, and I think sometimes when you looked at me, that was all you saw. A little girl needs her father.'

There was a moment of awkward silence in which Dani felt sure her mother must have realised the implications of her words. Layla had no father, not one that she knew, at least. Rightly or wrongly, Dani was responsible for keeping her from him.

'When you got pregnant, I'll be honest, I thought you'd done it on purpose. You wanted someone to love again because you didn't have him and you couldn't love me.'

'I thought the same about Dylan.'

'What? What do you mean?'

'I thought you got him so that you had something to love.'

Caroline shook her head. 'I thought he'd be good for you. Pets are supposed to help children cope with trauma. You couldn't talk to me; I thought maybe you'd talk to him.'

Dani laughed. 'Never got much back, that was the problem.'

She had never heard her mother talk like this before and hadn't known that she had made her feel so redundant. It had never been her intention, though Caroline's feelings had not been something she could consider, not when her own had been so overwhelming and had kept her so preoccupied. Her mother was wrong about so much of it, but how could Dani explain that it had never been a case of hating her, it was a case of hating herself?

'It was my fault,' she said.

'What?'

'His death. It was my fault.'

Caroline uncrossed her legs and turned to face her. 'Why would you ever think that?'

Dani had never said it aloud before, but she knew she was to blame for her father's accident. She had been nagging him about going on that skiing trip with the school, even though she knew it was too expensive and her parents couldn't afford to send her. Everyone else she knew seemed to have been somewhere further than the museum three miles down the road, and she had grown tired of always being different, the one who never did the things everyone else did, never visited the places everyone else went.

'That stupid skiing trip. I kept on about wanting to go.'

Caroline put a hand on her knee. 'You listen to me. What happened was not your fault, okay? Yeah, he wanted the best for you, of course he did, but it was nothing to do with that trip. Your dad was a good man. Better than most. But he could also be a bit of a prat, to be honest. The kind of prat who thought it was a good idea to climb scaffolding in a storm.'

She fell into silence, and under the weight of it, neither of them knew how to react. So they started to laugh, not because there was anything even remotely funny about the situation but because it felt like the only thing to do to stop themselves from crying.

'Your father would have been up on that roof anyway. He loved his job. I think half the time he went out to get away from me, so if either of us is to blame, it's me, not you.'

Dani placed a hand over her mother's, realising then that she couldn't remember the last time they had made physical contact. All she had wanted was for them to reach this moment, to understand each other a little better, and it was a shame for them both that it had taken almost a decade to get there.

'Do you know who's doing this?' Caroline asked.

Dani shook her head. 'But I promise I'm going to find out.'

TWENTY-SIX

ADELE

She timed her arrival home to coincide with Callum's, knowing he would be back around 5 p.m. He looked unimpressed to see her, his usual default expression whenever he got home to find her there, and turned up the volume on the radio in the garage as though he could drown the sound of her out before she had even opened her mouth to speak.

'Where's Ivy?'

'Gone to the park with Steph. I thought it'd give us a chance to talk.'

He narrowed his eyes and studied her with suspicion. 'About what?'

She hesitated, knowing how easily she could lose him from the conversation; his attention was already fixed upon the weights bench. She needed to know the truth, but she couldn't just ask him for it outright, not when she knew the way the house would implode in its aftermath. An involuntary image flitted into her head: Callum lying on the bench, her above him, pressing the weights onto his chest. Hearing his ribs crack as he fought for breath.

'The atmosphere between us.'

'I wasn't aware there was an atmosphere.' He held her gaze, his focus challenging her.

'I'm trying my best here.'

He said nothing, but the response was audible anyway – her best would never be good enough for him. She knew what he thought of her, and she was powerless to reverse his feelings or to convince him otherwise.

'Have you thought what this must be doing to Ivy? It isn't healthy for her, you know, living with us like this.'

'Then do us a favour and go.'

He was so cold, and yet Adele had always known this was who he really was. Watching him lift weights – one eye on his own reflection in the floor-to-ceiling mirror fixed to the far wall of the garage – it was obvious that the only person he cared about was himself. She felt a pulse tick in her neck, her frustration ready to bubble into anger. 'I'm not going anywhere,' she said defiantly, standing her ground. 'Not until I'm ready.'

Callum stood. 'This is my house, just remember that.'

'Paid for with my money.'

The tension in his jaw betrayed his reaction. She had never said it aloud before, though the truth had sat in awkward silence amid many conversations they had shared. He hated the fact that he was indebted to her, and he resented the control it represented.

'Your parents' money, you mean. I don't think you earned a penny of it, did you?' He stepped closer. 'Remember this, Adele – you are nothing in this house.'

The pounding in her chest had faded, her heart replaced by the slab of ice that sometimes resided there, protecting her from harm. 'Maybe to you. But Ivy loves me.'

Callum hated the fact that she and Ivy were so close. She had seen his expression when he walked into the living room to find them playing together, and caught the mumbled words spoken beneath his breath when he heard Ivy's laughter. Some bonds just couldn't be broken, and she would make sure theirs was one of them.

'She'll forget you soon enough.'

Adele shook her head and held his eye. 'Not if I take her with me.'

He smirked. 'You're not taking my daughter anywhere. Don't fool yourself into thinking the two of you have some sort of bond.' He stepped towards her and she flinched, but he held himself back, smirking at her reaction. 'Poor Adele,' he sneered. 'Are you scared?'

She glanced at her phone. Steph would be back from the park with Ivy soon, and Callum wouldn't do anything if there was a chance she might walk in on an altercation.

'You're doing it again, aren't you?' she said.

'Doing what?'

'Having an affair.'

His face contorted, and she wished others could see what she saw in him.

'You're a fantasist, Adele.'

'Don't try that. You won't gaslight me.'

He rolled his eyes before returning his attention to his reflection. 'What's her name?'

He dropped the dumb-bell, letting it smash onto the concrete at his feet. She backed away, but there was nowhere for her to go, and as he came closer, she found herself pressed against a shelving unit, unsettling the boxes and bottles that were stacked there.

'Whatever you think you know, it's nothing to do with you. I'm not answerable to you, Adele.'

From the other side of the garage door, they heard a sound on the driveway. Laughter. A child's voice. Ivy. Callum backed away and left the garage, and Adele followed, plastering on a fake smile and reassuring herself with a silent resolution that sooner rather than later, he would be made to suffer for his sins.

TWENTY-SEVEN

DANI

After finding the photograph of James in his company football kit it had been easy to find him. Seeing him again resurrected feelings she had tried to bury, and though she hated him for what he had done, most of her anger was directed at herself. It was obvious how arrogant he was – it was visible even in the way he walked to his car – yet when she had met him, she'd chosen to ignore what was right in front of her.

When he left the car park, Dani followed, hoping he'd be heading home. His route took her to the other side of Cardiff, to an affluent area in which the houses were three times the size of her mother's. As he pulled onto the driveway of one of them, she felt her heart sink a little further, anticipation nudging out her earlier anger. Why would he have risked this life for her?

There was no other car on the driveway, but Dani didn't know whether his wife drove, or if she might still be at work; she knew nothing about her other than the fact that she had made a poor choice when she decided to get married. She didn't even know whether they had kids. There were none in any of the photographs on his Facebook profile, though Dani realised this meant nothing. The thought of Layla having a half-brother or sister she knew nothing about ate away at her.

His wife might be in the house, and if it did turn out that she was responsible for everything, she wanted him to be there to witness her scheme unravel. She wanted the woman to feel the same shame that she had inflicted upon Dani, and to see the look on his face when he found out. She wanted to see him humiliated in front of his neighbours, just as she'd been humiliated in front of his friend. She remembered how it had felt when he had walked in on the two of them that day. She had only just started to trust people again, and James was the only man she had bothered with in a long time. The others before him had been nothing, one-night stands that she couldn't claim to be proud of, but she'd liked James, had thought he was different.

The thought that she might have got this wrong caused her heart to thud painfully in her chest. There was still a chance that James's wife hadn't done all these things and that Amy Davies was somehow responsible, and yet she hadn't been able to shake the look that had crossed the other mother's face in the park that day when she had mentioned the missing cat. That had been more than a performance for Dani's benefit. Amy hadn't had a clue what she was talking about. Dani knew she had to take the risk of being proven wrong, or the not-knowing was going to tip her nerves past breaking point.

Her mobile rang – it was her mother – but she cut the call and turned her phone to silent. Caroline would be wondering where she was, whether she would be back in time for Layla's bedtime, but Dani didn't care if Layla stayed up late.

When he got out from his car, Dani did the same and crossed the street.

'James. Nice to see you.'

His face dropped at the sight of her, the colour draining from his cheeks. He hadn't seen her in so long that he probably thought he'd got away with it.

'Sorry,' she added with an exaggerated wave of a hand. She leaned closer to look at the name badge pinned to his shirt. 'Ben. Nice to meet you.'

'What are you doing here?'

'I've come to see your wife.'

'You can't,' he said quickly, glancing at the house.

'Well one of us needs to tell her to pack this shit in,' Dani said, thrusting one of the flyers towards him.

As he studied the page, the colour crept back into his face. She wondered if it was embarrassment, a glimpse of shame for what he'd done and the way he'd treated her, though she doubted it. People like him had no conscience. She wondered how many others there had been.

'She didn't do this,' he said, passing the flyer back to her.

'Of course she didn't. I bet she doesn't have a clue where my mother's cat is either, does she?'

'Your mother's cat? What are you talking about?'

'What sort of psycho steals someone's pet?' She could feel her voice trembling as she spoke the words, anger and sadness balled into a knot of jumbled emotion.

'Wow,' he said, raising his hands. 'Whatever you're talking about, you're way off the mark here. My wife isn't involved in any of this.'

'Oh, you know that, do you? Hardly likely to tell you about it, is she?' Her voice was rising, anger jarring every word. The thought of Dylan trapped in a cage made her feel sick, and she swallowed back tears as she tried to push to the back of her mind involuntary images of what might have become of him.

'Look,' he said, his voice panicked, 'I'm sorry I lied to you, I really am, but whatever you think my wife has done, I'm telling you she hasn't. She doesn't even know about us, and I don't want her to find out.'

'I bet you don't.'

'You don't understand.' He stepped towards her and lowered his voice to a hiss. 'She's not well, she hasn't left the house in weeks. This wasn't her, okay.'

His words were punctuated by the sound of the front door. He backed away as though Dani had burned him, and she was left standing with the flyer still hanging from her fingers.

Her heart flipped when she saw the woman who hobbled out of the house on crutches. She wore loose tracksuit bottoms that looked two sizes too big for her, and even the chunky knitted cardigan that covered her could not hide how skinny she was. The most noticeable thing about her was the scarf she wore wrapped around her head, protecting the obviously bald scalp underneath.

Dani looked away, back to Ben, and his whole face was a plea. She might almost have pitied him. He was right: whoever had done those things to her, it wasn't his wife. This wasn't the woman Corey Sinclair had described.

'Everything okay?' the woman asked. She was looking at Dani expectantly, waiting for her to explain who she was and why she was standing on their driveway.

'Sorry,' Dani said, the word falling out of her mouth, because she was – she was sorry she had ever gone there. She was sorry she had got things so wrong. 'I was just asking for directions.'

When she glanced back at Ben, she thought she saw a silent apology somewhere in the look he gave her, but she didn't wait long enough to try to read it. She would never see him again – he would never know about Layla – and now she wondered whether she would ever find the person she was looking for.

TWENTY-EIGHT

ADELE

The bedsit was tiny and disgusting, the smell of marijuana and damp washing hitting Adele as she stepped across the mess of envelopes and leaflets that had been left to pile up behind the door. Leanne sat on the unmade bed, a pair of headphones covering her ears, her eyes closed. A cigarette dangled between her fingers, its smoke rising in a fine line into air that was grey and murky. Adele disturbed the cluttered coffee table, catching her knee on it and sending an array of debris falling to the stained carpet. Leanne opened her eyes and a hand flew to her chest, the other pulling the headphones from her head.

'Jesus, you nearly gave me a heart attack.'

'I did text you to say I was on my way.'

Leanne glanced at the phone on the bed beside her, and Adele noticed the stained sheet that looked as though it had never made acquaintance with a washing machine. 'Oh yeah.'

She wore a vest top and a pair of tiny shorts, so small that when she got up, Adele could see the bony contours of her pelvis. Her diet had always consisted of a concoction of water, air and toxic substances; she reminded Adele so much of someone else that every time she looked at her she felt a pain in her chest that stabbed as deep and sharp as a blade.

'How many more times are we going to do this?' Leanne asked as she crouched to the side of the bed and rummaged in the clutter that lay beneath.

'As many as it takes.'

'It went too far last time.'

Adele shot her a glare. 'I'll decide when it's gone too far.'

Leanne produced the belt. Adele had taken it there with her the first time they had arranged one of these meetings, not wanting Leanne to have to associate anything she owned with these acts that Adele regarded as a kind of punishment ritual. The very first time, Leanne had used a wire brush. She had hit Adele reluctantly, the contact barely marking her skin, but Adele knew enough of her history to understand how her rage could be drawn from her, gradually at first and then with vigour. It had taken little more than the mention of the stepbrother who had abused her as a teenager to get Leanne to react, and since then it had been cathartic for them both: Leanne expelling the fury she had kept trapped within her for over two decades; Adele made to suffer until the hurt was numbed and replaced with a void into which her guilt could be temporarily swallowed.

She lifted her top and lay face down on the floor, trying not to breathe in the disgusting smell of the dirty carpet. She couldn't bring herself to lie on the bed, not knowing who might have last been in it. Leanne might have made something of her life once – she might have been academic, she might have been beautiful, she might have been a million other things – but she was her own worst enemy. She basked in the squalor of her life, finding comfort amid its familiarity no matter how unappealing it might appear to others.

The bruises on Adele's back were fading, their deep purple having paled into a sickly green glow. She had asked Leanne to work on other areas – always those that would be unseen – but it was on her back where she felt it the most, and she needed to feel every inch of it. Her body tensed as it prepared itself. The first blow was always the worst. Even though she knew it was coming, that initial assault upon her flesh never failed to deliver a searing pain that burned through her and tore at her skin, but she needed it in the way a drug addict needed that first hit of a high, to remind her that she was still there, still alive, that blood was pumping through her veins. The second blow brought acceptance. This was what she deserved. Then with each one that followed, it eased; she was absent somehow, as though the pain was inflicted upon someone else and she was merely delivering it through her body to theirs.

Leanne had hated doing it at first, but it had become easier for her over time. Adele paid her for the beatings, and a silent acknowledgement had passed between them – that she was keeping Leanne from harming herself and protecting her, for one night at least, from the sweaty, leering men who climbed into her bed so she could keep the roof of that dump over her head. The first time Adele asked her to do it, she'd had to reassure her there was nothing sexual involved. Leanne had questioned her motives, but it seemed now that she understood why Adele needed to feel this pain. Why she needed to be punished. Their friendship – if it could be called that – had survived on respecting each other's addictions with a muted acceptance.

When it was over, she stayed lying on the floor for a few minutes, her mind blank in the way she had trained it to become.

'I don't want to do this any more.'

Adele winced as she turned onto her back. Leanne was still standing at the bedside, looking down at her with an expression that was part pity, part revulsion.

'Why not?'

'I just don't think it's healthy for either of us.'

'It's more than healthy for your pocket.'

Leanne shook her head. 'There's some stuff you need to deal with. You should get help… proper help.'

Adele got up from the floor and retrieved her top. 'I thought you were different. I thought we understood each other.'

Leanne shrugged. 'It's not going to give you what you need.'

Adele laughed, and Leanne flinched as though the sound might cut her. Adele gestured to the cluttered coffee table, to the stubs in the ashtray and the papers and lighter scattered beside it. 'Maybe I should try your approach. Does this give you what you need?'

'Don't pretend you're better than me, Adele. You might have quit your habit, but you still are who you are. You can't change your past, can you?'

In her head, Adele spat venom. She took one last look at the grotty bedsit and held the words back. Leanne was a lost cause; she always would be. She didn't need Adele to remind her of her reality.

She grabbed her bag and left Leanne alone, slamming the door to the flat behind her. But Leanne's words echoed, scratching at her consciousness as she absorbed their truth. Perhaps she was right. Maybe Adele was no better than her. Maybe they were just the same.

The little voice that sometimes spoke to her told her everything was going to be okay. She shut her eyes and forced it into silence. She at once loved and loathed that voice, both longing for it and trying to drown it out. *Everything's going to be okay.* It might once have been true, but Adele knew she was too far gone for that now.

TWENTY-NINE

DANI

She had only been to Elaine's house once before, to drop off some shopping. Josh's father, Martin, did a weekly shop for his mother, but when he'd gone on holiday the previous summer, Dani had done it instead. She hadn't been invited inside; Elaine insisted she could manage, so Dani had left the bags on the front step, feeling guilty as she glanced back to see Elaine lugging them in. Elaine seemed physically capable, but she hid a lot. Her husband had dementia, and she was his full-time carer. Martin stayed with his father on Friday mornings so that Elaine could spend time with Josh and take him to playgroup, but otherwise her days were confined to her home. Dani had never once heard her complain or even sound unhappy about the turn her life had taken, but there must have been times when she got tired and lonely. If Dani thought about it for too long, she started to fear old age as a place she never wanted to have to visit.

She pressed the doorbell and wondered whether she had done the right thing going there. Elaine was a proud woman and there was a reason she hadn't wanted Dani to set foot in the house before.

'Here's a lovely surprise,' Elaine said, opening the front door, though her face said something different, an expression of panic at Dani's unexpected arrival flitting across it. 'Everything okay, love?' She looked tired, her eyes red and bloodshot.

'I won't keep you,' Dani said. 'Did you get my texts?'

'Sorry, love. You know what I'm like with my phone, I'm bloody useless. Do you want to come in?'

Elaine stepped aside, but Dani was reluctant to enter.

'Trevor's not here,' Elaine said, reading her thoughts. 'He's in hospital.'

'Is everything okay?' Dani asked, realising the stupidity of the question. Of course everything wasn't okay. According to what Elaine had told her over the previous few months, Trevor's condition was deteriorating rapidly.

'Another lung infection. He can't fight them off like he used to. This is how it'll be from now on.'

Elaine was stoic in the face of a pain she wasn't going to give focus to, and Dani wished she had something helpful to offer. She got the impression that Elaine didn't want to talk about her life at home while she was away from it, as though playgroup and the people she knew there gave her a temporary escape.

'Come on in. You're cluttering up the doorstep.'

Dani followed Elaine into the hallway and closed the front door behind her. The living room door was ajar, a glimpse of Trevor's hospital-standard bed visible. He slept downstairs now, moved from the bedroom months earlier because he was no longer able to use the stairlift. The thought of what it must be like to have a life confined to one room – the life of an offender without having ever committed a crime – was too much for Dani to comprehend. She didn't know why, but she felt a sudden urge to cry, a sadness that gripped her chest and jumbled her thoughts. It was an uncharacteristic reaction she was becoming more prone to by the day.

'Are you going to the hospital today?' she asked, following Elaine through to the kitchen. 'Do you need a lift?'

'Thanks, love, but Martin's coming to pick me up in a bit. I was just going to make a cuppa – do you fancy one?'

'Only if you're sure I'm not keeping you. How's Josh doing? Is he feeling better?'

Elaine filled the kettle. 'He's fine, love.' She returned it to its stand. 'What do you mean, "feeling better"?'

'Last Friday. Adele said you couldn't make the playdate because Josh was unwell.'

Elaine brought two cups down from the cupboard and placed them on the worktop. 'I haven't spoken to Adele. She never mentioned you two meeting up.'

There was a moment of uncomfortable silence.

'It was only a trip to the park,' Dani said. 'Maybe she got mixed up.'

Or maybe Elaine had, she thought. She had a lot going on with her worries about Trevor, and Dani could see no reason why Adele would claim to have spoken to her if she hadn't. She didn't want to mention the almost-accident for the same reason. Though Layla was fine, Elaine would only worry if she heard about what had happened, and Dani didn't want to burden her with anything more than she already had to cope with.

'I think I know who sent that email, by the way.'

'Who?'

'One of the women from playgroup. Amy – the one whose son Layla pushed over the other week.'

Elaine's mouth fell open. 'The nasty cow. You sure? Why would she do that?'

Dani shrugged. 'They've never liked me, it was obvious. Don't have to worry about me or Layla corrupting their precious kids now, do they?'

'You and that girl of yours are going back to that group – she's not getting away with that. Leave it with me.'

When she left Elaine's house half an hour later, Dani went straight to the supermarket. Her mother hated food shopping and would often end up without half the things they needed for the week, so it had become easier to do it herself. Over the years they had fallen into their respective roles, with Caroline taking care of the cleaning and cooking, and Dani responsible for the washing and shopping.

She was at the far corner of the supermarket when she saw Ivy, the little girl's attention transfixed by a birthday cake shaped like a unicorn, with a horn of multicoloured sparkly sprinkles. She was wearing a summer dress with a Peter Pan collar and she looked strangely old-fashioned, like a child from the front of one of the sewing patterns Dani's nan used to have in her house. The thought of that house – the smell that lingered in the hallway, gas fire and toasted teacakes – pulled her into a grip of nostalgia that was unsettlingly out of place in the bakery section of Asda.

'Hi, Ivy.'

Hearing her name, the girl turned to her, and though Dani was sure she recognised her, she looked shy and sheepish, bowing her head as though Dani was a stranger. She looked for Adele, but she was nowhere to be seen. There were only a few other people in the aisle: a young couple deliberating over trays of cupcakes, an elderly man studying the best-before date on a fruit loaf, and a woman who was stretching to reach for a packet of jam tarts from the top of the shelving unit. If Ivy was with her dad, he was nowhere to be seen either, and Dani wondered if the little girl had wandered off, and whether she should take her to the customer service desk to find whoever she was with.

'Where's your mummy?' she asked her.

The woman behind Ivy gave up her struggle to reach the top shelf and turned her attention to Dani. 'Do I know you?' she asked, the words coated with a brittle layer of defence. She moved closer to Ivy and put a hand on the girl's shoulder in a protective gesture, as though Dani presented some sort of threat to her.

'No, I—'

She didn't finish her sentence, because Ivy turned to the woman and started tugging at her trouser leg, pointing at the cake on the shelf beside her. 'Mama! Ooh-corn.'

The woman was still looking at Dani, waiting for her to say something. Dani was lost for words. The girl was Ivy, there was no doubt about it, yet she had addressed this woman – a person Dani had never seen before – as Mama, and there was no possibility that the word was anything else.

'I… I'm sorry. I thought she was someone else.'

She smiled, but the look went unreturned, and she left the aisle hurriedly, almost bumping her trolley into an elderly lady in her haste to be away from the place.

She had put her list down somewhere, and now she fumbled half-heartedly among the bags for life hanging from the front of the trolley, wondering why her mother couldn't join the rest of the twenty-first century and WhatsApp it to her. When she failed to find it, she made up what she needed, barely considering whether the things she threw into the trolley might work together to make meals for the week ahead. She was preoccupied with avoiding Ivy and her mother, but her main thought lay with Adele. She racked her brain for memories of playgroup, trying to recall whether she had ever heard Ivy calling Adele Mama. The child hardly ever seemed to speak, and no, Dani couldn't remember ever having heard her say it. But if Adele wasn't her mother, then who was she, and why had she been lying all this time?

THIRTY

ADELE

Dani had spotted Adele as soon as she'd entered the salon, yet now she was hiding out in the back room, no doubt pretending to be too busy to come into the shop. Adele hadn't replied to the text she had received from her. No text could explain what she needed her to know, and she would prefer to see Dani in person, to watch the trickle of realisation as it filled her; to be there for the fallout it would inevitably bring.

A blonde woman sat at a desk just inside the salon, a large book open in front of her, her mobile phone close to hand. 'Do you have an appointment?' she asked Adele.

'No.'

She scanned the book. 'We might not be able to fit you in for another hour. Would that be okay?'

'Fine. I don't mind waiting, if that's okay. Is Dani in today? I'd like her to do it if possible, please.'

'Has she done your hair before?' the woman asked, eyeing Adele speculatively.

'She's been recommended by a friend.'

The woman raised an eyebrow and showed her to a chair.

Adele sat and flicked through the pages of an old magazine while she waited for Dani to come out, faking an interest in a feature about the most flattering hairstyles for women over forty. She was certain Dani was not busy out the back but was merely feigning activity just to make her wait. After twenty minutes, she went to use the toilet and spotted Dani standing in a small makeshift staff room, scrolling on her phone. She didn't see Adele pass, and it was another thirty minutes before she finally came out.

'Wet cut?'

'Please.'

Dani gestured to the sink area at the back of the salon, and Adele followed her to a chair, where she tied a black apron around her neck. She imagined the younger woman behind her, the apron cords long enough to wrap around her throat, Dani pulling tighter, tighter still, until she cut off the supply of blood to her brain. She settled into the chair and the image slipped away as she tipped her head back, her hair falling into the sink.

'Temperature okay?' Dani asked, moving the flow of water across her head.

'Fine.'

Dani soaked Adele's hair before applying shampoo. Adele felt the tension in the other woman's fingertips, the reluctance in her movements as she massaged it into her skull. There was hesitancy in every circular motion; Dani didn't want to touch her. She had touched the hair of so many strangers, people she had never seen before, people she might never see again, but this time it was different. She no longer trusted Adele, someone she had grown close to, even thought of as a friend. Adele needed to regain that trust.

Dani rinsed out the shampoo without speaking, before asking whether Adele would like conditioner. She told her she would, and Dani repeated the process, dragging the lotion through her hair, snagging on a knot that she worked loose with her fingers. Once the water was turned off, Adele opened her eyes, but Dani was out of sight behind her. She imagined her reaching for a towel and placing it over her face, leaning across her to press it against her nose and mouth as she smothered her shuddering body until the air dried from her lungs.

'Okay,' Dani said as a prompt for Adele to sit up. She towel-dried her hair vigorously, digging her fingertips into Adele's scalp. They were playing cat and mouse, both aware of the other; one cautious, the other all too knowing.

At the cutting chair, Dani adjusted the height of the seat. 'Just a trim, is it?'

Adele nodded.

Dani dragged a brush through the wet lengths of hair. 'Doesn't really look as though it needs cutting,' she said, and met Adele's eye in the mirror, silently questioning what the other woman was doing there.

'I got your text,' Adele said.

She had received it the previous evening.

I've just seen Ivy. She was with another woman she called Mama.

There was no question mark, and Adele wasn't sure it required a response. The truth was going to come out sooner or later, and in a way, it felt easier that she had been spared the task of doing it herself.

'So why didn't you reply?'

'I wanted to speak to you in person. It didn't seem right explaining in a text.'

Dani reached to the trolley for a pair of scissors. 'Go on then,' she said. 'Explain.'

She ran a comb through Adele's hair, and Adele felt it scratch the bare skin at the back of her neck. She dragged it down for a second time, then stopped. Adele watched her in the mirror, the young woman's eyes fixed on the back of her neck. She had seen the tattoo.

'Everything okay?'

Dani set to work again. When Adele still didn't speak, she leaned forward and met her gaze in the mirror. 'You're not her mother, are you?'

Adele shook her head. There was a flicker of something in Dani's expression, as though she had expected this but was still shaken by the admission. Perhaps she'd expected her to lie, though Adele had never lied to her about anything other than how she had come by her bruises.

'Ivy's my niece. I never actually said I was her mother, Dani – you just assumed that was the case.'

Dani hesitated. Adele imagined her memory tripping back through their conversations like fingers thumbing the pages of a flip book. She could return to them as many times as she liked, but unless she made her own alterations to the past, she would find Adele was right.

'You never corrected the assumption.'

It had felt good to have Dani believe she was Ivy's mother. It had felt good to be one, if only for a while and if only in a world of make-believe. There was an expectation of mothers – a set of characteristics ascribed to any woman fulfilling the role. Mothers were warm and kind and reliable. They could be trusted.

'Why didn't you just say? It wouldn't have made any difference.'

'I don't know. I'm sorry.'

Dani continued to cut Adele's hair, her focus on her work. 'Bit weird, though, don't you think?' she said. 'To let people believe you're her mother when you're not.'

There was something admirable in her determination, some grit that might have almost made Adele like her. But Dani was dangerous, her anger bubbling at the edges of her self-control, just waiting to spill over, and Adele knew only too well what this young woman's vitriol was capable of.

'Can we talk? Another time, I mean – not here, somewhere private. I'll explain then, I promise.'

Dani looked briefly as though she might consider it. 'It's none of my business,' she said flatly.

Adele sat silently as Dani continued to trim the ends of her hair. She was right: it didn't need cutting. She'd had it done at a hairdresser's a couple of miles from here just a few weeks earlier.

'I got you something,' she said eventually.

She waited for Dani to stop cutting before reaching down to her bag and taking out a wrapped package. She had tied it with string and tucked a card beneath the knot. Dani didn't take it from her; just glanced down before looking back at Adele in the mirror.

'It's an apology. Please.'

With obvious reluctance, she took the package and placed it on the trolley at her side before returning to Adele's hair.

'My baby died.'

Adele felt the cold edge of the scissors glance the back of her neck as Dani reacted to the words. She stood still, her head bent, unable to make eye contact.

'That's awful,' she said eventually. 'I'm so sorry.'

Was she really sorry? Did she speak those words because they were expected of her, or did she mean them with the sincerity of a mother who might be able to imagine how it would feel to lose her child?

Dani continued to work with the scissors, snipping and trimming her way from right to left until eventually she stood back, reached for a mirror, held it at an angle and asked if Adele was happy with what she'd done. Adele pictured herself lunging forward and smashing her forehead against the glass, seeing her shattered reflection through the blood that ran into her eyes. She

saw herself reaching for a shard of glass and turning it upon Dani
like a knife edge.

Her baby was dead. Dani said she was sorry. But was she really?
She should be. She was the one who'd killed her.

THIRTY-ONE

DANI

She couldn't argue when Tracy told her Adele wanted her to do her hair, not when she was already walking on such thin ice where her boss was concerned. Tracy was still unhappy about the flyers and the negative attention they'd brought to the salon, because despite the fact that she'd been able to take them down before opening, a few of the customers had still somehow known about them and a couple had had no issues with asking what they referred to. The incident with Mrs Bracknell had been her penultimate strike, and it occurred to Dani that perhaps Tracy liked her more than she had ever let on, when plenty of other employers would have already got rid of her.

She made her way straight home from the salon when her shift finished, trying to distract herself from thoughts of Adele and the strangeness of their exchange by wondering whether Travis was okay. The tattoo parlour had been closed for the past couple of days, and though she had replied to his email about his brother, she had yet to hear back. If she'd had his phone number, she would have tried to call him, but they had never got as far as exchanging numbers.

The tattoo at the back of Adele's neck had unsettled her. Butterflies were not uncommon tattoos, but the sight of them always provoked the same reaction, forcing an uneasy roll of nausea in the pit of her stomach. She had never noticed it there before, though perhaps Adele's hair had always kept it covered. She didn't seem the type to have a tattoo, though it occurred to her that she didn't know what 'type' she expected that to be.

When she reached her street, she saw a car parked at the side of the road a few houses down from her own, and a tall young woman, dark-haired, leaning against a sports car as she tapped out a message on her phone. She looked familiar, but it was only when she glanced up that Dani realised who she was, recognising the air of superiority as though it was something visible that she had painted her skin with. Maddie Gardiner.

'Danielle.' Maddie dropped the phone through the open window before stepping away from the car. She wore heels that were impossibly high and a pair of jeans so tight Dani wondered how she had managed to drive while wearing them. As she got closer, Dani could make out the lines in the thick make-up she wore. Maddie was beautiful, but not quite in the way her sister had been. She had always had to try harder; she must have known that it was easier for Eve, and when they were younger it must have bothered her. It was cold in someone else's shadow; Dani had spent enough time in Eve's to know, always wanting to be beside her and yet always somehow lagging behind, never quite getting the sun on her face. She assumed it was worse as a sibling, but as an only child, she didn't know. There were times she would have loved a sister, but once she saw the trouble they brought, she decided that maybe the loneliness of a solo childhood was preferable.

'What are you doing here?' She heard the tremble in her voice, and she hated herself for it. As a teenager, she had always been intimidated by Maddie, but she wasn't a teenager any more.

'I need to talk to you about Eve.'

Her chest tightened. She hadn't seen Maddie in years, not since before she last saw Eve, but no amount of time could have passed for her to be ready for the conversation Maddie wanted.

'I'm so sorry about what happened. Someone from school told me.'

Maddie's jaw tightened. Dani hated that look. She knew what it said because she had seen it enough times from other people. Maddie wore the expression so well. She had always thought she was better than Dani; she'd thought her sister was better than Dani and had wondered why Eve bothered with a girl from the estate. Dani hadn't missed the snide remarks Maddie would make about her shoes or her school bag – they were always delivered in a tone that made them unmissable – or the way she talked down to her as though she was stupid.

'What happened between you two?'

Her words slammed Dani in the stomach like a punch. She had known she would ask but hadn't expected the question so soon. 'Nothing.'

'Don't lie,' Maddie said, and Dani saw her temple twitch in anger as she fought back tears. 'A couple of weeks before she died, Eve started talking about the prom again. She hadn't mentioned it in years, and then a few weeks later she was dead.'

It didn't sound like a question, yet a space was left in the air between them, some gap it appeared Maddie expected Dani to fill.

'What are you trying to say?' Dani asked.

'I'm trying to say it seems a bit of coincidence, don't you think?'

'What did she say?' Dani wasn't sure she really wanted to know, but curiosity got the better of her.

'She started going back over what happened at the prom. She seemed suddenly fixated by it, saying it should never have happened. What should never have happened, Dani?'

'I don't know. I'm so sorry about everything, I really am, but you're looking for answers I don't have.'

Dani started walking, but Maddie blocked her path.

'No one was as close to my sister as you were, Dani. If she was involved in what went on that night, you would have known about it.' Maddie studied her, trying to gauge her reaction. 'You do know something, don't you? What did you do, Dani?'

'I've got no idea what you're talking about. Whatever you're hoping for, you've had a wasted trip.'

Dani tried to get past again, but Maddie grabbed her by the arm.

'You'd better let me go,' Dani said, her voice lowered warningly.

'Or what? You'll do something to me as well?'

Dani shook her arm loose of Maddie's grip. 'Are you suggesting I'm involved in Eve's death? Are you mad? I hadn't seen her in years, not since your family moved to Bath, but now I'm supposed to have done what? Killed her?' The words spilled from her mouth, tumbling over one another in their haste to escape. 'She was my friend, Maddie. I loved her. I know you did too and I'm sorry for everything, I really am, but I had nothing to do with what happened.'

Before Dani knew what was going on or how she was supposed to respond to it, Maddie suddenly lurched against her and began sobbing on her shoulder. Dani's arms hung limply at her sides, not wanting to touch the other woman, but she knew she should, if only to stop herself from looking like a heartless cow, so she raised a hand and smoothed Maddie's hair as she cried against her.

Maddie's weight shifted, and she pressed her head against Dani's. 'I know you're involved in this,' she said quietly into her hair, her sobs subsiding. 'And when I find out how, I will kill you.' She pulled back, kissed Dani on the cheek for the benefit of anyone watching, then waved goodbye as she headed back to her car, her lips turned into a smile but her eyes cold.

Shaken, Dani had no doubt she meant exactly what she'd said.

THIRTY-TWO

ADELE

It was gone 11 p.m., and Steph and Callum thought Adele was asleep upstairs, like a child who had been sent to bed and was too fearful of the consequences to get out from beneath the duvet, because that was how things tended to be in that house – she was held to ransom by a self-appointed king despite being the foundations upon which his castle had been built. Callum wanted to control her, and he hated her because she couldn't be controlled.

'It was supposed to be temporary.'

His voice had developed a chiselled tone in recent weeks, increasingly brittle as his charity extended into something that threatened to become more permanent. He had never made much secret of his feelings towards his sister-in-law, and she had never wanted to move into that house either. Necessity had driven her there, and though it was inconvenient it had served a purpose.

'A couple of weeks, you said.'

Adele slid down to the next step – the only way to stop the staircase creaking and drawing attention to her presence there, on the edges of a conversation they thought was only between them. She had made her way down almost to the hallway, their words growing clearer as she neared the exchange.

'I know, but I can't just leave her on the streets, can I?'

Callum expelled breath noisily, the sound of a disgruntled horse being pulled in a direction it didn't want to be led. 'She wouldn't be on the streets, though, would she? She's got plenty of money to get her own place.'

They were in the kitchen; Adele could tell from the occasional scrape of a chair leg on the tiled floor and the echoey quality of their voices as they bounced around the room's modern, minimalist interior. A few days after moving her stuff in, she had stuck a drawing Ivy had done (more a squiggle that was cute merely for the fact that it was her hand holding the crayon) on the fridge door, but it had quickly been whipped away by Steph, who professed to hate clutter. At some point during the years they were apart, her sister had changed. In his marketing of the lifestyle that this place would secure them, Callum had sold Steph a lie, one she had bought into unquestioningly and was now blinded by.

'I'm not sure she has, though, has she?' Steph said, her voice lowered, the words like a hiss. 'She signed nearly everything over to me.'

Callum laughed, but the sound was a sneer, an audible display of his contempt for Adele. 'Don't be so naïve, Steph. Do you really think she didn't keep something back for herself?'

He was right; Adele had made provision for herself and for the future. Steph had been so shocked at the offer she had made to sign everything over to her when their father had died that she hadn't waited to hear details. She had been blindsided by this place, a house she had been eyeing for some time but had never thought she might be able to afford. They could have done it alone, at a push, but it would have meant a large mortgage and a financial commitment that would have looped a noose around their necks until they neared their seventies. Adele's generosity – her sacrifice – had funded the life they had longed for without the heavy debt to accompany it.

What use was money to Adele now? There was no one to share it with, no one to spend it on, and anyway, she had never considered herself a materialistic sort of person. The more she saw of her sister's changing ways, the more she was grateful that she wasn't like her. Signing over a large portion of her half of the inheritance had bought something that couldn't be ordered on the internet, and her sister's appreciation of the debt had been demonstrated in a loyalty that had secured Adele a temporary home amid a setting she had needed. But why shouldn't she have protected herself? Life was difficult enough, and one thing money always bought was choice. Besides, she was no less entitled than her sister.

'I'm not saying she didn't,' Steph argued, 'but it's not as much as you seem to think.'

There was a louder scrape of a chair across the kitchen tiles as one of them stood. Adele slipped further into the hallway, edging towards the kitchen door.

'When will you see her for what she is?' Callum snapped. 'She's just using you.'

'I've been pretty useful too, don't you think?'

Steph and Callum were both startled by Adele's appearance in the doorway. Steph's cheeks coloured, but Callum remained impassive, eyeing his sister-in-law with defiance.

'Quite expensive to hire a nanny these days,' she added. 'Think of all the money I've saved you.'

'He didn't mean—'

'He meant everything,' Adele said, cutting Steph short. 'It's okay. I'm a big girl, I can take it.' She smiled at Callum, enjoying his silent anger.

'When are you planning to leave?' he demanded.

'Soon,' she told him. 'Very soon. I'm just sorting out a few last things and then I'll be out of your hair.'

'There's no rush,' Steph said quietly.

Callum glared at her. 'Actually, there is.'

Adele reached into her dressing gown pocket and took out her phone. She tapped in her passcode, went to her gallery and found the photograph of Callum and the mystery woman she had seen him with in the tapas bar.

'He's doing it again,' she said, passing the phone to her sister.

She watched as Steph studied the image. She saw her face change, the twitching of her mouth that revealed her fears.

'I'm sorry, Steph.'

Steph handed the phone back without looking at her. 'I'm going to bed.'

'What?' Adele stepped aside to block her path to the door. 'You're not just going to let him do this to you again, are you?'

'Goodnight, Adele.'

'Don't be an idiot, Steph. You know what he is – he's done it once and he can do it again. What more evidence do you need? I saw him with another woman.'

The room was silent for a moment, the air between them thick and claustrophobic. Callum's expression had morphed from bewilderment to smug satisfaction, no doubt aided by Steph's reluctance to see what was right in front of her. Steph stared at the floor, downcast in an internal battle between what she wanted to be real and what she knew to be the truth, because if she dared to be honest with herself just this once, she knew that Adele was right and that this was something she had seen coming.

A slow smile began to spread across Callum's face, and his eyebrows lifted as he declared, 'I'm sure you did, Adele.'

Steph's eyes moved towards her husband with reluctance. Adele didn't enjoy doing this, but her sister needed to know who she was married to.

'Shop assistant?' Callum said. 'Colleague? Woman from two doors down?' He turned to Steph. 'I've been seen with a lot of other women this week. I work with quite a few.'

'You work with this one, do you?'

He took the phone from Adele and glanced at the photo.

'And?' he said nonchalantly before passing it back.

Adele made no secret of the fact that she had never liked Callum. He was smug and self-satisfied, believing the world owed him, and he had never been good enough for her sister. He had known that money would head his way once her parents died, and he had waited for the chance to swoop on the inheritance, parasitic in his desire to feed off someone else's life's work. He had claimed his infidelity had been a one-off, putting it down to the pressures of work and the ongoing fertility treatment that had nearly caused a split between them on more than one occasion. Desperate to hold onto the appearance of a perfect marriage, Steph had bought into his empty excuses.

'Who is she then?' Steph asked. The hope that this was all some big misunderstanding was visible in her eyes, in the way she held her head, and yet doubt had crept into the corners of her mouth.

'Just a woman from work,' he said without looking at her. His focus was still on Adele, contempt seeping from him.

'I don't recognise her,' Steph replied flatly, though there was no reason she should have recognised someone Callum worked with.

'We'll talk about it later,' Callum said, and the dismissiveness of his tone made Adele want to scream. The cheek of the man, that he believed for even a moment he could just sweep this aside and sweet-talk Steph into submission, though it had no doubt been done a thousand times before.

'Talk about it now,' Adele suggested.

He glanced at Steph and shook his head; not an outright instruction – he wasn't quite brazen enough to attempt to control her like that in front of Adele – but sufficient to plead for her support.

'Who is she?' Steph repeated.

Adele's heart surged with respect for her sister; she had been forced to take sides and she had chosen Adele's, her loyalty making itself known in her refusal to be silenced.

Callum lingered over his answer, a certain indication that he was about to lie, because no one ever needed to hesitate over the truth.

'Her name is Diane Nicholson. She's a private investigator.'

The words hung in the air a moment, refusing to fall into place, a jumble of letters that left a juddering echo between Adele's ears. A private investigator? For Steph? And then she realised. Not for Steph. For her.

'My turn.' Callum went to the sideboard, where his phone was plugged into its charger. He unlocked it, swiped the screen and held it up in front of Adele so she could see the photograph selected: a picture of her and Dani, taken outside the church hall.

'She's been taking Ivy to a playgroup once a week,' he told Steph, who was watching them both, her focus moving from one to another as though gripped by a tennis match.

'Playgroup?'

Steph was clearly hurt; she hated having to work full-time, but they had chosen to spend the inheritance on the house, putting everything into making it the *Ideal Home*-style property she believed would guarantee her happiness. She could have gone part-time if they had stayed where they were – she could have afforded to give up work for a while to spend more time with Ivy, if that was what she had wanted – but she had made a choice and now she resented her sister for having the time she didn't and for sharing it with Ivy in a way she wasn't able to.

'We made a deal.'

'No,' Adele reminded her, jabbing a finger at Callum. 'He dictated a set of rules. That's not the same thing at all.'

Steph looked as though she was about to cry, but Adele found herself unable to feel sympathy for her.

'She should be around other children more,' she added.

'You're not taking her for her benefit, though, are you?' Callum interjected. 'Who's the girl?'

'What girl?' Steph snatched the phone from Adele and studied the photograph.

'She's been using our daughter,' he told her.

Steph looked up. 'I trusted you.'

'Yeah,' Callum scoffed. 'She'd already proven herself trustworthy, hadn't she? She killed a woman, Steph, or have you forgotten about that? She's unstable.' His sing-song tone cut through the air, its venom slicing at any effort Adele might have made to make her sister understand.

'Don't play that card,' Adele said, hearing the implication of his words. 'You've been happy to allow me to look after your daughter for months. Not concerned about Ivy's safety, despite how "unstable" I am.' She spoke the word with inverted commas, mocking him with the repetition. 'Ivy's safe with me, Steph – you know she is. If you didn't believe that, you would never leave her alone with me.'

Maybe it wasn't entirely true. Steph loved this life – the detached house, the bespoke fittings, the expensive car, the buzz of her job – even, perhaps, a little more than she loved her only child. She had waited for years to conceive, but once the reality of motherhood was there, the day-to-day drudgery of the role had quickly lost its appeal.

'Who is she?' Callum asked again.

Steph looked at Adele expectantly. She could have told her, but she would never understand; they were sisters, yet they were totally unalike, and any attempt at explanation would have been like pouring words into a well and watching them disappear into its depths as if they'd never existed.

'She's a friend,' she told them. 'Just a friend.'

It was true; or at least, there was an element of truth in it until recently. In the sense of keeping one's enemies close, Dani really was a true friend.

'You know,' she added. 'Just like Amanda Clarke was just a friend.'

Callum lunged towards her. Steph was faster, predicting the exchange as it happened and blocking his route to Adele. 'Don't do anything stupid,' she warned. 'She's not worth it.'

The words cut through Adele with such force that Steph might as well have plunged one of the kitchen knives into her stomach.

'It was one night, Steph, you know that. I could have lied about it, but I didn't. I told you everything, and we've been making it work, haven't we? Everything was fine until *she* moved in.'

Adele waited for her sister to defend her, but it didn't happen.

Callum looked at her over Steph's shoulder. 'I want you out of this house. First thing tomorrow.'

Adele smiled, trying to hide the pain of the invisible blow her sister had landed. 'Gladly.'

THIRTY-THREE

DANI

That night, Dani received a text from Adele. *I'm sorry*, it read. *Have you had a chance to start the book yet? You should read it. It says so much more than its words.*

The book that Adele had given her at the salon sat on Dani's bedside table, curiosity forcing her to keep it there. Layla had picked it up earlier that evening, drawn to the illustration on its cover: a rag doll with plaits at either side of her head, sitting with her head bowed forward. It wasn't a new book; the pages were worn at the edges and there was a stain on the back that looked like an old tea ring.

She didn't have time for reading, not while so much was racing through her mind, her thoughts in a turmoil with the reverberations of Maddie's words. How could Maddie possibly think Dani might be involved in Eve's death? It was madness, all of it, and yet she'd seemed convinced by every word she had spoken. The police were talking about an altercation. Did Maddie really believe that Dani and Eve had fought before she had died?

Layla was asleep on the bed beside her, snug in a pair of recently washed Disney princess pyjamas that still smelt like fabric conditioner. Her hair was fanned across the pillow like a peacock's feathers, her pale skin pinched pink at her cheeks. Sometimes Dani let her sleep in her room rather than in her own bed so that she could cuddle her while she slept. She looked forward to these peaceful moments when she could just lie beside her daughter and absorb the beauty of her, because whatever else she might have failed at, Layla was the one thing she had managed to get right.

And yet so often she felt as though she was failing.

The most beautiful thing about Layla was her innocence. When did it end? Dani wondered. There must have been a time when Caroline had done as she was doing now, lying beside her daughter and marvelling at the little life that was yet to be lived. Had she noticed Dani's innocence gradually leave, easing in the way her baby features had, or had its absence come as more of a shock, one day there and one day not? At some time, in some faraway life, Dani had been just like Layla, until one day she had become the kind of girl who wished harm upon another.

Her thoughts spilled back towards the night of the prom; the night that represented the death of her friendship with Eve. Everyone had looked amazing. Eve's mother had bought her a dress from a boutique in Swansea, the kind of shop that women bought their wedding dresses from; they'd travelled down twice to choose it, staying overnight in a hotel on the second visit so they could go back to the shop to make sure it was the right one. It had cost hundreds of pounds, and when Dani had seen it a couple of weeks before the prom, she'd felt a knot of jealousy in her stomach that made her hate Eve just for the slightest of seconds. She always had everything – the best clothes, the most money, the highest grades.

Caroline had blamed Dani's father for what she always referred to as their 'shit creek situation'. He'd had no life insurance, presumably because dying at the age of forty-three had never been a part of his agenda. Caroline hadn't worked while Dani was young, but after her husband's death she went back to the supermarket where she'd been employed before Dani was born, resenting every minute she spent behind the till and reminding her daughter of it regularly.

Dani had bought her own prom dress with savings from her job at the garden centre, and though it cost a tiny fraction of what Eve's parents had spent on hers, her mother still felt it necessary to tell her what a waste of money it was. She'd already been charging Dani rent by then – she had started paying towards food and bills as soon as she got her first job, at the age of fourteen – and rather than commend her for being hard-working and frugal, Caroline scoffed at her for being stupid and trying to be like everyone else.

Dani had felt frumpy in the floor-length dress she'd chosen. She was a bit overweight, and standing there with the middle pulling across her stomach and her bare arms on show for all to see, she had realised why all the other girls had been crash-dieting for the previous month in a bid to look their best on the day. When Eve's mum had come to the house to give her a lift, Dani had shuffled self-consciously to the pavement, yanking at the fabric that kept getting twisted at her hips and putting all her focus on not being the girl who was going to take an inevitable and graceless tumble in her heels.

'You look nice,' Eve said through the open back window, but Dani heard the sneer in her voice before the expression became visible on her face seconds later. She didn't know what Eve's problem was. She looked incredible, like a high-fashion model from the pages of a glossy magazine, but beneath the perfect exterior there was this ice about her, as though she was intent on finding trouble.

When Dani got into the car with her, Eve's mum told her how lovely she looked, managing to sound a lot more sincere than Eve had. She liked Mrs Gardiner, she always had. She just seemed normal, whatever normal was. There were times when Dani had been jealous of the life Eve had, frustrated with her when she moaned about her parents and the pressure they apparently put on her – things like curfews and revision – thinking how nice it would be for her own mum to care about any of those things, and how nice it would be to have a father who was still alive. Caroline wasn't awful – Dani had never thought that. She was just a bit absent sometimes, despite being there.

When they arrived at the hotel, half their year was gathered in the car park, posing for selfies and laughing in groups. Dani had texted Scarlet in the car but hadn't heard back, so assumed she hadn't looked at her phone. They had found her not long after arriving; she'd been standing at the entrance holding hands with Rhys Paterson, and before they got close enough for them to hear her, Eve had leaned towards Dani and whispered, 'We should so do what you suggested.' Dani had tried to laugh off her words, but she wished then that she'd never said anything. It had been a joke. She hadn't meant it.

Desperate for a distraction from the memories of that night, she reached for the book Adele had given her. It was called *The Little Doll* – Dani had never heard of it – and if it was meant as a gift for Layla, it seemed a bit old for her. Layla rarely sat still long enough for Dani to read to her, and her interest in books was still yet to go beyond trying to tear pieces from lift-the-flap pages.

She turned to the front page and began to read. *A little doll lived all alone in a doll's house made of cardboard...* She looked at her daughter's sleeping face, the rise and fall of her chest, and felt a surge of love so intense it was almost painful. *It was lonely in the doll's house, quiet and empty...*

There were fingerprints at the corner of the page left by grubby hands, and Dani wondered why Adele had given her something so worn and battered, something that might once have been precious to someone. There was a red pen mark at the bottom of the page, and as she continued to read, she spotted another, as though someone had been making corrections.

Sometimes the little doll felt sad and she longed for a friend to talk to...

Dani stopped reading, put the book on the bed beside her and turned to curl her body around her sleeping child's. Silent tears stained her face, her body shuddering as sadness escaped her in a flood. She let it wash over her as, like a child, she cried herself to sleep.

THIRTY-FOUR

ADELE

Adele avoided Callum that morning, not going downstairs until she knew he had left for work. When she went into the kitchen, Steph was sitting at the table, her laptop open in front of her. Ivy was sitting on the floor nearby, playing with a wooden grocery set.

'I've packed most of my things.'

Steph looked at her apologetically. 'I'm sorry,' she said, though she didn't sound it. 'It was only meant to be temporary, though, wasn't it?'

'Of course,' Adele said, forcing cheeriness into her voice. 'And I know I've outstayed my welcome. I'm sorry it's caused problems between you two – I never meant for that to happen.'

Ivy got up from the floor and wandered over to her, wrapping her arms around her legs and squashing her face to her knee.

'Good morning, gorgeous,' Adele said, crouching to her niece's level. 'Well, that was unexpected and lovely.' She felt an involuntary tear threaten to slide from her left eye. No matter what anyone else might have thought of her, Adele could be confident that Ivy at least loved her. 'Who's looking after her this morning?'

'I've taken the day off.'

Adele glanced at the laptop. What Steph meant was that she wasn't going into work and would do what she needed to from home, while poor Ivy was left to amuse herself all day.

'Let me take her on one last trip to the park.'

Steph grimaced. 'Callum said—'

'Are you answerable to your husband?' Adele snapped. 'What is this… 1952?'

Steph raised an eyebrow, but it was obvious Adele had hit a nerve. Callum could have taken the day off work to look after Ivy; Steph's job was more lucrative than his. Of course, he wouldn't do that, not when being a man seemed to mean his job was more important than hers would ever be.

'Go into work for the morning, do what you have to do, and you can come back at lunchtime. What do you think? I'll leave after that, I promise. Callum won't know anything about it.'

Steph looked back at her laptop. 'I can probably get this done here…' she started.

'But you'd get it done in half the time in the office,' Adele finished for her.

Steph sighed as she weighed up the options. 'Are you sure? I don't want you to feel I'm taking advantage.'

Adele bit her tongue. Her sister had been taking advantage the whole time Adele had been staying with them; one more morning was unlikely to affect her. She and Callum had saved thousands of pounds in childcare costs, and it increasingly seemed that so long as their bank accounts were healthy, they were happy. In a way, Adele was grateful that they had used her. She loved spending time with Ivy. Children were always preferable to adults.

'Go,' she said, pointing towards the door. 'Before I retract the offer.'

Five minutes later, Steph was gone. Adele took Ivy up to her bedroom to get her dressed in appropriate clothing, and while she was there, she gathered the things they would need: wet wipes, nappies, a change of clothes. Once the bag was packed, they went back downstairs in search of snacks.

Adele sat Ivy on the kitchen worktop while she filled her water bottle, and as the little girl sat silently watching her screw on the lid, the familiarity of her features stole Adele's breath. She retrieved her phone and took a photograph of her, Ivy even managing to smile on cue when asked to.

'You and your cousin would have got on so well,' she said, pushing Ivy's hair behind her ear. 'She was so much like you, you know. Beautiful and loving.'

Ivy smiled, though Adele realised she had no idea what she was talking about. It made her sad to think that the child would never remember this time they had spent together.

'She would have loved you so much, just like I do.' She kissed the top of Ivy's head. 'Right, missy. I've got a little surprise arranged for you. Would you like to go on a playdate?' She lifted her down. 'Come on then. Let's go.'

She took Ivy outside and strapped her into the toddler seat in the hire car before getting the petrol can out of the boot and returning to the house. She had filled it the previous afternoon, anticipating that her move from the house would be imminent. If Callum wanted to test her, it was only fair to show him just how unstable she could be.

The kitchen seemed the obvious place to start, the heart of the home and Steph's pride and joy. Adele unscrewed the cap and took a last look at the garden, lamenting the fact that Ivy would no longer run and play there. Never mind. There would be other places for her to play, in a life her parents would have built themselves rather than just taking.

Steph's words rang in her ears. *She's not worth it.* She might have pretended to be a loving, supportive sister, but Callum was wrong: it was Steph using Adele, not the other way around.

In the living room, she retrieved one of Ivy's favourite soft toys, placing the fluffy white cat by the front door so she could take it to her when she went back to the car. She thought of Dylan, feeling a momentary pang of remorse for what she had had to do. Certain things were necessary. Like this, she thought. She went back to the living room to douse the sofas with petrol before moving out into the hallway and soaking the coats. In the kitchen, she took a lighter from her pocket, flicked it and let it fall to the ground. There was a hot whoosh of flame, and she stood for a moment, watching as it quickly spread. Then she picked up the cat and left the house.

THIRTY-FIVE

DANI

She was sweeping up the snow-white curls of Mrs Beckett – an octogenarian who had visited the salon for a cut and blow dry once a month, always on a Thursday, for as long as Dani had worked there – when the fire alarm went off. It was shrill and continuous, and poor Mrs Beckett had to put her hands over her ears, her hearing aid no doubt amplifying the already deafening noise.

Dani stopped what she was doing, propped the sweeping brush against a chair and raised her shoulders at Nadine, the stylist who was cutting Mrs Beckett's hair; in the time she had been there, she had never heard the fire alarm either, and neither of them knew what the procedure was, other than that they should probably go outside. There was a fire drill poster stuck to the wall by the back entrance to the salon, but Dani had never given it more than a passing glance and didn't know where the designated meeting point was – or whether there even was one.

Mrs Beckett swivelled around on her chair and asked for someone to turn the alarm off just as Tracy came back into the salon, the two-pint bottle of milk she'd popped out to buy wedged under one arm, her mobile phone in the other hand.

'We need to get everyone outside,' she said, putting her phone in her pocket and the milk on a spare chair before offering Mrs Beckett a hand up. 'It's probably nothing to worry about.'

Dani and Nadine waited for Tracy and Mrs Beckett to leave first before following them across the car park. A member of staff from Greggs was lingering by the doorway, drawn there by the alarm, and a moment later Travis appeared from the tattoo parlour. Dani hadn't realised he was back at work. He crossed the car park when he saw the women from the salon there.

'Everything okay?' he asked Tracy.

'I've called 999 as a precaution, but I can't see anything.'

'Want me to take a look?'

She batted away the offer with a waved hand. 'Thanks, but they won't be long, I'm sure. Better to be safe than sorry.'

Travis caught Dani's eye. 'You okay?'

She nodded.

'I'm sorry,' he said, as he moved closer to her. 'I only got back to work this morning. I was going to come and see you later.'

She smiled, not quite believing it. 'Is your brother okay?'

'He was knocked off his motorbike. He came out of a coma yesterday.'

'Oh God, I'm so sorry, I had no idea.'

'Well why would you? I didn't message you back, did I?'

'Is he going to be okay?'

Travis nodded. 'It was touch and go until yesterday, but he's shown signs of improvement. I stayed to be with my mum, she's been a mess.'

'I bet. I'm so sorry,' she said again. 'If there's anything I can do to help, just let me know.'

'Come with me for that drink this weekend? I just want to do something that feels normal, you know?'

'With me? Probably won't be normal.'

'I'll email you,' he said. 'I quite like this not-having-your-number business. Feels a bit old-fashioned.'

'Courting. My nan used to say that.'

'Is that what we're doing then?'

'Have to see how this drink goes first, won't we?'

'Dani.' Their flirtation was interrupted by Tracy, who was beckoning her back to the shop.

'I'll message you later,' Travis told her, and she felt his eyes still on her as she made her way back to the salon.

Three more customers were waiting for now-overdue appointments, and Mrs Beckett's hair had been air-dried into a frizz any poodle would have been proud to call its own. Tracy offered her the cut for free, which quickly halted any complaint she was about to put forward.

Once Dani had finished sweeping up and making cups of tea to pacify impatient customers disgruntled by the delay in their appointments, her shift was over and she couldn't wait to get home. The weather had changed, dark skies moving in to cloud the blue; perhaps she would take Layla to the soft play centre for an hour or two, assuming she wasn't already too tired after her morning at nursery.

The house was quiet when she got back. She found Caroline in the back yard, pegging clothes on the line. 'I wouldn't bother with that,' she said. 'Looks like it's going to rain.'

'And good afternoon to you too, Danielle,' her mother replied without looking at her.

'Where's Layla?'

'With you, isn't she?'

Dani felt her stomach drop. 'You were supposed to be picking her up from nursery.'

'You said you'd do it. You texted me.'

'No I didn't, Mum. For God's sake.'

She went back into the house for her bag, but when she looked for her phone, it wasn't there, and she realised she must have left it at the salon. With a strangled scream of frustration, she took the car keys from her mother's handbag. The nursery fined parents who were late to collect their children, and it was already nearly an hour since Layla's session should have come to an end. People made mistakes and plans became confused, but Dani was concerned that this would look like neglect.

When she got there, she rang the bell and waited for a member of staff to answer.

'I'm so sorry I'm late,' she said. 'There was a mix-up with my mother – she was supposed to come and collect Layla, but she thought for some reason that I was doing it.' She reached into her bag for her purse. 'I'll pay you for the extra hour.'

The woman raised a hand to stop her. Dani couldn't remember her name; she didn't see much of her as she was usually inside the building at drop-off and pick-up times. But she didn't need to know her to realise there was something wrong with her reaction and the way she was looking at her.

'Layla's not here.'

'What do you mean, she's not here?'

'She's already left.'

For a moment, Dani was thrown into a vacuum that sucked her into silence. The noise of the children inside the nursery faded, then the silence was replaced with a screaming that filled her head. The other woman's jaw slackened at the implication of Dani's reaction to her words.

Tara, the woman who ran the nursery, came over, a small red-haired child clinging to her leg.

'How's your mother doing?'

Dani felt it like a punch to her gut – a heart-pounding moment in which the world seemed to rotate too quickly around her, a gravity that was too strong pinning her feet to the ground, keeping her immobile. The woman whose name she couldn't remember was saying something, but Dani couldn't hear it, every other sound drowned by the scream that continued to ring out inside her head, a scream that could not make itself audible even if she had tried to release it. Layla was gone. Someone had taken her.

Tara ushered them both into the office, keeping the conversation away from the rest of the nursery.

'Where's Layla? Where's my daughter?'

'You texted me,' Tara began. She fumbled with her mobile, her finger swiping the screen as she searched for the conversation thread. 'Here.' She passed Dani the phone.

Mum's had a fall, the message read. *I'm at the hospital with her – we won't be back in time to pick up Layla. My auntie will be coming to get her.*

Sorry about your mum, Tara had replied. *Hope she's okay. Are any of the staff familiar with your aunt?*

No – good point, sorry. I'll send you a pic.

Dani scrolled on. Adele smiled back at her from the screen. She felt fear snake through her veins and cool her blood. 'I didn't text you any of this. There's nothing wrong with my mother – someone stole my phone.' *And now she's stolen your daughter*, said a voice in her head. 'How could you have let this happen?'

Tara took the phone back with a shaking hand. 'Do you know her?'

'Yes.' Though the truth of it was, she didn't know her at all. Was she really who she said she was – was her name even Adele? Dani realised she didn't know her surname. She didn't know whether the house she had been to with Layla was really where Adele lived. All she had ever had from her was a phone number, stored on a phone she now couldn't access. 'I mean, I thought I knew her, but I don't really…' She stopped and tried to catch her breath, but she could feel herself shaking, her darkest fears making themselves known one by one in a film reel that played in high definition at the front of her mind. 'Call the police.'

Tara turned to the desk and reached for the office phone.

The other woman looked at her anxiously. 'She got into a car, I think… I'm not sure.'

'She doesn't drive,' Dani snapped, but of course that might not be true. And someone else might have been driving for her. Helping her. She couldn't believe anything Adele had told her. She had lied – as good as lied – about being Ivy's mother. Had her daughter really died, or had that been another lie to keep Dani on her side and disguise her true intention to take Layla from her?

THIRTY-SIX

ADELE

Layla cried relentlessly for twenty minutes, repeating the word 'Mama' on an endless loop as Adele left the city and made her way onto the M4. It has been easy to take her from the nursery. Once Layla had seen Ivy, she had gone with them willingly, probably expecting a trip to the park to follow. The wailing that had started once they were in the car now tore at Adele's nerves and managed to send even a usually placid Ivy into a state of agitation.

She pulled the car over into a lay-by and gave Layla a bag of crisps, its pacifying effects seeming to Adele a sad reflection of the relationship between mother and daughter, that one might be so easily distracted from thoughts of the other. She wondered whether the same would apply to Dani. Of course, she knew how much Dani loved her daughter. She would be frantic by now, distraught with worry about where Adele had taken her and what she might be planning.

'No more tears now,' she said, wiping a hand across Layla's forehead and pushing her hair from her sweaty skin. 'We're going on a playdate. It's going to be lots of fun. You can play with the toys my little girl used to play with. Would you like that?'

Layla studied her questioningly, but she was calmed by the words. Satisfied that the promise of new toys to play with might keep her subdued for the rest of the journey, Adele returned to the driver's seat. She had told Dani she didn't drive, but she had never told her she couldn't. In nearly eight years she had only driven a handful of times, each time when there had been no alternative. She hated driving. Just being behind the wheel of a car brought back memories she tried to keep buried, and her hands gripped the wheel tighter now as flashbacks flitted across the screen in front of her, replaying moments she didn't want to be forced to relive.

A dark night. A tunnel of trees enveloping her.

They had argued. Arguments had been rare; what was more common was avoiding one another in a pretence at normality, in the daily routine of waking, eating, working, sleeping. The routine was his, of course; any sense of order or purpose had long ago gone from Adele's existence, each day a new vacuum into which she was sucked down and held, barely keeping her face above the surface to allow sufficient oxygen into her lungs. She had eaten sometimes; she had slept occasionally. When she looked back on that time, she realised there had been arms around her keeping her afloat – Brandon's arms – though she had been too absorbed by internal pain to feel them there. But there had been a limit to his strength, to the length of time he could endure the weight of her.

'When is all this going to end, Adele?'

He hadn't heard his words in the same way Adele heard them. He was used to working with time frames, looking for answers, searching for reasons – he had wanted everything neatly packaged into a sequence that might offer an indication of when she would get better. He had never used the phrase 'snap out of it', though sometimes she heard it in the silence between them. The truth of it was, she had resented him for not being like her. His life moved on when her own was stalled. He had no idea what it was like for her. Nobody did.

'End?' she had repeated. 'I don't know. Do you want a date? I'm sorry, but you knew who I was when you met me.'

Brandon had sucked in his cheeks and pressed his fingertips to his temples. 'We've got to try to get back to normal at some point.'

Her drinking had got worse, she knew that. She might have done something about it months earlier, but she felt as though she was now past the point of being able to control it by herself. There had been something else at work, an addiction that was bigger than she was, and she was weakened by the need for alcohol, for its magical ability to make everything seem better, if only in the short term.

The truth of it was, Brandon hadn't known anything about her when they met. Adele had come to think of her life as a book, the kind that featured past and present in alternating chapters, the only difference being that her chapters were marked Grey and Blue. Her blue-sky chapters were the phases of her life in which everything seemed simple and clear, when she knew what she wanted, and she didn't hate herself for all the things she wasn't. Then the grey clouds would roll overhead, heavy and oppressive. She would exist beneath them for the time they stayed, not really living but just there, just being, and she couldn't help that everyone who knew and loved her would be dragged down with her beneath the weight of them.

A look had passed between them, something silent and tragic that acknowledged the bare fact of the thing: there was never going to be the normal he was so desperately awaiting. Maybe there might once have been the glimmer of a promise of one, but the foundations on which it had been built had slipped too far from beneath Adele for her to claw herself back, and she doubted she had the energy to do so even had she wanted to. He had met her during a blue-sky phase. He had been lured into a life with her under false pretences.

'There is no normal,' she said.

When she'd got up from the chair, she'd stumbled and hit her shin against the coffee table. She might have been drinking, but she wasn't so drunk that she missed the look he gave her. They had grown in frequency over the years, a slight tensing of his jaw morphing into a flinch when she breathed too close to him, and she knew what he suspected, that ignoring the problem had only made it worse.

'You need to speak to someone. Please.'

She had heard it before. He thought she needed help, professional help; he was tired of his pleas being ignored. Sometimes she wondered whether the help was to benefit him more than her, to make his life easier so that the burden of her no longer rested with him.

'You don't get it, do you? I can't stop. I don't expect you to understand it, but this isn't about me, Brandon, it's about something outside me that I have no control over. You want me to be this perfect wife, this perfect mother, and I can't do it, okay. I just can't give you what you want.'

With a single swipe of his arm, Brandon had sent the photo frame that rested on the mantelpiece crashing to the floor. The glass had smashed on the laminate flooring, shattering into tiny shards at her feet. She had never seen him lose his temper before. In the fifteen years she had known him, his anger had never extended beyond muttering a curse at a fellow driver. Throughout everything, he had been the solid one, the support on which she relied. But who did he rely on?

'Have you heard yourself?' he had asked, his words shaking with his anger. 'Have you actually listened to the nonsense that comes out of your mouth? You have a child. You have responsibilities. When are you going to grow up and stop playing the "poor me" card, Adele? Your life is good, don't you see that? There are people who would give everything for just a slice of your existence, yet all you do is abuse it. Don't you think there are days I feel like stopping too? I don't want to work every day just to get old and bitter and wonder if there might have been something better that I missed, but that's life, Adele, and guess what – we're all heading the same way. So just grow up, get help, and stop putting us through all this shit.'

The slap had been sudden and sharp, leaving an angry red mark that flared on his cheek. As soon as she had done it, she wanted to take it back, but it was too late. Neither of them had ever been violent to the other before. A line had been crossed, a boundary that he must have believed obvious, that had never needed to be drawn. Before he had a chance to say any more – things she knew she couldn't bear to hear – Adele fled the room and slammed the front door behind her, taking the car keys from the hallway drawer on her way out.

It had been her fault, all of it, but she couldn't see that at the time, not with her vision blurred by a fog of alcohol in which she'd willingly immersed herself, her safety net from all the things she wished to escape.

She didn't think she had drunk that much. The news reports claimed she had been on a binge – a bottle of wine and half a dozen vodkas – but she never believed it could have been that much, not when she had sobered up so quickly afterwards. It was the sound that had sobered her. The lack of sound. There wasn't the screeching of tyres that might have been expected, the crunch of metal or the hiss of the car's engine as it thundered to a stop. There was little more than a dull thud, and then nothing – just a silence that seemed to roll out ahead of her, a void in which the past and everything that had gone with it evaporated behind her, and the future – that foreign country feared for all its uncertainty – stood before her, shrouded in a cape of darkness. She was suspended there between the two: one life ended, another just begun.

Of course, it wasn't a case of just one life having ended; there was also the life outside the car, the one lying inert at the roadside. Still sitting at the wheel, Adele couldn't possibly know then that the person she had hit – man or woman, she didn't know which – was dead, not for definite, and yet somehow she already did, could feel it in the way she felt other facts, with a finality that left no room for doubt.

She couldn't get out of the car. She knew she had to – there was no running away from this – but she was too weak to pull the door handle, too detached from her own body to find the strength to heave herself out. She wanted to go back. She listened to the sound of Brandon's anger in her ears, to the echoes of the words his broken heart had written, to the pleas that had gone before that night, all left ignored, as though she had thought somewhere in her subconscious that there might be another time, another life, for her to put right all her wrongs. That they would heal, in time, and she would get better, in this life or the next.

In that moment, she would have given anything to go back there, to the recriminations and the fury, if it had meant undoing what she had just done.

At last she had stepped from the car. There had been a rustling in the leaves somewhere to her right, a bird fluttering amid the trees or a squirrel scuttling in its search for a late-night snack, and the sound was so beautiful, so everyday, that she could have cried at the normality of it.

She hadn't seen her at first. There was nothing in front of the car but the coal-black road winding ahead of her. She had seen her bike first, crumpled on the grass verge, its back wheel bent as though it was made of rubber rather than metal. When she'd stepped closer, she'd seen something staining the crossbar. Blood.

The woman had been knocked so far that her body had landed near the hedgerow, flung into the shadows at an angle Adele knew no one could have survived. She was young, maybe mid twenties. No fluorescent strips on her clothing; no helmet on her head. No chance of surviving the force of the impact.

The next time Adele had seen Brandon, she had been released on police bail. She'd known what would happen, that it was just a matter of time between then and the trial, and he knew it too. She would have no choice but to plead guilty, not when her guilt was so undeniable. He couldn't look at her. In those months that followed, they floated past each other like ghosts. They slept in different beds, spent their time in different rooms; spoke only when it involved something relating to their daughter, who became increasingly withdrawn and spent most of her time when she wasn't at school in her bedroom.

Now Adele dragged herself from the fog of the past and glanced in the rear-view mirror at the two girls sleeping on the back seat. She was already a killer. No matter what Tim or anyone else told her, she would always be regarded by the world as one. Perhaps, then, it didn't matter how many more deaths she was responsible for.

THIRTY-SEVEN

DANI

There were two officers standing in the living room: a man with grey-flecked hair receding at the temples and a much younger woman who was wearing more make-up than Dani would have worn on a night out. She was standing so close that Dani was able to see the terracotta line of foundation that curved under her chin, and she found herself distracted by it, using it as something else to focus on, something other than the thought that Adele had taken her daughter.

DC Lewis watched with scepticism as Dani scanned the pages of the book Adele had given her. 'What are you looking for?'

'Just wait,' she told him, her voice fraught. 'Please.'

She had a scrap of paper beside her, the ripped envelope of a utility bill addressed to her mother. Each time she saw a red pen mark, she wrote down the letter that was above it. She hadn't noticed the previous night, but the marks continued right up until the end of the book end. She had thought them some type of correction, but it was quickly clear that she was wrong. After three letters, she realised she had been blind to what had been happening right in front of her.

'Oh God.'

'What?' DC Lewis stooped forward to look at what she had written. Letters had formed words, and the words revealed a message.

Eve and Dani. They did it. U owe me this.

'Oh God, I've been so stupid.'

'What?' Caroline asked. 'What have you done, Dani?'

Her mother's mascara was smudged from crying. She was blaming herself, as though feeling she should have somehow known that the text she received from Dani's phone was not in fact from Dani.

'She gave me this. And it's here in black and white.'

'What is?'

'Can you get a location on my phone?' Dani asked, ignoring the officer's question. 'Or on Adele's?'

'Someone's working on it,' PC Cartwright said, casting her superior a glance. 'In the meantime, you need to explain to us exactly who this woman is and why you think she's taken Layla.'

'What do you mean, "in the meantime"?' Caroline chipped in. 'How long is it going to take?'

'Mrs McNamara,' DC Lewis said, 'we know you're worried about your granddaughter, but the most helpful thing you and Danielle can do right now is tell us everything you know.'

'Well, brilliant. I don't know anything.' Caroline looked accusingly at Dani, who felt the room close in on her as three pairs of eyes focused on her, waiting for an explanation.

'You remember Scarlet?' she said, speaking directly to her mother, trying to imagine there was only the two of them there. 'I think Adele is connected to her somehow.'

'Who's Scarlet?' asked PC Cartwright.

'Dani's friend from school,' Caroline told her. 'She killed herself.'

The words stabbed Dani in the gut. Scarlet's suicide might have been anticipated by those closest to her – a history of self-harm, an eating disorder, a mother who had died while she was a child – but there had been something specific that had tipped her over the edge of the precipice on which much of her life had balanced, and it was Dani who had nudged her from the cliff edge. Dani and Eve.

'We did it,' she said, the words expelling themselves in barely a whisper. 'Eve and me. We killed her.'

Another glance was exchanged by the officers.

Dani ignored them and kept her gaze on her mother. She had never told Caroline what had happened, too ashamed to admit her part in it. All the things that had occurred in the aftermath of Scarlet's death – the abandoned university place, the one-night stands – Caroline had put down to the shock of the suicide, but as time went on, her patience with Dani's reaction had started to wear thin. She would remind her that Scarlet had been a troubled girl. Dani hadn't known her that long. She had her own life to get on with, one that she deserved to live.

But did she? Dani wondered. Did she really deserve it after what she'd done?

Scarlet had briefly been their friend. She'd started at their school midway through Year 12, which seemed a strange time to change schools, right in the middle of A levels, but she told them that her dad had taken on a new job that had meant them moving. Eve had latched onto her first, and Dani remembered the jealousy she had felt at the time, how until then it had been just her and Eve, no one else to infiltrate their partnership. Looking back, she knew why Eve had made such a sudden move towards Scarlet. She was pretty; prettier, perhaps, than Eve herself. In an act of keeping-your-enemies-close, Eve had befriended her so she could control the threat she posed.

'Where's your phone?' Dani asked.

Caroline found her mobile and passed it across, and Dani searched for the video of prom night that could still be found on the internet. She pressed play and handed the phone to DC Lewis, waiting as the two officers watched it. She hadn't seen it in years, but the shame it brought was as hot and real as though the events it displayed had occurred just the night before.

She could replay it in her memory without having to see it again. Scarlet came into view of the camera within moments, stage right, as though photo-bombing the intended main point of focus. Whoever had been behind the phone (Freddie Carmichael, if she remembered correctly – proud of his camera skills when he uploaded the video to the internet, but less so when the police got involved) had pinned his attention on someone else at first, but when the girl in the red dress staggered into shot, he was soon distracted.

The officers watched as Scarlet danced on screen, and Dani was reminded of that song she used to hear at her nan's house when she was little, only there was no romance in what was being viewed and there were unfortunately plenty of people there with the lady in red. It quickly transpired that the girl in the red dress was not dancing; she was staggering. Her arms began to flail and her head lolled back so that she was staring wide-eyed at the ceiling of the hotel function room. Before anyone had a chance to intervene (though Dani couldn't recall anyone looking as though they were going to do so), she grabbed a passing member of staff and wrapped her leg around his like a dog about to take a piss on a lamp post. Sniggers could be heard; the odd word could be made out between the sneers. *Mess… state… embarrassing.* Dani gulped down a lump that had formed in her throat, because she knew now how it felt to have people comment on you when they were ignorant of the facts.

'The girl in the red dress, that's Scarlet. The video was all over the internet after prom night. I was jealous of her – the boy I liked right the way through school had asked her to go to the prom with him. Eve spiked her drink. It was me who put the idea in her head, though.'

It was a condensed version of what had happened, an edit from which the details had been cut. Dani looked away from her mother, unable to face her reaction.

'So where do you think Adele comes into this?'

'I don't know.'

She sat down on the sofa and put her head in her hands. She could only assume that Adele was a relative of Scarlet's, and now she wished she had seen sooner what was happening right in front of her. All the times she had thought James's wife was out to seek revenge, there had been someone else intent on righting a wrong she had caused. But who *was* Adele? Scarlet had no family other than her father, and he had died eighteen months after her suicide. A heart attack. A broken heart. Another death Dani had inadvertently caused.

'Oh God.' The words came out strangled in a sob.

'What?' Caroline said.

'She talked about him. That night she came over here, when you were out, she spoke about Scarlet's dad. Losing someone close to her. It was him. She told me at the salon that her baby had died. I thought she meant an actual baby. I never thought…' The possibility that Scarlet had lied reared its head. 'Scarlet can't have been her baby – she said her mother had died. Why would she make up something like that?'

The words left her in a confused jumble, barely making sense to her own ears.

'Who do you think she is, Danielle?' DC Lewis asked.

'You need to find Layla,' she pleaded, her voice fraught with desperation. 'Please. Adele is going to do to me what I did to her. She's going to kill my baby.'

'Danielle.' PC Cartwright placed a hand on her arm to calm her. 'This isn't making much sense. You need to explain everything you think you know.'

'But I don't know!' Her voice rose to a shout. An image of Eve passed behind her eyes; an imagined snapshot of her that Dani had seen so many times since reading of her death. Eve hated water. She remembered again that on the few occasions they had been to the beach together as teenagers, Eve had never gone near the sea.

'Oh God,' she said again, and the words this time were filled with fear. Tears followed, unforgiving and unashamed.

The doorbell rang. Dani rushed out into the hallway and opened the door to be met with a woman she didn't know, though it took only moments for her to realise that although she didn't know her, she had seen her before. A supermarket aisle. Ivy.

The woman turned back to glance at the police car parked on the opposite side of the road. 'They're with you?'

Adele's sister. She had said that Ivy was her niece – perhaps this was one thing she hadn't lied about. It made sense that Ivy was related to her, considering how much access Adele had to her.

'Where is she?' Dani asked breathlessly.

'She mustn't see the police,' the woman told her. 'I don't know what she'll do.'

Dani looked back into the house. DC Lewis had come out into the hallway and was watching them. 'You know where they are?' she asked, her voice lowered.

The woman nodded, an unspoken message passing between them, and in the silence, Dani heard enough to know that whatever else happened, she had to face Adele herself. She didn't need to think twice about the threat of possible danger, not when Layla needed her now more than ever.

'Let's go,' she muttered, and before the police officer could intervene, they were at the woman's car. Dani saw her mother in the wing mirror as she clipped in her seat belt; heard her calling her name from the pavement and saw the two officers chasing after the car as it sped from the street.

'You're Adele's sister?'

The woman nodded.

'Please tell me you know where she is.'

THIRTY-EIGHT

ADELE

The house stood alone at the end of a lane where nothing had changed since she had last seen the place. Time had stopped there, everything as it had once been, years ago in another life. An old-fashioned black dustbin stood on the driveway, its lid propped to one side, filled with rainwater. On the path that led to the side gate, a rusty bicycle lay forgotten, its pink frame aged brown. There had been a basket once, used to transport soft toys and snacks, but it was gone now, the way of most things, abandoned somewhere and never to be seen again. Bottle-green paint flaked from the wooden frame of the front door; they had intended to treat and repaint it, but it was one of many jobs they had never got around to. Adele had been reluctant to change too much. Her childhood lingered in this house, the memories of it like ghosts in its corners, and she could never bring herself to dust them away or gloss over their shadows.

Both girls were asleep in the back of the car, lulled into slumber by the motion and duration of the journey. Adele carried Ivy in first, then Layla, placing both girls undisturbed on the rug in the living room before going to the kitchen. She had left the treats in an empty cupboard, and now she took them to the garden. She opened the door of the summer house and threw some inside before returning indoors and going upstairs.

Scarlet's room – Adele's before her – was exactly as she remembered it. The nail varnish stain on the carpet by the chest of drawers was still there, the pink smear dried into a scrubbed smudge that had faded over time; the corkboard hanging behind the door was still adorned with curled and yellowing concert and cinema tickets stuck there with drawing pins. Above the bed was a montage of photographs, a gallery of faces smiling and pouting; some she recognised instantly, others she had to pull from the recesses of her memory. She scanned the images in turn, recalling how happy her daughter had been there, when life had been good, her childhood untouched by the darkness that she had brought to it.

She stopped at a photograph of four young girls, early teens, their arms around each other's shoulders as they all pulled faces for the camera. A blonde, a redhead and two brunettes, one of them Scarlet. She was leaning forward, head tilted to one side, her tongue sticking from the corner of her mouth and her eyes rolled skywards as though mid laugh. She'd had friends then, Adele thought. Not friends like Eve and Danielle, but true friends.

She stood at the window and looked out onto the garden, which narrowed as it met the stone wall behind which ran a stream. The large hydrangea with its oversized pink flowers was still to the left of the lawn, which was now overgrown and overrun with weeds. She saw Scarlet – six years old, a large 'birthday girl' badge pinned to her party dress – running between the flower beds, screeching as her friends chased her with water balloons, and then she was gone, the vision of her evaporated as though she had never been there at all.

In the two years she had been back in Wales, Adele had returned to the house just twice. Once upon a time she had planned to spend her life there, but without Scarlet there was nothing to return for. Just being there was painful. Brandon had been right – she'd had everything, but it had never been enough, not while her demons had lived there with her. Her probation officer, Tim, had told her that going back to the house would be cathartic, a part of the healing process, but he hadn't really understood her, not like he thought he did. She was too broken to ever be repaired.

Her thoughts were paused by a sound from downstairs. She went back to the living room, but both girls were still asleep, their arms flung out so they were nearly touching. In a different life, the two sleeping girls might have been Adele and Steph. She could see them now as they had once been – a den constructed from dining room chairs and blankets assembled in the middle of the living room, their bare feet outstretched to catch the heat from the three-bar fire – and when she closed her eyes, she could almost hear herself, some distant echo of the past reaching out to speak to her.

Theirs had been an idyllic childhood. Their father was an estate agent who'd moved into property development, an original self-made man, and their mother was an artist who worked from a studio at the back of the house. She was always there when Adele and Steph got home from school, able to schedule her work around her family; they were safe and happy, the type of life Adele wanted to emulate for her own children in a future that had seemed so far away back then it might as well have existed on a different planet. Her parents had encouraged both their daughters to follow their dreams, and when, aged five, she had talked of being a nurse when she was grown up, her mother had bought her a kit complete with the paraphernalia required for the role.

Getting pregnant at nineteen had never been part of her parents' plan for her, or hers for herself, and the discomfort she had felt in her own skin when she had seen those two red lines on that stick could still be felt now, so memorable was the lack of control the moment had brought with it. She had felt a shift around her, the earth tilting on its axis, the tectonic plates moving so that her world was split in two: her old life receding from her, a new one drifting ahead.

She had been midway through a nursing degree. There had been so many things she had wanted to do, so many places she had wanted to see, and yet somehow she had always known that she would never do and see them while the grey days continued to squat beside her.

'It's your life,' her father had said with a shrug. 'You've got to do what you think is best for you.'

There had been a moment of awkward silence before he turned his attention back to his newspaper. Her mother was sitting on the chair opposite, a coffee cup clutched in both hands, her eyes fixed on the window as though some fascinating scene was playing out on the driveway. Eventually, she had looked back at the room.

'Would you like another cup of tea, Brandon?'

Their reaction might have been different had Brandon not been present. She had wanted him there with her to save herself from the full weight of her parents' disappointment, which she knew would make itself apparent soon enough once her stomach started to swell and the promise of a grandchild became less avoidable. They had liked Brandon from his first visit – what was not to like? At twenty-seven he was young to be a detective constable, and since meeting Adele just over a year earlier, he had bought his own home in Swansea. He was well educated, polite and well mannered – all the things Adele imagined were on her parents' checklist for any potential future son-in-law.

Any trepidation they might have felt about the arrival of a baby had melted once Scarlet was born. Brandon had fallen instantly in love, as had Adele's parents, and they had spent those first few months together in the family home, with Brandon commuting for work. It was only for Adele that the love hadn't come instantly, not in the way everyone talked about. Scarlet had been placed into her arms at 8.14 on a hot, sticky Wednesday evening in August 1997, a day Adele had spent in a state of near delirium after being in labour since Monday night. Brandon had been there throughout, offering sips of water and words of encouragement that had mostly done nothing but infuriate her. The words 'I'm never doing this again' had left her on more than one occasion, and she had meant every one of them. Forty minutes after making her noisy, red-faced entry into the world, Scarlet had fed from Adele's breast, but she felt nothing other than emptiness, as though sadness was being drained from her with every suckle.

She had witnessed the love between Brandon and Scarlet as soon as he held their daughter. Watching his eyes fill with tears and the way Scarlet's tiny fingers gripped his thumb, Adele had been grateful for the connection, hopeful that perhaps he would succeed with their child where she already seemed to be failing. But it would come, in time, she thought. She would feel different soon.

Less than two weeks later, with Brandon back at work earlier than expected and still in bed following a Saturday night that had seen him work late on a domestic murder case, Adele had paced the living room trying to soothe an over-tired Scarlet who had been awake half the night screaming with hunger. She had bobbed on and off the breast restlessly, not getting what she needed, Adele's anxiety making them both increasingly panicked. She hadn't had any formula in the house – she had thought this was all supposed to come naturally, and no one had told her otherwise – and when Scarlet had eventually fallen asleep on her chest, exhausted by the violence of her screams, Adele had slumped on the sofa in front of the television and cried at the news footage playing out: the crumpled car, the dead princess; the dreams that lay crushed around her.

She returned to the present, distracted by Layla, who sat upright, scanned her surroundings and immediately began to cry. Adele picked her up and Layla struggled against her for a while, her cries soon waking Ivy, who rubbed the tiredness from her eyes and looked around her with eyes only half adjusted to wakefulness.

'Come on now,' Adele soothed, trying to calm a still fretful Layla. 'Would you like to see the new toys?'

'Mama,' Layla whimpered, her voice pitiful. 'Want Mama.'

'Mama will be here soon.'

She led the children to the staircase and followed them upstairs, directing them to Scarlet's room. 'Go on,' she said, gesturing to the toy box. 'Have a look.'

As the girls amused themselves with dolls and a collection of wooden farmyard animals – Layla once again easily pacified – Adele returned to the window and to the ghosts in the garden. By the time Scarlet had turned six, they had been living in the house for nearly three years. It had been her parents' idea; Steph was at university by then, studying journalism at Sheffield, and theirs was a family home, they said, too big for just the two of them. Steph had been furious. Their parents had signed over another of their properties to her so that neither daughter would be favoured financially, but it wasn't the same, she argued – it was her home too, and she was being penalised for not getting herself knocked up. Their relationship was strained for a while, but when Steph's life moved on and she got a job with BBC Wales, her frostiness towards Adele began to thaw.

Adele and Brandon had been happy there. Theirs had been a blessed life, the kind so many wanted for their children, and yet it somehow hadn't been enough for her. Nothing would have been enough for Adele, not when her brain sucked the light out of everything in the way it did. She'd had everything and nothing, and now nothing was what she was left with.

In her pocket, her mobile rang again. She didn't bother to take it out this time, knowing that her sister's name would flash from the screen as though her ear had been burning at Adele's thoughts of her. She waited for the call to end before returning her attention to the girls, who were still occupied with the contents of Scarlet's toy box.

She didn't need to speak to Steph; she would see them soon enough.

THIRTY-NINE

DANI

Dani had no idea whether she could trust the woman sitting next to her, but she was her best hope of finding her daughter before it was too late. The thought that she had inadvertently caused all this kept clawing at her brain, and if anything happened to Layla, she didn't want to live any more. Was that how Adele had felt after Scarlet's death?

'Where has she taken her?'

'Them. She's got Ivy as well. She sent me a photograph of the two of them in the back of a car.'

Knowing that both girls were with her made Dani's anxiety worse. Adele was dangerous and calculating; there was no guarantee that being related made Ivy safe from whatever she had planned. Ivy was no more responsible for her aunt's crimes than Layla was for Dani's.

Dani watched Steph fiddle with her phone before it hooked up to the car's Bluetooth system. 'Call Adele,' Steph instructed. They waited in silence as the phone rang, but it went unanswered.

'Both the girls were okay?'

'They were fine.'

'I don't understand. Why has she taken Ivy?'

'For this, so I'll bring you to her. I know where she is, I think. She's gone home.'

'Home?'

'Just outside Carmarthen. It's where we grew up. She wants me to take you there.' Steph glanced at Dani, apologetic. 'She won't hurt your daughter. She wants you to think she will, but she won't. Adele could never hurt a child, trust me.'

But Dani couldn't trust her. Steph was delivering her like a parcel to a woman prepared to use children as bait. Perhaps Adele wouldn't hurt Layla. If she wished harm upon her, then wouldn't she have let that van hit her the day at the park? Instead, she had risked her own life to save her. It wasn't Layla she wanted; it was Dani.

'You sure about that? She abducted my mother's cat and sent me razor blades in a bunch of flowers.'

The car juddered as Steph reacted with a start to the words. 'What?'

'You heard me. She sent a photograph of him locked in a cage. She's probably killed him by now. And she's left me with this little souvenir.' She held out her hand to show Steph the scars that now patterned her palm. Steph glanced briefly before looking away, her face flushing pink as though she herself had been responsible for the injuries.

It seemed to Dani that a person capable of abducting a cat and then a child might be more than capable of harming one or both.

'We need to let the police know,' she said, reaching for Steph's phone.

'No!' Steph snatched it from her and dropped it into the driver's door pocket. 'I'm sorry,' she said, realising the violence of the act. 'I just don't think it's a good idea. I'm not sure how she might react.'

'You just said she'd never hurt a child,' Dani reminded her, though the look on Steph's face suggested she was no longer sure of anything.

'What's this all about?' Steph asked. 'Why is she doing this?'

'Scarlet,' Dani said, barely able to get the word from her tongue. She watched the other woman's reaction as she spoke the name, saw the tension in her jaw that revealed her connection.

'What about her?'

'Adele blames me for her death.'

That book. She had wanted Dani to find its secret message, for the realisation of what she knew to hit her in the gut with all its implications. Scarlet had left the message for Adele. She had wanted her mother to get revenge for what Dani and Eve had done.

Steph gripped the steering wheel tighter. 'Scarlet killed herself.'

The words cut at Dani – she guessed that was their intended purpose – but she could see they did the same to Steph. The two women sat in silence for a moment, their focus fixed on the road ahead. Steph was waiting for Dani to tell her something she suspected the other woman already knew. She must be aware of more than she was letting on. How else would she have known where to find Dani?

'There was a video of Scarlet. It was recorded on someone's phone at the sixth-form prom. It went round the internet.'

'Did you film it?' Steph asked.

'No. But… it was my idea to spike her drink.'

It didn't matter how many times she reminded herself that she hadn't meant it. It was her fault. If she hadn't spoken those words, Scarlet might still be alive. She imagined Layla sixteen years from now, how she might look, what sort of young woman she might grow to become. What if a so-called friend did the same to her? How might Dani react if she was faced with the girl who had contributed to her daughter's death?

They were on the dance floor, Eve's arms resting on Dani's shoulders. She moved closer, her face turning towards Dani's. 'I've done it,' she said, speaking the words into her ear.

Dani had pulled back, still smiling. 'Done what?'

'Scarlet.' The word had been so quiet it was almost simply mouthed. 'I've spiked her drink.'

Dani had pulled away and let Eve's hands drop from her. She had scanned the room for Scarlet but couldn't see her. There were a few couples among the crowd that had gathered on the dance floor – a corner of the room marked out from the rest by perilously slippery tiles – though it mostly consisted of groups of friends self-consciously moving with the music or raising arms above heads to take awkwardly posed selfies.

Dani had said it a week earlier, as a joke. Scarlet was going to the prom with Rhys Paterson; the news had burned like a wasp sting at first, but Dani had liked him for long enough by then to know nothing was ever going to happen between them. She didn't blame Scarlet for saying yes. She just thought she needed to lighten up a bit. She didn't think Eve would take it seriously.

Then she'd spotted her. Her drink was in her hand, the glass held away from her as she leaned in to say something to Miss Francis, their head of year. Her backless dress had slipped lower, revealing a small butterfly tattoo on her spine. Dani didn't know what to do. Had Scarlet already drunk from the glass? She couldn't just go over and snatch it from her – how would she explain that? She would end up looking guilty of something, suspicious at the very least, and perhaps Eve was only teasing her anyway, just to get a reaction from her. She had been in a weird mood all evening. She wouldn't really have done anything.

'I said to Eve we should put some vodka in her drink,' Dani told Steph now, ashamed at the memory. 'I never meant it, and I never thought Eve would go ahead with it. I didn't know what she'd put in her glass, not until later.'

She could have stopped her, though. For the past four years she had lived with the knowledge that if she had only intervened, distracted Scarlet somehow, she might still be alive. She had assumed

Eve had put vodka in the drink, but it was only later, once all eyes were on Scarlet and her erratic behaviour – the stumbling into people and the batting of arms that made her look as though she was under attack from something only she could see – that she realised something was badly wrong. Vodka didn't make people behave that way, not even someone who wasn't used to alcohol.

'We all knew Scarlet wasn't drunk that night,' Steph said, not looking at Dani. 'She hated alcohol because of what it had done to her mother. Adele had a problem for years.'

Whatever Steph's thoughts about what Dani had told her, she was managing to restrain her feelings beneath an exterior of calm control. Dani knew she herself wasn't capable of doing the same. She wanted her daughter back. She would kill for her if necessary.

'She told us her mother had died when she was young,' she said.

Steph flinched at the words. 'Her dad moved her away to start a new life. After the accident, he knew Scarlet would be stigmatised for it.'

'Accident?'

'Adele hit a cyclist in her car. Killed her. She'd been drinking when it happened.'

Dani tried to remember the conversations she'd had with Adele, filtering through each one in search of some clue that might have been dropped among them, but there had been none. She had talked of guilt and regret... was this what she had been referring to?

'She went to prison?'

Steph nodded. 'She served almost five years of a six-year sentence. She's been on probation until recently. I think they've signed her off now.'

There was so much that didn't make sense, and Dani's head hurt with attempting to piece together so many broken fragments of fact to make a complete truth.

'How did you know to come to me?'

'Adele has been living with us since she came out of prison. My husband wasn't happy about it, but she's my sister and she needed me. Anyway, he hired a private investigator. I didn't know anything about it, not until last night. He said he knew Adele was up to something. He had a photograph of the two of you together.'

'Me? Where?'

'Outside a church hall. Then I realised she'd been using my daughter to get to you. Ivy was probably the reason she was so keen to stay with us.'

Dani said nothing. She thought of Adele in her home, left alone with Layla while she went to collect her mother. A thought hit her. Had Adele spiked her mother's drink? Perhaps Caroline hadn't been lying when she had claimed to have only had two ciders. Had her mother had a drink before leaving the house that evening? She racked her brain, but she couldn't remember.

'It seems she found your friend Eve, too.'

Dani felt sick. She had always known Eve would never go close to water; Maddie's suspicions were justified after all. She *was* involved in Eve's death, despite never meaning to be.

'The private investigator only got back to Callum with all this earlier today. She's been looking into links between you and Scarlet, and when she found out about Eve's death, she tried to find a link to Adele.'

'And she found one?'

Steph tried to call Adele again, but this time it went straight to answerphone.

'Eve and Adele attended the same yoga class in Bath.'

Dani pushed back against the headrest and tried to chase the screaming demons from her thoughts. Adele had exacted revenge right in front of them, finding a common interest and then a fear. For Eve, it had been water. For Dani, the fear was of something happening to Layla.

'But you said she's been living with you. How was she going to yoga classes in Bath?'

'She moved out for a little while at the start of the year, for about six weeks or so. I thought she was in Carmarthen sorting out the house to finally sell it, but she must have been in Bath.'

The conversation she'd had with Maddie replayed itself in Dani's mind. Hadn't she said that Eve had started talking about prom night again not long before she had died? Had she realised who Adele was, and was that why Adele had killed her?

Steph was interrupted by her phone, the name Callum flashing up on the dashboard screen.

'Where are you?' asked a male voice.

'M4. I think I know where they are.'

'I think you should pull over.'

'Why? What's happened?'

'Please, Steph, pull over somewhere safe.'

'Callum, just tell me what's happened! Is it Ivy?'

Dani watched Steph's hands tighten around the steering wheel, the same fear gripping them both.

'No, it's not Ivy. It's Adele. Christ, Steph… she's torched the house. One of the neighbours called me.'

Steph's face contorted, though she tried her best to conceal her reaction from Dani. 'Okay,' she said to Callum, as though he had just asked her to pick up some milk on her way home.

Dani was finding it impossible to process everything that was happening. She had no idea where her daughter was or whether she was safe, and no clue whether the woman sitting next to her could be trusted to take her to her. All she could do was hope.

FORTY

ADELE

When Scarlet was a little girl, her favourite way to spend an afternoon was to set up a tea party in her bedroom, a tartan picnic blanket spread out on the carpet and the miniature china tea set Adele had bought for her seventh birthday laid out with the precision of a Michelin-starred restaurant, the spoons lined up alongside the dishes and the handles of the milk jug, teapot and teacups all turned at the same angle. The same soft toys would attend each party – Cleo the cat with the multicoloured fur and shiny bead eyes, Rebecca the rag doll with the brunette bunches, and Tommy the teddy, a raggedy old bear that had belonged to Adele when she was a child. Every animal, doll and teddy Scarlet owned was named alliteratively, and each would be kept in the same place, her habits of order and routine apparent before she had reached junior school.

If Adele had noticed the signs of her daughter's obsessive nature, she'd chosen to ignore them. Everything had to be just so, and when it wasn't, Scarlet responded with a disappointment she tended to internalise, seeing each and every failure at perfection as a reflection of her own inadequacies. With hindsight, Adele knew she herself was to blame. But hindsight had never been of help to anyone, and the knowledge of her fault had never left her, not even when Leanne had tried to beat it from her.

While Ivy and Layla played, Adele looked for Cleo, Tommy and Rebecca. She couldn't find them anywhere, so could only assume that Scarlet had taken them with her when she and Brandon had moved. It was comforting to know that she had chosen to hold on to a memory of her childhood that was coloured and shaped in some way by her mother's presence.

She took the girls downstairs to the garden, and after allowing them to burn off some energy running around, she led them to the summer house. Cobwebs were strung across its ceiling and the smell caught in the back of her throat, but neither child seemed to mind, their little trip now seeming more of an adventure. Adele returned to the house to gather some toys, and after giving them to the girls to play with, she slid the bolt across the door, quietly locking the pair of them inside. She went to the shed, where all her father's tools and gardening equipment was still stored, much of it now rusted. Finding a hammer, she took it back to the house with her. She heard the distant sound of crying as she walked through the kitchen, but she ignored it as she had taught herself to, having to fight off the ghost of a crying child most of the nights she failed to find sleep.

Back in the bedroom, she unearthed the tea set from a box at the bottom of the wardrobe. She laid it out on the blanket she spread in the middle of the floor, setting four places: one for her, one for Steph, one for Dani, and one for the Russian dolls she had taken from Dani's bedroom. She imagined they had some personal relevance or sentimental value – why else would a twenty-two-year-old woman keep them on show like that?

She checked the time. It was nearly five thirty, and they would be here soon, just in time for a tea party.

Sure enough, less than twenty minutes later, she heard a car on the driveway. She went downstairs, taking the hammer with her, and heard Steph's voice calling to her as she waited behind the living room door.

'Adele!'

Then Dani's voice, filled with an intoxicating, heady mix of exhaustion and fear. It was everything Adele had hoped for.

'Layla!'

'She's in here,' she called.

Dani burst into the living room, Steph following close behind. Her mouth fell open at the sight of the raised hammer in her sister's hand.

'Adele, don't do this. Things have gone far enough.'

'Do what? I just want you to go upstairs.'

Dani glanced at Steph as though seeking her approval.

'Where are the girls?' Steph asked.

'Just go upstairs.' Adele stepped forward, brandishing the hammer, and Dani turned, almost falling into Steph as she tried to get back into the hallway.

'I swear to God, if you've hurt Layla—'

'You'll what?' Adele challenged. 'You'll kill me? I'm already dead, Dani. You've already done it, remember?'

She kept the hammer raised, ushering the women back into the hallway and up the stairs.

'She didn't kill Scarlet,' Steph said as they reached the landing. 'I know it's not what you want to hear, but it's the truth. Scarlet had already tried to kill herself twice.'

Adele turned and swung the hammer. Steph stumbled backwards and the hammer smashed into the wall, bouncing back with the force of the blow and sending Adele staggering. Dani made a grab for Steph to stop her falling, and she collapsed into her, breathless and terrified.

'Where are the girls?' Dani asked.

'In Scarlet's room.'

Adele watched her made-up face pale at the mention of Scarlet's name.

'I'm coming, Layla!'

Adele ushered the two women along the landing with a threatening wave of the hammer. Her sister dutifully did as she was told, clearly aware of the consequences if she didn't. Dani tripped forward as Adele jabbed the hammer into her lower back, then followed Steph.

'I thought we could have a little tea party.'

Steph turned to her. 'What has happened to you? Are you insane?'

'Shut up and sit down.'

With the obedience of somebody forced to comply through fear, Steph sat down on the floor. Reluctantly Dani did the same.

'Where are the girls, Adele?' Steph asked, her voice thick with fear. 'You said they were in here.'

Adele smiled, ignoring the question as she picked up Scarlet's teapot and poured each of them a cup of imaginary tea, aware of the looks passing between her sister and Dani, relishing the uncertainty her behaviour was creating. They thought she was crazy, that she had lost her mind, when the truth was that she had never been in greater control.

'Have you missed them?' she asked Dani, gesturing to the Russian stacking dolls. She would have put money on the honest answer being 'no'. She suspected Dani hadn't even noticed they were gone. She didn't seem the sentimental or appreciative type.

'Do you remember we talked about these a few years ago?' she continued to Steph, picking up the doll and turning it in her hands. 'While you were trying for Ivy and you were reading all those fertility books.' She looked at Dani. 'They're traditionally known as matryoshka dolls, representing motherhood and symbolic of family.' She twisted the doll's middle, cracking it open to take out the next. 'The doll within a doll not only symbolises pregnancy but also reflects the generations,' she went on, as though quoting from a textbook, 'with one mother leading to another and then to another. Each one carries on the family legacy. Where did you get them?'

Dani studied her with contempt. Her hands were balled into fists at her sides, ready for possible retaliation. 'They belonged to my grandmother.'

Adele opened the next doll and removed its contents, repeating the process until all six were lined up on the carpet. 'It's easy, though, isn't it, to destroy a family?' She reached for the hammer and raised it above her head before bringing it down on the smallest of the dolls. The wood smashed into tiny pieces, and her mouth twisted into a look of mock sympathy. 'You just remove a unit. And what happens to this one?' she said, pointing to the next in line. 'Her baby is gone. She's left hollow. Empty.' She raised the hammer again and brought it crashing down.

'Stop this,' Steph said softly, her voice laced with a quiet threat.

Adele smashed the next doll and then the next, until they were all broken, nothing left of them. 'Sad really, isn't it?' she said, enjoying the tears that had filled Dani's eyes. 'That you can't keep them safe forever.'

'I am sorry for what happened,' Dani said. 'More than you'll ever know. If I could go back and change things, I would, but I can't, and I hate myself every day for it. I never meant what I said, and I never thought Eve would go through with it. If I'd known Scarlet was so vulnerable—'

'If you had known she was going to hang herself, you mean?'

The room fell silent at the words. On so many sleepless nights, Dani had imagined what Scarlet's poor father must have walked in on. What part of his daughter had he seen first? Her feet? Her face? She had tried and failed over and over to escape the re-enactment that had played like a horror film in her head; the message became a little louder and a little clearer every time, until eventually it deafened her. It was her fault. She was a killer.

'You ruined her life,' Adele said flatly.

'Is that true, though?' Steph chipped in. 'You'd already done that for her.'

'I loved Scarlet,' Adele said defensively.

'You had a funny way of showing it. All those times you could have been a mother to her, a proper one, you were too busy playing the martyr. Too preoccupied with drowning your sorrows at the bottom of a bottle. Poor Adele, with all her demons. Really? What were they, Adele, because no one seems to know to this day. Do *you* even know? Or were they just an excuse for you to treat everyone who cared about you like shit?'

'You don't know what you're talking about,' Adele said through gritted teeth.

'Everything Brandon said to me about you was right. Spoilt, ungrateful, privileged. You were the same when we were children, always believing yourself hard done by in some way. Do you remember when I wouldn't give you the bag of chocolates one of Mum's friends had given me for my birthday? I shared them with you, didn't I, but it wasn't enough for you – you wanted the lot. And when I caught you trying to take them from my room, do you remember what you did? Hit yourself in the face hard enough to bruise your eye socket and then told Mum and Dad that I'd done it. That's you all over. You've always had to have more.'

Adele laughed. 'Is that why I signed everything over to you then?'

'You didn't do that through generosity – you did it for control. Buy me out so I'm eternally grateful, so that I feel obliged to do anything you ask of me. Callum saw through it straight away.' Steph paused. 'You can't have everything and everyone the way you want them, Adele. Life doesn't work like that.'

'Says she with her huge house and her Instagram career.'

'Is that what all this is about? Jealousy? Torch the house because it isn't yours? Ruin my life because you screwed up your own?'

Adele lunged at her and grabbed her by the throat. Steph staggered back and fell against the wooden frame of Scarlet's bed, and as the two sisters grappled there, fighting for breath against the other's hands, Dani took her opportunity to run.

FORTY-ONE

DANI

She was sure Layla was there, somewhere in the house; she had to find her before it was too late.

'Layla!'

She called for her daughter repeatedly as she pushed open doors and checked wardrobes, but it quickly became clear she wasn't upstairs. She heard a dull thud from Scarlet's bedroom, then a silence she didn't want to allow herself to interpret. Instead, she hurried down the stairs. She had noticed the phone on the hallway table when she and Steph had entered the house, and she hoped it was connected to a working line. She lifted the receiver and was grateful for the sound of the dial tone, her fingers shaking as she called 999. She didn't know the name of the house, but she had noticed a road sign when they had turned off to get there. Hopefully, the directions she gave would be enough to lead the police to them.

In frantic tones, she explained who she was and that her daughter had been kidnapped. Once the call was ended, she checked the cupboard under the stairs before going into the downstairs bathroom. She turned at a noise behind her. Steph was in the doorway, her top ripped and her hair messy and knotted from the struggle. The bruises around her throat were already visible.

'Where's Adele?'

'I hit her with the lamp. We need to find the girls.'

'Is she dead?'

'I don't know. Let's just hurry.'

They headed to the back of the house, Steph checking the living room as they passed. When she got to the kitchen, Dani saw that the door to the garden was open. It led out onto a small square of concrete slabs, followed by a wide expanse of grass – the kind of garden she could never imagine owning but that Layla would have loved. The thought of her daughter twisted her heart, and she called her name as she stepped into the garden.

Ahead of her was a wooden summer house, old curtains, brown with age, hanging limply at the windows. She hurried towards it and unbolted the lock that had been screwed to the top of the door. The smell of cat urine and wet fur hit her in the face. Ivy and Layla were sitting huddled against each other on the damp floor, crying. Layla was cradling something in her lap, and as Dani's eyes adjusted to the dark, she realised it was Dylan.

'Mama.'

Layla put the limp cat down and rushed to her mother, wrapping her arms around her legs. Dani crouched to hold her, pushing her sweaty hair from her face and whispering into her ear that she was all right, that everything was going to be okay, though she wasn't convinced by the words. There was a whimpering noise, and she realised that it was Dylan. He was alive.

She turned back to look at the house. Where was Steph?

She beckoned Ivy to come to her. 'It's okay, sweetheart. You're safe now.'

She took Layla by one hand and reached to Ivy with the other. Both girls were shaking, their fingers warm and sweaty in Dani's. As she led them out of the summer house, she looked up. Adele was standing at the back door of the house. She held a knife in her hand, its blade covered in blood.

Steph, thought Dani, and a tsunami of thick bile rose in the back of her throat. 'Let them go,' she said, pushing the girls behind her as she moved back towards the summer house. 'None of this is their fault.'

'I know that,' Adele said, stepping out into the garden. 'It's your fault, Dani. All of it is your fault.'

Dani shook her head. 'I never wanted to hurt Scarlet.'

'You killed her. You might not have put that rope around her neck, but you may as well have kicked the chair from under her. She was already so fragile – you must have seen that. All she wanted was to be loved. She thought you and Eve were her friends, didn't she? That's what pushed her over the edge.'

'Eve put the drug in her drink,' Dani spluttered, but she heard the words for what they were – a tattle-tale's 'she did it' that might as well have been delivered with the stamp of a foot and the indignant folding of her arms across her chest. 'I mean... I'm responsible, okay, I know I am, but there isn't a day that's gone by when I haven't thought about Scarlet and hated myself for what I did.'

Adele tilted her head to one side as she came closer. 'Poor Dani. You play the victim card so efficiently. You act up to the stereotype expected of you – girl from the poor end of town, no expectations, no prospects – yet you know it's not true. You had opportunities, didn't you? You just chose not to take them. That's the difference between you and Eve. Ruthlessness. She moved on when you couldn't. Am I supposed to thank you for your guilty conscience? Do you think it excuses you somehow?'

'No, but...'

Layla was gripping onto the back of Dani's trousers, as though she knew what was coming next. 'Everything is okay, Layla. Listen to me,' Dani said, looking down at her daughter, desperately trying to keep the child's attention on her and not on Adele. 'You're okay. I promise.'

'You're such a convincing liar,' Adele said.

'So are you. I thought you were a friend.'

Adele raised her hands, as though Dani had made her point for her. 'And now you know how Scarlet must have felt. Not nice, is it?' She stepped closer. 'So where do we go from here? Because my daughter wants me to avenge her death, but I'm only halfway there.'

Layla had let go of Dani's hand, and Dani grabbed it again, grasping it in her own. 'Just don't let them see it. Please.'

Adele gestured to the summer house. Dani crouched down beside the girls and smiled, fighting back the tears that threatened to escape her. She didn't want them to be scared. She didn't want them to see just how scared she was. 'Let's play a game,' she suggested. 'Hide-and-seek? You go into the summer house and I'll come and find you.'

Layla had yet to grasp the concept of hide-and-seek; whenever they played it at home, she would call to her mother before Dani had even counted to five. She couldn't understand that knowing where she was would make the game pointless before they started, but one thing she did seem sure of was that the summer house was a place to which she didn't want to return. Her fingers squeezed around Dani's, refusing the instruction.

'Please, Layla. Be a good girl for Mama, okay? Dylan needs you to look after him.' Dani kissed her head and then gave a big smile, as though everything was a lovely game. 'Go, go, go!'

Layla took Ivy by the hand, and the two girls headed back into the summer house. 'Just be quick,' Dani said, pretending to slide the bolt across. If Adele was going to kill her, she didn't want the girls to be left trapped inside there and unable to get help. She wondered where the police were, and whether Steph was dead.

Adele came towards her, the knife held out level with her stomach. Dani tried to swallow her fear, but she felt warm urine run down the inside of her leggings. She needed to hold Layla just one last time.

'You don't want to do this, not really,' she said, her voice shaking. 'You could have hurt Layla if you'd wanted to, but you didn't. You could have killed Dylan, but you didn't do that either.'

She flinched as Adele stepped forward, expecting her to lunge at her.

'Take it,' Adele said, turning the knife so that the handle faced Dani. 'You're right, I can't do this again. I should never have killed Eve.' She stopped just feet away from Dani, who eyed the weapon warily. 'Go on. I mean it. Take it.'

Dani knew Adele was playing a game, but she had no idea what her next move would be. Her bewilderment was allowing Adele all the control; this was clearly exactly how she had planned it.

'I don't want it.'

'Take it, or I'll take the girls.'

Dani leaned towards her and took the knife, bracing herself for the struggle she felt sure would ensue. It didn't come. She held it in front of her at arm's length, trying not to focus on Steph's blood glistening on the blade.

'Everyone knows what a temper you have, Dani. And killing is so much easier the second time around. You've done it once – you can do it again.'

Dani didn't see what was coming until it was too late. Adele rushed towards her, her arms reaching around Dani as though to embrace her. Dani felt her arm shudder, and Adele's head lolled onto her right shoulder as the knife thrust into her stomach. Her grip tightened on the handle as though she was unable to let go, fear rooting her to the spot.

There was a low moan next to her ear, and then Adele moved, her head tilting back to look at her. She took a ragged breath. 'Now you begin to pay.'

Dani stepped back, at last releasing her grip on the knife. As she moved away, Adele staggered and collapsed to the ground. Dani stared down at her body, at the knife embedded in her stomach and the blood that stained her own hands. She started shaking, an uncontrollable shuddering that consumed her as she stepped back and stumbled towards the summer house, where she could now hear both girls crying. She could also hear the distant sound of sirens becoming louder. Layla's voice, terrified, called to her, but she couldn't go to her, not like this.

'It's okay, Layla,' she said, trying to steady her voice. 'Mama's coming, I promise. You're safe in there, sweetheart. Just five minutes more.'

She slumped against the wall of the summer house and pressed her bloodied hands to the grass to stop herself from collapsing. The blood on her hands, the fingerprints on the knife… Adele had got what she wanted in the end. Hot tears rolled down her cheeks as she listened to her daughter's frightened sobs, and she apologised to her over and over as she waited for the police to arrive.

FORTY-TWO

ADELE

No one had ever visited Adele in prison. Her parents were both dead, and Steph had her excuses: it was too far to travel, she was busy with work, she was having fertility treatment. Brandon didn't come. He hated her. He'd never said it, but he didn't need to. Adele had cost him everything – the home he had loved and the job he had put his life into. The family that had meant everything to him, despite it having never truly existed. After Adele was sentenced, he had quit his role as a detective. Being the husband of a woman serving a six-year sentence for causing death by driving under the influence of alcohol didn't do much to aid his credibility, so he had stepped down and taken on a desk job, which he had continued until Scarlet's death. Eighteen months later, Brandon was also dead.

That Tuesday, Adele had expected to wait in her cell as she did every week, reading while Leanne sat in the visiting room with her cousin. They had an hour together, an hour that to Adele felt like an eternity but for Leanne probably passed in a heartbeat. She tried to conceal the sound, but every Tuesday night Adele would hear Leanne crying in the bunk above, her sadness stifled in sniffles like a child kept sleepless by the lingering shadows of a nightmare. They had been living their respective nightmares. For Leanne, it had been the cravings and the withdrawal; for Adele, it was the solitude.

She hadn't seen Scarlet in nearly three years. Her daughter had always been slim, but now she was skinny, her collarbones prominent and her skeletal frame obvious even beneath the loose clothing she wore. She was only seventeen – her eighteenth birthday was two months away – yet she looked so much older, aged by weight loss and by sadness that clung to her like a cheap perfume.

There had been no smile for her mother as she took a seat opposite.

'It's so good to see you,' Adele said.

Scarlet had scanned the room, eyeing each of the other prisoners and their visitors in turn. 'It's not really like what you see on TV, is it?'

'Not really. The food's just as bad, though. Like aeroplane food, but without going anywhere.'

There was no reaction. Scarlet shifted uncomfortably in her seat. Adele waited, wondering why she had come after all this time to then sit there and say nothing. Having her close was enough, and yet it wasn't – she wanted to reach across the table and touch her, to hold her in her arms as she had done when Scarlet was younger.

'Is everything okay?'

Looking at Scarlet had been enough to tell her it wasn't, but Adele didn't want to mention her daughter's weight loss for fear of inadvertently exacerbating her condition. Scarlet's obsessive behaviour with food had started a year or so before the accident, first with becoming picky over which foods she would eat, before progressing to refusal of entire meals. It was normal for girls that age to start worrying about how they looked, wasn't it? And yet Adele hadn't noticed how quickly Scarlet's interests had developed into issues, too preoccupied with her own demons to recognise those that now plagued her daughter.

Addiction. She had never said the word because it didn't apply to her. Leanne was an addict. She couldn't go without. The prison doctor had prescribed her methadone, though it didn't seem to reduce her need for the real thing. Adele didn't need alcohol, only during those grey sky phases that had darkened her days intermittently for as long as she could remember. Even as a child, a depression had fallen upon her sometimes, something heavy and lingering that she couldn't name and wasn't able to describe. It had kept her distracted. Blinded.

'How's school?'

'Finished,' Scarlet had answered flatly.

'University next?'

'Depends on my grades.'

'I'm sure you'll do great.'

The words had sat in the air between them, weightless and without substance. Adele had no idea whether Scarlet would do well or not. Scarlet had been bright as a child, but a lot had changed since then.

'Are you still going in for drama?'

Scarlet had rolled her eyes and shaken her head, not bothering to try to hide her frustration. 'That was a phase,' she said, as though she was an elderly aunt reminiscing over a wayward period of her youth, rather than a young woman with her whole life ahead of her.

Adele had waited, but she had to prompt Scarlet for further information.

'Psychology.'

'Oh,' she said, surprised at the change of direction her daughter's interests had taken.

'You could pretend to be more enthusiastic about it.'

'Sorry. I think it's a good choice, I just didn't expect it, that's all.'

'I find that kind of thing interesting. What makes people tick. Why people behave as they do. Why they do the things they do.' Scarlet held her mother's eye, the accusation, the recrimination evident in everything left unsaid.

What answers could Adele give her? She couldn't explain to herself why she had done the things she had, let alone to form the reasoning into words of any coherence. There was a darkness in her, one she had never been able to escape. The only time she had managed to push it away, if only temporarily, was when alcohol obscured the pain and sent her into a muted numbness.

'I got a tattoo,' Scarlet said suddenly, standing from her seat and turning to lift her T-shirt. A small colourful butterfly had been inked onto her skin, fluttering near the base of her spine. 'What do you think?' she asked, turning her head.

Scarlet knew that her mother hated tattoos. Adele guessed that was why she had gone and had it done. She was trying to test her, knowing that while she was stuck in that prison, she was denied any parental control.

'It's pretty.'

Scarlet's disappointment in her reaction was obvious as she sat back down. 'I've always liked butterflies. Imagine just being able to fly. To have that freedom.'

Adele said nothing. Whatever explanation Scarlet hoped to draw from her mother, Adele couldn't bring herself to give it to her. Sitting in that room during visiting hours, Scarlet's words sounded heavy with intent. Later, Adele realised they had been. Just not in the way she had at first assumed.

Scarlet lowered her head. 'Why was I never enough for you?'

The question was loaded with resentment. A nearby visitor glanced at Adele, her attention staying with her for a moment too long, as though the conversation that was about to play out at their table already promised to be more interesting than that at her own.

The words hurt, but they were the truth. Nothing was enough for Adele, and yet all she wanted was freedom, from the sadness that had crept into her bones and now kept her weighted, and from the feeling of hopelessness that had entwined itself into her

DNA. Brandon had called her self-pitying. He had been right, she supposed. But he couldn't change her. Nothing could, or so she had thought.

'It isn't you. It was never you.'

And it was true. After those first few sleep-starved months of relentless screaming and colic, something had changed. A love like no other she had ever felt before had eased its way into her skin, filling her with a warmth that was more intense than any flood of alcohol could ever offer. There had been no warning of its arrival, no signs that might have eased the guilt she felt at her initial ambivalence. The love was absent and then it was there, and it felt then as though everything should have looked and felt so different.

'I asked you to stop. Dad asked you to stop. We begged you, Mum, but you just wouldn't listen. If you'd only listened…' Scarlet stopped and reached into her bag. 'Remember this?'

She unfolded the sheet of paper and put it between them so that Adele could read it. She didn't need to. A glance was enough for her to realise what it was. Scarlet must have gone through her things; she couldn't even recall where she had hidden it all those years earlier. Her ten-year-old daughter had given it to her after one particularly heavy drinking session, leaving the letter on the bedside table. She must have been into the bedroom while Adele slept; she must have seen her face-down on the duvet, the remains of the previous evening's sick crusted to the side of her face.

Dear Mum, I hope this letter wont make you sad. I love you and I wont to help you and that is why I am writing this. I hate it when you drink. You are the worlds lovliest person when you are sober but when you are drunk I am sumtimes scared of you. Daddy says its not you its the drink that makes you like it but it makes me sad when you are sad and I just want you to be happy. I want to help *you but Daddy says you cant help sum one who doesent want to help themself. Please stop drinking mum. Love from Scarlet xx*

She remembered her initial reaction of denial as she read the letter in the fog of a raging hangover and a headache that felt as though she had been trampled by a horse. Those weren't the words of a child: they were Brandon's words, overheard and repeated, and she was angered at the thought that he had probably encouraged their daughter to write it. Now, her reaction was different. She was sorry for what she had allowed herself to become, and ashamed that she had let her daughter see her in such a state. Scarlet deserved better. She had always deserved better.

Scarlet reached into her bag for something else. A book. Adele's heart stuttered at the sight of it. *The Little Doll.* They had read it together when Scarlet was a child, over and over, one of her daughter's favourites.

'You used to love this book,' she said with a sad smile, picking it up and studying the cover. 'Is it the same copy?'

Scarlet nodded. 'You should read it again,' she told her. 'It says so much more than its words.'

Adele closed her eyes, and for a moment she was no longer in that prison. She was in a bedroom painted pink and white, the curtains pulled back and the window open to let in an evening breeze that cooled the heat left from the summer's day. Scarlet was sitting on the bed beside her, all bare limbs in a Disney princess nightie and newly washed hair that smelled of strawberries. 'Which story would you like?' Adele asked, and Scarlet pushed herself from the bed to go to the bookcase, returning to her mother with the same book they had read every evening for that past fortnight.

'I'm sorry,' she said, opening her eyes.

'What for?'

'For everything. You deserved better.'

Scarlet studied her blankly, her face betraying no reaction to her mother's admission. 'There's always time to make amends,' she said eventually. 'It's never too late.'

She stood, and Adele watched as she left.

Three days later, Scarlet was dead. Brandon found her hanging in her bedroom, a makeshift noose formed from a scarf tightened around her neck. The night she heard the news, Adele read the book for the eleventh time since her daughter's visit, noticing for the first time that the seemingly innocuous red pen marks spelled out a message.

FORTY-THREE

DANI

Steph was alive. She had needed emergency surgery, but a week after the attack she was through the worst and on the road to recovery. When the police had arrived, they had found Dani still sitting beside the summer house, Adele on the ground in front of her, Layla standing silently to the side. Dani hadn't noticed her daughter leave the summer house – she hadn't realised she was standing there – and it worried her just how much Layla had seen. Would she be traumatised by the events she had been witness to, by being locked up in the summer house, by seeing Adele's body, the knife, the blood that stained her mother's hands?

For the past four years Dani had believed herself a murderer, and now she really was one. Acceptance had filled her quickly, like water being poured into a glass; of all the ways she might have anticipated she would feel, this sensation of numbness would never have been something she expected. She wondered if this was what Adele had felt, this sensation of being removed, as though she was above her own body, observing a life she had once known but now didn't recognise. An old life and a new life. A before and after.

She had been to the hospital and had left a card for Steph, though she hadn't wanted to see her. It was too soon, and perhaps there would never be a need for it. If Steph hadn't survived the attack, Dani realised her own fate might have been very different.

A day after her surgery, Steph was able to tell detectives what had happened that afternoon at the house. This coupled with the private investigator's findings – and with the link they quickly made to Eve's death – meant that Dani was absolved of any crime, though it seemed to her still that she was far from innocent.

Eve's family had been told about Adele's involvement in their daughter's death. CCTV images of Adele near the place where Eve had last been seen alive were found, though there was no physical evidence to prove that it was Adele who had been involved in the altercation detectives believed had taken place. Adele's email account and call history had been accessed and were being investigated, so it would only be a matter of time before police were able to connect the pieces to create a picture of what had happened to Eve on that final evening. Dani had received no message from Maddie, no apology for her suspicions that Dani had been with Eve before she'd died. Perhaps she still regarded her as complicit in her sister's death, and maybe she was justified in that.

Two weeks after Adele's death, Dani stood in the park and pushed Layla on the swing. She had been tempted to drive to a different town and find a new park to go to, this one plagued with memories of Adele and everything that had happened, but she knew that running away would never lead her anywhere. Unless she was going to uproot Layla's life and her own, find a new job and a new place to live somewhere far away where no one knew them, she was going to have to work at moving on where they were. There were worse places to live, she supposed, and this was Layla's home. She had a duty to make life as normal for them both as she could.

She glanced up and saw her mother returning from the ice-cream van. She lifted Layla from the swing and carried her over to one of the benches. She dug the wet wipes from her bag, knowing that a single cone with a flake had the potential to require at least half a packet.

'She's okay,' Caroline said, sitting beside Dani.

'Was I looking at her again?'

'You haven't stopped looking at her for a fortnight. You're going to burn a hole in the side of that poor girl's head.'

Caroline had been the same with Dylan, barely letting him from her sight. Dani had half expected her to put him in a handbag to take him to the park with them. Like the rest of the family, he had been shaken by his ordeal, but physically he had come away from it unscathed.

Dani smiled. 'Thanks, Mum.'

'What for?'

'The ice cream.'

Caroline laughed. 'I thought you were about to give me some profound speech about how much I mean to you.'

'Nah, you're all right.'

Dani swiped a wet wipe across Layla's chin, catching a blob of ice cream before it had a chance to fall off and land in her lap.

'You still haven't told me how it went the other day.'

'There's a reason for that.'

'You going to see him again then?'

'His name's Travis.'

She had been for a coffee with him two days earlier, taking Layla with her. After everything that had happened, she didn't want to let her daughter out of her sight. One day she was going to have to, but not just yet. Travis had seemed more than happy for Layla to join them, and had played with her in the café, taking a book from the bookcase in the corner and reading it to her as she sat beside him. Dani had watched them silently, wondering as always whether she had done the right thing.

'Yeah, so…?'

'So maybe, yeah. Stop fishing.'

They sat quietly for a moment; the silence interrupted only by Layla's noisy slurping of an ice cream that was melting faster than she was able to eat it.

'You ready?'

'As ready as I'll ever be.'

Caroline cleaned Layla's face and hands, and the three of them made their way to the car. Within minutes, Layla had fallen asleep in her seat in the back. Dani sat anxiously in the passenger seat, the flowers resting at her feet. Outside the cemetery, Caroline cut the engine. 'I'll wait here.'

Dani took the flowers from the floor. 'I won't be long.'

She already knew where the headstone was. She had only been there once before, vowing that she would never return, unworthy to be anywhere near the place in the darkness of what she had done.

Scarlet Miller
August 1997–June 2015

No quotation from a poem; no parting message from a grieving father.

Beneath it, a second name and date had been added.

Brandon Miller
January 1969–December 2016

She placed the flowers at the base of the headstone and smoothed the palm of her hand across it, wiping away the wet leaves that had stuck to its surface following the previous night's rain.

'I'm sorry. I'll always be sorry.'

She sat there for a while in silence, time passing, for once, as though it meant nothing. She knew she would have to begin to forgive herself, for Layla's sake if not her own, but she realised that doing so would be a long and lonely journey. She had travelled similar routes before, she thought. She could do it again.

When she got back into the car, Caroline's hand moved to her knee. 'You don't believe it yet, but you're going to be okay. Everything is going to be okay, you'll see.'

Dani acknowledged her words with a nod and turned to look at her daughter in the back seat, still lost to a peaceful world of sleep. For the first time in a long while, she allowed herself to believe that her mother might be right.

A LETTER FROM VICTORIA

Dear Reader,

I want to say a huge thank you for choosing to read *The Playdate*. If you enjoyed it and want to keep up to date with all my latest releases, just sign up at the following link. Your email address will never be shared, and you can unsubscribe at any time.

www.bookouture.com/victoria-jenkins

I wrote *The Playdate* during a year that was difficult for all of us in so many ways – a year in which bubbles, tiers and masks became a part of our everyday lives, and playdates temporarily became a thing of the past. Stuck in our bubbles, we become absorbed within our own circumstances; for me that has been life in lockdown with a toddler and a newborn. To every parent who has struggled with isolation, loneliness, home-schooling, tantrums, sleeplessness, depleted creativity, absent energy, working from home amid the chaos – you are still going, and you are doing a brilliant job, the most important job in the world.

When you become a parent, you have an imagined version of how life with children will play out. There you are, all soft-edged in your daydreams of cradling your beautiful babe-in-arms, who is neatly swaddled and cooing contentedly. When he or she arrives, you are overwhelmed with an all-consuming love that is like nothing you've ever felt before. It is beautiful... and it is exhausting. The glossy magazines and Instagram-ready parenting blogs look nothing like the scenes taking place behind your door, to the extent that you start to wonder, am I doing this right? Dani is a young single mum, flawed but doing the best she can for her daughter. I hope that readers root for her, not because she is exceptional in any way, but because she is like so many of us – not always getting it right, but always trying to put right the wrongs.

Although Adele is the villain, I hope there is sympathy to be found in her circumstances. Like Dani, she makes some poor decisions in her younger years, and she suffers the consequences of her mistakes. She is capable of kindness and shows Dani compassion, albeit as a means of getting closer to her to wreak havoc upon her life. Arguably, it is not Dani she hates, but herself, and in plotting her revenge, she can temporarily escape her own guilt and responsibility.

I hope you enjoyed *The Playdate*; if you did, I would be grateful if you could write a review. I would love to hear what you think, and it makes such a difference in helping new readers to discover my books for the first time.

I love hearing from my readers – you can get in touch on my Facebook page, through Twitter, on Goodreads or my website.

Thanks again,
Victoria

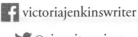 victoriajenkinswriter

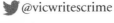 @vicwritescrime

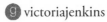 victoriajenkins

ACKNOWLEDGEMENTS

Firstly, a big thank you to my editor, Lucy Dauman – it has been a pleasure working with you on this book, and I hope there will be many more to come. (The off-topic conversations about *Bridgerton* and book titles have also been entertaining and have helped break up the lockdown tedium!) As always, thank you to my agent, Anne, who saw something in my writing nearly five years ago (where did that time go?) and has been stuck with me ever since.

Thank you to all my family, who continue to support me, as always, and endure my moments of self-doubt. We have lost so much time over this past year, but we will make up for it soon (and you can have the kids while Steve and I go to the pub, so be careful what you wish for!). My biggest thank you is to my pair of naughty noodles, Mia and Emily – I would have got this book written in half the time if it wasn't for you two, but the process wouldn't have been nearly so much fun. Thank you both for brightening the dark days – this book is for you.